Memoirs of a Confederate Gentleman

Thomas William Tear

Tate Publishing & Enterprises

Published by Tate Publishing & Enterprises, LLC
127 E. Trade Center Terrace | Mustang, Oklahoma 73064 USA
1.888.361.9473 | www.tatepublishing.com

Tate Publishing is committed to excellence in the publishing industry. The company reflects the philosophy established by the founders, based on Psalm 68:11,
"The Lord gave the word and great was the company of those who published it."

Published in the United States of America
ISBN: 978-1-61739-969-5
1. Fiction; Historical
2. Fiction; War & Military
11.02.07

DEDICATION

For Dorothy Dean Tear Heldman

Aunt Dot, who taught me: "Always believe in yourself. Treat everyone with the same respect that you would desire. Good manners will open doors that money and power will not. And most importantly, question, listen, and learn."

"The thing that bothers me the most about dying is the thought of all the really great books I will never read."

D. Heldman, August 1974

I know, Aunt Dot, I know!

ACKNOWLEDGMENTS

No book is ever written that does not require the patience, understanding, and support of the friends and family of the author. The writing of any book is indeed a community affair.

First and foremost, I must thank Sherry Wallen, a dear friend and knowledgeable reenactress whose persistence and love of the hobby got me involved with living history reenactments. Sherry, your friendship has enriched not only my life but many others as well.

I would like to thank my companions in this grand adventure: Karen Jessee and Roxanna Hurst, who, for dinner party entertainment, created the wonderful characters of Josephine and Aunt Effie and then allowed me to take liberties and expand on them for the book.

I would like to thank my partner, Ed Ward, who has been a chauffeur, tour guide, and research assistant to me. Ed, who never complained and who waited patiently as I spent hours tramping around historical sites and dusty museums all over the South and Ed, who listened patiently as I read and reread chapters and revisions to him on those long road trips to Charleston.

Thank you, Barbara Lewis, for your encouragement and for years of friendship. I will never know how you always came up with just the right book or information at exactly the time I needed it.

Thank you to Linda Packard, Sue Kenny, and Diana Wojnisz, who read pages and pages of unedited materials and offered their help, suggestions, and encouragement.

Thank you, Carol Hardy Stewart, for lots of great conversations, but one in particular that proved most helpful.

Thank you to Rob Gibson of Gettysburg, Pennsylvania, wet plate photographer extraordinaire, for permission to use the photo of Charles, Josephine, and Aunt Effie.

I would also like to thank the citizens of Charleston, South Carolina, who shared their knowledge and love of their city with me. And to the docents and employees, both in the museums and behind the scenes, thank you for your efforts to keep history alive and for your enthusiasm and willingness to share.

Thank you to Jack Thompson, author of *Charleston at War*, for his superior knowledge of all things Charleston.

A special thanks to Charleston resident Caroline Gilman, who, when she returned home to Charleston in 1865 and found flowers blooming, penned, "I could not help thinking yesterday, as I saw flowers…that they set a good example politically. But then, flowers have no memory."

And last, but not least, thank you to everyone at Tate Publishing for their help, expertise, and for giving me the opportunity to share this story.

Thank you all so very much, for without the help of all of you, this story would never have been told.

TABLE OF CONTENTS

July 12, 1987

McGuire, Josephine Margaret

Charleston residents were saddened to learn of the passing Tuesday of Miss Josephine Margaret McGuire, formerly of Grand Oak Plantation. Miss McGuire was predeceased by her parents, Hardy S. and Margaret (nee Harris) McGuire. She was the granddaughter of the late Major Charles Everson McGuire and Josephine St. John McGuire. Miss McGuire was born July 4, 1900, at Grand Oak Plantation. She was the fifth generation of her family to reside at Grand Oak where she lived until her death.

Miss McGuire was an active member of Saint Michael's Episcopal Church and member of the D.A.R., the Daughters of the Confederacy, and the Charleston Historical Society. She was a former president of the Charleston Women's Garden Club and served on the board for many years. Miss McGuire leaves no direct descendants but is survived by several cousins and many long-term friends. Her tireless support of local charities and fundraisers will be greatly missed. There will be no viewing. Friends may call at Saint Michael's Church, Charleston, between 10:00 and 11:00, Saturday morning. Services will commence at 11:00. Interment will follow in the churchyard at the conclusion of the service.

March 25, 1988

A rare chance to own a piece of history
By Brenda A. Scott of the Post and Courier staff

Charleston—Have you ever wanted to own a piece of history? Here is a rare opportunity. Next Saturday, April 1, will mark the end of an era for one of the Ashley River's great antebellum homes. The plantation known as Grand Oak and all of its contents will be sold at auction.

Captain Charles Everett McGuire bought the land in 1797. Grand Oak was completed in the early 1800s. The estate has been the family seat of the McGuire clan for five generations.

According to family legend, the home Captain McGuire constructed for his new bride was built on the site of an ancient live oak. It was from this oak that the house took its name.

During the Civil War, the captain's grandson, Major Charles E. McGuire, owned the home. The Union Army used the grounds as a field hospital, camping around the house after two days of fighting nearby.

Tradition says that it was the hospitality of the major's wife, Josephine St. John McGuire, aided by the ladies of the family that kept the Union Army from burning the home.

The estate has long been known for its collection of rare and historic plants and trees. The original gardens were laid out in 1802 by Captain McGuire's wife and greatly expanded by his daughter-in-law, Louisa Everson McGuire.

In recent years, the estate and grounds, under the direction of their last owner, Miss Josephine McGuire, have gained national prominence for their stunning collection of camellias and azaleas. Miss McGuire was a passionate and knowledgeable gardener and a past president of the Charleston Ladies Garden Club. She frequently opened her home and gardens to the public for various charitable events.

Miss Josephine Margaret McGuire, the last living descendent of the captain, died four months after the tree was felled by a storm last June.

In accordance with Miss McGuire's wishes, the estate and its contents will be auctioned off, and the money will be used to endow several of her favorite charities.

All of the household furniture and fixtures will be sold. Among the items to be auctioned are cut-crystal chandeliers from France, fine gilt mirrors, numerous oil paintings and portraits, five complete sets of china, silver flatware and serving pieces, oriental carpets, a fine Charleston rice bed, chairs, settees, a mahogany dining room suite that seats twenty, a matching pair of Hepplewhite sideboards, and objects too numerous to mention. The sale will run from 12:00 noon to 7:00 p.m. Saturday, April 1, and resume at 12:00 on Sunday, April 2.

For further information, directions, or to request a catalog, please contact Sotheby's Auction House, Charleston.

Prologue

My passion for stories about places and times gone by was handed down to me like a precious heirloom by my grandmother on my father's side. When I was a child, I would sit with her in the front parlor of her house on the last Monday of each month as she waited for the ladies from her garden club to arrive for tea. The ladies would usually arrive all at once, filling the front hall. They seemed to me to be a flock of feathered hats and white gloves. We would hear them clucking among themselves as Aunt Maude took their coats and ushered them into the parlor, where Grandmother and I waited.

I had a small, child-sized chair that had been bought just for me. The chair would be carried into the parlor and placed beside Grandmother's chair before her guests arrived. Here, I would sit in my Sunday-best suit and wait patiently as Grandmother poured tea and conversed with her friends. The ladies discussed the weather, the neighbors, their flowers, their neighbor's flowers, and what a "big little man" I was getting to be. Finally, when all the news had been discussed, recipes shared, and tea and refreshments consumed, the ladies would depart as they had arrived: in a flight of white gloves and feathers.

Once the last guest had flown from the entrance hall, I would beg Grandmother to get out the old Chinese box filled with photographs and letters. I would then pester her to tell me stories about what she fondly called "the olden days."

Grandmother would call for Aunt Maude, who would come puffing, no doubt from the pantry, where she would have been putting away the teacups and saucers and polishing the silver service.

Aunt Maude would arrive red-cheeked and breathless, smoothing a few wisps of gray hair from her face.

"Yes, Mother," she would say.

"Maude, dear, would you please bring to me the Chinese box from the linen press in the hallway?" Grandmother would ask.

In a few moments, Aunt Maude would return bearing the large cedar wood box, which contained old pictures and mementos from days gone by. The box had come long ago from China; it had been a present from one of her uncles, who had gone there on holiday to see the Great Wall. The box was lined in faded beige silk that was patterned with butterflies and plum blossoms. A sturdy lid of matching silk fit neatly over the top of the container.

Grandmother would set the box on her lap and gently remove the lid. The scent of cedar and lavender would perfume the air. We both would take a deep breath and inhale. Grandmother would look down at the box of old letters and pictures, and she would smile lovingly at the faded sepia images as though they were smiling back at her. I used to love to watch her face; it seemed to change, and there would be a faraway look in her eyes as if she were seeing people and places that nobody else could see.

There were many curious items inside, things like little locks of hair, some tied with faded ribbon, others braided into pretty designs. There were old buttons and small scraps of fabric. There were medals from wars fought long ago in far away places. And there were many old photographs. The photographs were not like the ones we took with Grandfather's "Kodak Brownie." They were made on little glass plates that were kept in small leather-bound cases with smooth pieces of dark blue or red velvet facing the picture. Grandmother called these "ambrotypes." Some of the pictures were made of tin; others were mounted on neat pieces of cardboard with fancy gold edges. A calm peacefulness would overtake Grandmother as she began to handle the faded, yellowing scraps of paper and cardboard.

"This was my mother, your great-grandmother…" she would begin.

As much as I loved my grandmother's stories, it was Grandfather's sister, my great-aunt Isabelle, who was the official family historian. Much to my grandmother's chagrin, Isabelle loved to tell things as they were.

Aunt Belle, as the family called her, lived in an oversized white wedding cake of a house on the outermost edge of the city of Charleston, South Carolina. Her residence had been a wedding gift from her father pending her marriage to one Whitney Hamilton. Construction was begun in 1918. The house had been designed in the Italian renaissance style and was constructed of the very best materials that money could buy. There was an abundance of porches and high windows.

Built for entertaining, the downstairs reception rooms were large and spacious. The public rooms had fourteen-foot ceilings to help keep them cool during those long, sultry summer days and nights.

Upon its completion, Aunt Belle and Uncle Whitney set out on a honeymoon trip around the world to purchase the furnishings for their new home. When they returned from their trip, they lost no time in gaining a reputation for entertaining the very smartest set in town. For many happy years, their residence was known for its hospitality.

With the crash of 29, the Jazz Age came grinding to a halt. The endless river of money ceased to flow, and the parties stopped. Uncle Whitney died ten years later in 1939, and whatever funds were left seemed to disappear with him. By the time I was old enough to remember anything, Aunt Belle and her once beautiful house had fallen into a state of elegant decay.

When I was in my early teens, in the late 1960s, my parents would ship me off to Charleston for a week or two every summer to see dear Aunt Belle. Looking back, I suppose this was not out of any great love on the part of my parents for the woman, but more a desire to make sure we were remembered in the will. Everyone in the family was sure that there were still millions squirreled away somewhere in a box or a drawer.

Mom and Dad would say, "Poor Aunt Belle. She never had any children of her own. To whom would she leave all of that money? It might as well be one of us."

Actually, I looked forward to my visits to Charleston. Aunt Belle and I got along very well. I remember a dainty, fine-boned woman, in her late sixties, with an amazingly smooth, round face and large, brown eyes. She had a crown of perfectly coiffed silver hair and spoke with a pleasing genteel drawl. Her gnarled hands were always bedecked with the last of the diamond rings Uncle Whitney had given her. Those hands always seemed to be a little too large for the frail woman pouring tea from a slightly tarnished silver teapot. Here, amidst the faded grandeur of her once elegant house, Aunt Belle, wearing a strand of pearls and a ruffled floral print dress, would hold court with me, her cats, and Sadie, the black lady who came every day to dust and fix lunch for Miss Isabelle.

Aunt Belle loved to talk about the history of Charleston. Like most of the women in town, she could recite a complex litany of genealogies connecting all of the people in town through several generations and just as many states. I liked to think of Aunt Belle as a collector of unusual personalities. At one time, she had filled her home with the great, the humble, and the eccentric. Her guests would laugh and mingle in her drawing rooms in the evening but would look in the opposite direction when they saw each other on the street the next morning.

She would go on for hours with stories about the people—some famous, some scandalous, but none boring—who had come through the big double front doors. There were congressmen and clergy, sinners, and saints.

Often included on the guest list was a senator who scandalized polite society by bringing his mistress from Louisiana to a reception at the house, and a portly woman, named Mrs. Davenport, who dyed her hair and smoked cigars.

Mrs. Davenport gave piano lessons and rented rooms to single ladies, who, it was rumored, entertained gentlemen callers in the upstairs rooms of their landlady's house.

Another frequent visitor was a tall, swarthy man named Captain Henry, who walked with a limp. Aunt Isabelle never knew why he was called Captain, for he did not own a boat and never went near the water. A rumor once circulated that he was descended from a famous pirate who had terrorized the Carolina coast until his capture. This remote ancestor had been hanged in the public square, and the family denied him for many years.

It would seem that even her staff was eccentric. In those days, it took a staff of four, with as many as twenty brought in for parties and special occasions, to run the house. Aunt Belle's maid was said to be both deaf and mute, and yet there never seemed to be any problems communicating between them. I once heard a rumor that the story of Miss Evelyn's disabilities had been a ruse cooked up by Aunt Belle and her for the benefit of the towns-folk, who, believing she could neither hear or speak, felt free to discuss things they did not want repeated to other parties in front of her, things Evelyn later repeated to her mistress.

I kept in touch with Aunt Belle over the years. After I had graduated college and was working at my job in the city, I became very interested in Civil War history and started attending reenactments.

My interest in this particular area pleased Aunt Belle immensely, and she would send me yellowing clippings from the *Charleston Post and Courier* from time to time, articles she thought I might find interesting.

While I enjoyed all of the news items, there were two that captured my imagination. Both of these articles arrived in the same envelope with a letter from Aunt Belle one day in the early spring of 1988.

The first item was an obituary of an old acquaintance of Aunt Belle's; the second article had been written almost ten months later. It was a story about the sale of an old family home. The home had belonged to the woman mentioned in the obituary.

In her letter, Aunt Belle mentioned that she had visited the home many times when she was young and that she remembered how beautiful the old house had been and what a shame it was that after five generations and two hundred years, there were no relatives left to pass the estate on to. I had no idea how these neatly folded, yellowing clippings were about to change my life.

After reading about the auction sale at Grand Oak, I thought it might be a good excuse to fly down to Charleston. Once I arrived, I could attend the auction and visit Aunt Belle, who had turned eighty-nine that January.

I rented a convertible and drove to Aunt Belle's from the airport. The late spring sun was warm on my back as I cruised the old familiar streets lined with moss-draped oaks. I smiled to myself, and memories of those lazy summer days of my adolescence came flooding back to me. The trees were a lot bigger. There was a little more paint missing here and there on the house. The china blue wisteria had overgrown the porch and invaded the once lush lawn. Some things, however, had not changed; the same ancient red-and-white tabby cat rose to greet me as I climbed the front steps. I reached down and scratched her graying old head.

"Hello, Tobias," I said. "Where's your mistress?"

Tobias just purred in welcome as the front door creaked open.

"Mista Thomas, is that you?" came a thin, high voice.

I immediately recognized the voice as belonging to Sadie, Aunt Belle's housekeeper.

"Hello, Sadie." I smiled.

"Why, Mista Thomas, it is you, and look at you. You's all grown up now. Come in, come in. Miss Isabelle will be so glad to see you."

I followed Sadie into the coolness of the large entrance hall. I sat my bag down on the faded oriental carpet and inhaled the humid mustiness of the old house. The scent mixed with another pleasant familiar smell. "Sadie, is that your famous peach cobbler I smell?"

Sadie looked at me and grinned. "Yes, sir, Mista Thomas. You sho have a keen sense o' smell. Peach cobbler always was yo favorite. When you was little, you used to come a runnin' from wherever you was hidin' as soon as you smelled it cooking. You'd pesta me until I gave you a little taste."

I smiled at Sadie. It sure was good to be back in Charleston after all of these years.

"Miss Isabelle's in the front parlor," said Sadie. "She don't get up the stairs so good anymore, so we moved her bed and things into the back parlor downstairs. You go in and surprise her, and I'll bring some tea, and maybe we can find you a little bit o' dat cobbler."

I opened the double doors and stepped into the first of two parlors, which exactly mirrored each other. There, in front of a window, in a large, overstuffed chair, sat Aunt Belle. Like one of her cats, she was napping in the afternoon sunlight that came streaming into the room through the open draperies. I stared down at my grandfather's sister sleeping so peacefully in that chair. She had gotten older and seemed so small and frail. She still wore her pearls, and that silver hair was still perfectly groomed.

Not wanting to scare her, I leaned close and said softly, "Aunt Belle."

Her large brown eyes flew open, and she sat up with a start, saying, "Oh! Oh!"

"It's okay, Aunt Belle. It's Thomas. I'm sorry; I didn't mean to scare you. Are you all right?" I asked.

"Merciful heavens! You gave me quite a start," she said. "Just let my catch my breath."

Aunt Belle sat up in her chair and smoothed her cotton dress over her lap. "What a pleasant surprise. What are you doing here?"

"Oh, nothing special. I just came to visit my favorite aunt," I said, as I leaned over and kissed her.

"I see," Aunt Belle replied. "I take it you got the newspaper articles I sent you."

"Yes," I answered.

"And you just happened to arrive in Charleston the day before the big sale at Grand Oak?"

"Why, Aunt Belle, you make me sound so mercenary. Do I need a reason to visit my favorite person in the whole world?"

"Come now, you wicked boy! I know this is more than just a friendly visit to an old lady. I wasn't born yesterday. You forget I know you pretty well. I know you wouldn't miss the chance to poke around in an old house, especially one like Grand Oak."

We laughed together at the conspiracy; we both knew Aunt Belle was right. She knew the articles she had sent would inspire me to visit Charleston for the sale.

"We will have to get an early start, you know," said Aunt Belle. "I expect half the county will show up."

"What time did you have in mind?" I asked.

"I would suppose there will be a lot of dealers there too, buying up the good stuff and driving up prices," continued Aunt Belle, ignoring my question.

"I suppose so," I said.

At that moment, Sadie walked in carrying a tray of tea and cobbler. She sat it down on a table in front of us.

"Can I get you all anything else?" asked Sadie.

"No thank you, Sadie," said Aunt Belle.

We sat in the front parlor of Aunt Belle's house and reminisced together. Aunt Belle wove stories about the great house known as Grand Oak and its two-hundred-year history, which, it appeared, would end with the demise of the great tree from which the house took its name and the death of its last mistress, Miss Josephine.

The next day dawned sunny and pleasant. We awoke with the first light at 6:00 a.m. The sale did not start until noon. Nevertheless, Aunt Belle wanted to get there early.

It took us about an hour to drive out to Grand Oak. At that early hour of the morning on a Saturday, we had the roads all to ourselves.

We drove over bridges and past the suburban sprawl. Eventually the tract houses and mini malls gave way to the beautiful South Carolina countryside that I remembered from my youth.

The country landscape was brilliant beneath the warm spring sunshine.

The rising sun made mirrors of the lakes and rivers. Here and there, wisteria vines, having escaped or survived the gardens that they had so long ago graced, grew to fantastic heights. They blanketed anything in their path with fragrant blue flowers. We flew past azaleas and dogwoods dressed in a kaleidoscope of color. Everywhere we looked, the trees and lawns were bathed in green so bright it seemed to blind our eyes.

After driving about forty-five minutes, we came to a bend in the road.

"Slow down. It's just around this bend," said Aunt Belle.

As we rounded the curve, two brick piers supporting a huge pair of iron gates came into view on the right.

"Turn here," said Aunt Belle.

I turned the car into the mile-long driveway lined with centuries-old oaks, and I was filled with anticipation.

As we neared the end of the driveway, a man with an orange flag motioned us to the left into a parking area.

There we saw a white tent, where we registered and got our number in order to bid on items in the auction. A round, pleasant woman with sun-flushed cheeks assigned us our number and wished us a pleasant day. She pointed us in the direction of a path across the grass leading to an ancient camellia hedge.

We walked across the lawn and through a gate framed on either side by the largest camellias I had ever seen. The stately, old shrubs gave way to lush, green lawns dotted with tiny, white flowers. The sight before me took my breath away. There, on a slight rise, framed by four massive oak trees, sat Grand Oak!

The house sat on the edge of a reflecting pool so still it appeared to be a mirror. It was hard to imagine that this was the back of the mansion, for the custom when the house had been built was for the front of the house to face the river.

We walked through beautiful gardens filled with exotic flowers to the front of the house. The oak tree from which the house had taken its name was no more than an impressive stump between the mansion and the lethargic river. The big house was still guarded by an impressive grove of moss-draped oaks, which had been planted when the house was built.

The furnishings being sold had been removed from the house and set up in neat rows on the front lawn to allow prospective buyers a chance to examine them up close before the bidding started. Aunt Belle and I walked up and down the orderly rows of beautiful old furniture, stopping here and there to admire the bounty of the collection amassed by five generations of one family.

"The wealth of Midas spread here on the lawn," I said.

"You mean Croesus," corrected Aunt Belle. "Midas turned everything he touched to gold. Croesus was the king who amassed limitless wealth."

I realized, of course, that she was right; Aunt Belle was always right.

"It still seems such a shame," I said. "All of this history, all of those family members who cherished these things, and now the people are all gone, and their memories are scattered on the lawn to be picked over by strangers."

"That's the point," said Aunt Belle. "These are just things. We never really own things; we are just guardians of them for the next generation. It is our job to keep things safe and cherish them and, when the time comes, pass them on to the next generation. That's what is happening here right now. Think of all of the people who will be made happy today, and how they will add their own history to the things they will buy here. And don't forget the money from the sale, which will go to charity. Think of all of the good that will come from that."

With that comment, I realized how wise and wonderful Aunt Belle really was. I remembered with regret those first summers my parents had shipped me to Charleston in the hope of securing things from Aunt Belle, and I was thankful that our friendship had long ago passed beyond the value of things.

Once we had looked at all of the furnishings that were to be sold, we went into the house. We wandered from room to beautiful room.

We looked through the same glass windows into the same gardens that the McGuire family had looked for five generations. We marveled at the beautiful, curved, double staircase that led to the upper floors. We admired the woodwork and carved plaster ceilings hung with beautiful crystal chandeliers, which soon would be removed to hang in new homes.

Aunt Belle reminisced about how the rooms had once looked filled with the furnishings that now occupied the front lawn.

"I met your Uncle Whitney in the ballroom here," said Aunt Belle. "I thought he was quite the handsomest man I ever saw. I knew after that first dance that I would marry him. So many happy memories. I hope whoever buys the house doesn't tear it down. I suppose Grand Oak is a lot like my house; she has lived a lot and seen a lot of history, but it will take a lot of love and money to fix her up the way she used to be."

I shuddered at the thought of the old mansion being torn down and replaced with a housing development.

"She has survived this long. I am sure that she will last a while longer," I said.

"I certainly hope so," said Aunt Belle. "We are losing bits and pieces of our history every day. It's such a shame, but very few people today have the money to maintain a piece of property like this, and the people who do have the money want to build something new and flashy near the ocean. Those houses won't be standing after a good Charleston hurricane. This house, though, has withstood floods, hurricanes, earthquakes, and even the Union army. Why, I don't expect there is much which could bring it down!"

"I hope you're right about the house. I hope it survives," I said.

At that moment, the plantation bell rang loudly, signaling the start of the auction. Aunt Belle and I returned to the front lawn, took our seats in the shade of one of the old oaks, and waited for the bidding to begin.

The bidding went on for hours; there were old family portraits and the usual assortment of tables and chairs, silver, china. There was a beautiful Charleston rice bed with a matching wardrobe and an exceptional old Chippendale settee whose back legs had been repaired. I watched as item after item was sold, but for some reason I cannot explain, it was an old steamer trunk that caught my eye. The trunk was about twenty inches deep and three feet wide, and it stood two feet high. It was made of an unidentified wood and lined in cedar, and the outside was covered with brown leather, over the top of which were heavy darker brown leather straps that could be pulled down and locked. There was a tarnished brass plaque on the top inscribed with the initials *C. E. Mc.*

As the assistants lifted the top of the trunk to show the contents, I was assailed by memories of my grandmother lifting the top off the old Chinese box. Inside the trunk were old newspapers; magazines; a faded, moth-eaten, yellow sash; an old, worn belt with a belt buckle that had the initials *CS* in raised letters on the front; and old family papers. I knew I had to have this trunk.

"Lot 224," began the auctioneer. "A campaign trunk probably belonging to Charles McGuire, who fought in the War Between the States. It is filled with bits and pieces of history waiting to be discovered. Can we start the bidding at four hundred dollars? Do I hear four hundred dollars?"

I immediately began to raise my hand, but Aunt Belle grabbed me by the wrist.

"Don't be in such a hurry," she said. "Let's see who bids on it first."

"Come now, ladies and gentlemen. Let's not be shy. This trunk once belonged to a Confederate officer. It has good solid construction and is lined in cedar. Why, it can be used for quilts or all sorts of things. Can I get four hundred dollars?"

"I'll give you fifty," a voice in the back said.

"Sir, I'd rather put a note in it and float it down the Ashley River for fifty dollars," replied the auctioneer.

The crowd broke into amused laughter.

"Remember, ladies and gentlemen, the proceeds here today go to charity. Let's not be stingy."

"Seventy-five dollars," said a second voice.

"That's better," said the auctioneer. "I have seventy-five; do I hear one hundred? One hundred?"

A distinguished-looking lady wearing a wide-brimmed hat bid one hundred dollars. I have one hundred from the lovely lady in the hat. Thank you, madam. Do I hear one twenty-five?"

"One twenty-five." It was the first man again.

"Now, Aunt Belle? Now?" I asked. I was eager to get into the spirit of bidding.

"Be patient. Let's see where this goes. Best not to seem too eager," cautioned Aunt Belle.

"One fifty," said the lady in the hat.

"One fifty. Do I hear one seventy-five?" said the auctioneer, looking in the first man's direction.

The man shook his head no. The second man offered a bid of one seventy-five. The auctioneer looked to the lady in the hat. She bid two hundred.

"Two hundred. I have two hundred. Do I hear two twenty-five? Remember, ladies and gentlemen, it's for charity. Do I hear two hundred and twenty-five dollars for this treasure chest full of Confederate memories?"

A man in the third row bid two twenty-five. The auctioneer looked to the lady in the hat. "Do I hear two fifty?"

The lady in the hat shook her head no.

"Going once for two hundred twenty-five dollars to the gentleman in the third row. Going—"

"Now, Aunt Belle. Now? I'm going to lose it," I pleaded.

"Sit back and watch how it's done." With that, Aunt Belle raised her hand and held up the numbered card we had been given.

"Two hundred and fifty. I have two hundred and fifty. Thank you, madam. Do I hear two seventy-five?"

"Two seventy-five," the man in the third row said.

"Do I hear three hundred?" The auctioneer was looking directly at Aunt Belle, who nodded her approval.

"I have three hundred. Do I hear three twenty-five?"

The man in the third row started to raise his hand, but Aunt Belle shot him one of those freezing looks that only a Southern woman can give, and the man shrank in his chair. Aunt Belle settled back in her chair, confident in her victory.

"Going once, going twice, sold for three hundred dollars to the lady with the pearls!" said the auctioneer as he banged his gavel down.

"Fantastic," I said, hugging Aunt Belle. "I can't believe we got it!"

Aunt Belle looked pleased with herself as if there had never been any doubt in her mind that she would have won the bidding.

My flight for home left at eleven o'clock the next morning. I woke early and said my good-byes. I boxed the trunk up, took it to the UPS office, and mailed it home to myself. The trunk arrived at my house two days after my return. I opened it and glanced through the top layer, and sure enough, it seemed to be filled with old newspapers and cloth. My curiosity temporarily satisfied, I put the trunk in a corner of my office and resumed the work that had piled up on my desk during my trip to Charleston.

For the next couple of days, as I strived to meet my deadlines, I tried to ignore the trunk in the corner. It sat there mocking me, whispering my name then laughing at me. Finally, I could stand it no more. *Deadline be damned*, I thought.

I unhooked the leather straps and opened the trunk. Exploring its contents was like finding a time capsule. I took each of the items out and laid them on the floor around me. Only then did I come to realize what I had purchased.

What had appeared to be worthless old bits of moth-eaten cloth wrapped in unwanted newspaper were actually pieces from an old Confederate uniform.

I discovered a faded, yellow sash, which had seen a good deal of wear, but the tassels on either end were still in good condition. The trunk also contained a pair of much-worn white leather riding gauntlets with eagles embroidered in gold thread on the cuffs and a leather sword belt with a shoulder strap. Attached to the belt was the original two-piece C. S. belt buckle.

In addition, in the trunk was a brass bugle with a black ribbon tied around it. The initials *H. S.* were inscribed on the side of the bugle. There was also a leather wallet, the old-fashioned kind, not like the ones we carry today. It contained two hundred and thirty-seven dollars in Confederate money.

However, the most extraordinary thing I found was an oval box made of tin and covered with brown leather. The box had a brass plaque on the top, which bore the initials *C. E. Mc.* I opened it to find that it was lined with faded, worn, black velvet and contained a pair of gold epaulets, the old kind, which were called "shoulder mops." They still gleamed brightly as if they had just been polished. The epaulets were made of brass, and the fringe was made of coiled brass wire.

Compared to the other items in the trunk, they were in strangely good shape, except for one, which looked as though someone had scratched across the top of it with a round file.

There was, however, one more surprise in store for me. As I looked into the now-empty trunk, I realized that something just did not look right.

On the outside, the trunk seemed to look deeper than the inside. I examined the inside closely. On either end, about eight inches down, I noticed two leather handles, which I had assumed to be just reinforcement to keep the outside handles from pulling through. I pulled on both handles at once. To my surprise, I found the whole lining came out like a box within a box.

There in the compartment, hidden in the bottom, were the following items: a gold pocket watch with a chain and a fob. The chain was woven with what appeared to be a very fine reddish colored thread. I couldn't identify the material.

There was a tintype portrait of a bearded man wearing a Confederate uniform and another beautiful tintype of three handsome people in a gold frame. The man in the middle was obviously the same man in the smaller image. He now wore civilian clothes. Two fashionably dressed women accompanied him.

There were also three more tintypes from the same era and a handwritten diary, the front of which was embossed with faded gold letters: *J. A. St. John McGuire.*

In the bottom of the box there were three more diaries that had belonged to a Euphemia Everson Scott, two leather satchels containing pages and pages of handwritten notes, and a notebook, on the front of which was handwritten, *Memoirs of a Confederate Gentleman.*

Over the next few weeks, as I started to read the notebook, I realized that it had been written by Major Charles McGuire, who had owned Grand Oak Plantation during the Civil War. The diaries that accompanied it had been written by his wife, Josephine, and his aunt, Euphemia Scott. I would later come to realize after reading the documents that these were the same three people who appeared in the tintypes included with the letters.

I could scarcely believe my luck at this find. My first instinct was of course to try to return these items to the family. However, I remembered that there were no living relatives, which was why I had the trunk in the first place.

It became obvious to me that the major had at one time been planning to write a family history. For whatever reason, he never finished his story, and the diaries and notes had all been put in this trunk and forgotten.

Now over one hundred years later, thanks to the wonderful written record of their journey through a most remarkable time, the major and his family were alive again in my imagination. I resolved not to pack these wonderful people up and return them to a dusty old trunk. I decided that I would finish the major's story and share it with the world so that he and his family might live on in this book.

For the sake of simplicity and continuity, I have decided to tell the following story through the major's eyes. It was, after all, his work on the notebooks in the trunk that reached across the years and inspired me to tell his story. This meant combining Josephine and Euphemia's diaries with the notes and writings of Major McGuire. The letters and diaries that his family kept, which he read later, would allow the Major to speak as an observer of events he did not witness but would have known about based on the communication that he shared with his loved ones.

I have tried to stick to as much of the original text and vocabulary as possible. The problem that I encountered was that the style of writing in the Victorian times was very verbose and flowery, making it necessary to reword some of narratives to make them more interesting to the present-day reader. I apologize to the major for liberties I found necessary to take and to the reader for words, which although in common usage in the 1800s, might be offensive in our politically correct times. It is not possible to accurately portray the philosophies and passions of those living in the Victorian era without using some of the words, beliefs, and phrases that were common in those times. To truly understand how our predecessors lived, we must view the world through their eyes; to omit their cultural dialogue in order to cater to our current sensitivities would be like omitting the spices from cooking. Here then, in the words of Major Charles Everson McGuire, are the *Memoirs of a Confederate Gentleman*.

CHARLES

Looking back on my eighty-six years in this world, I feel a sense of wonder. Could all of those events really have happened in one man's lifetime? I remember the beautiful golden days of my youth. We measured time in hours. Now as time flies by, we measure time in years.

I was born at Grand Oak Plantation, on a sultry summer night in 1823. When the midwife told my grandfather that his daughter-in-law was carrying a boy, he insisted that the child be born at Grand Oak. Grandfather always got his way.

Grandfather had come from good solid, Scottish stock. His parents had immigrated here in 1747 after they had lost their land and titles due to political misalliances. When grandfather turned eighteen he left South Carolina and sailed to England to learn the textile and weaving trade. When his mentor died without an heir, grandfather inherited a considerable sum of money and the woolen mills he had been running. His fortune made, he returned to South Carolina in 1798. Six months later, he met and fell in love with Grandmother.

Grandmother's family had been in South Carolina and Charleston as long as there had been a South Carolina. Her Christian name was Charlotte Anne Rutledge, but the family called her Lottie. Her blood ran as blue as indigo, and her pedigree went as far back as anyone could remember.

Hoping to impress Miss Lottie's father and convince him that he was a worthy suitor, Grandfather purchased a large tract of land on the Ashley River. He bought the land from a cantankerous Scottish national known as Robbie McGregor. It was rumored that there was some sort of deception and a lot of alcohol involved in the transaction. The truth is lost to history, but the plan worked. Grandfather received Lottie's hand in marriage, and our family has called this land home for over eighty years.

The land grandfather had purchased was home to an ancient live oak known as the council oak. It was the largest tree in the state. The Indians had used it as meeting point before the white man had driven them westward. Grandfather took Miss Lottie and her chaperone on a picnic to see the site. Grandmother wrote in her diary about the first time she saw the oak.

> It was indeed the most beautiful spot I had ever seen, and the tree was certainly the grandest oak I had ever beheld. I told Charles so, and I said that I could spend forever there!" And then, Charles made me a proposition. He said, "If you will agree to marry me, I will build you a house right here in the shade of this tree, a house the likes of which Charleston County has never seen. I will build for you a house as grand as this oak!"

Grandmother went on to write that she accepted Grandfather right then and there. True to his word, Grandfather built a house the likes of which Charleston County had not seen. The plantation was called Grand Oak, after the tree. The mansion would take over three years to complete. My grandparents moved into the unfinished house in September of 1801, just in time for the birth of my father.

Grandfather liked the idea of having all of the male heirs born at the plantation. He told me stories his father had told him about our Scottish ancestors and their ancestral lands in the old country. I believe that he felt he could establish a new feudal dynasty on the shores of South Carolina. I was to be the third generation of that plan.

And so in the last month of her pregnancy, Louisa Rose Everson McGuire, her maid, two servants, the attending midwife, and my father, Thomas, sailed up the Ashley River to Grand Oak. They were met at the dock by the house servants, two of whom carried Mother up to the house in a sedan chair. Father followed with the servants from Charleston. The slaves who lived at the plantation carried the rest of the trunks up to the big house.

When mother's sister, Euphemia, found out that Grandfather had insisted that Louisa come to the country for the delivery, she was furious. Euphemia was on her honeymoon, taking the cool air in Newport, Rhode Island, when the news of what Grandfather had done reached her. She immediately packed up her belongings and her maid and sailed for Charleston, leaving her surprised husband to make apologies to their friends in Newport.

Euphemia arrived at Grand Oak one week later. She was relieved to see that Grandmother was there with Louisa and that the captain had procured a decent midwife. Grandmother explained to Euphemia that her husband was not going to let anything happen to the woman carrying his grandchild. Euphemia thought that his priorities were a little misplaced. She was indignant. She felt as though grandfather viewed her sister as nothing more than one of his breeding mares, but she held her tongue. There was nothing left to do but wait. Fortunately, the wait was not long. Everything went smoothly, and I was born in the big Charleston rice bed in the front bedroom at two o'clock in the morning on August 21.

As a child I was unaware that we lived any differently from anyone else. I thought that everybody lived in a big house with an army of servants to grant their slightest whims. I knew nothing of poverty or mistrust, nothing of hunger or fear. It seemed to me that the entire world had been created only for my pleasure and enjoyment. I was not spoiled; there were chores and responsibilities, to be sure. Grandfather made sure of that. "Children with responsibilities become responsible adults," he would say. I was well aware of my place in the order of our neat little world. Still, life held an easy grace and a beautiful symmetry; the future, it seemed, could only promise more of the same.

We lived at Grand Oak from late March until mid-May when we would leave and head back to Charleston until October. In October, we would return to Grand Oak for the harvest. We would stay in the country until January, returning to Charleston for the start of the season.

Grand Oak house may have been the largest residence on the river, but the plantation was far from the size of our neighbor's holdings. The plantation consisted of the original eight hundred and fifty acres Grandfather had purchased from Mr. McGregor and an additional five hundred and twenty-four acres Grandfather had purchased from a neighbor. This brought our total to thirteen hundred seventy-four acres. Of that, total seven hundred fifty were cleared for crops. Also on the estate was a stable that would accommodate eight mules, twenty-four of grandfather's prized horses, and a dairy barn big enough for fifteen cows.

Much of our cultivated land was devoted to cotton, sea isle cotton. Sea isle cotton was prized for its extra long fibers, which made high-quality fabric. The cotton we grew could be sold to our mills in England. In addition to cotton, we grew corn, wheat, and hay. The latter would feed the animals through the winter.

A portion of the remaining acreage was kept as pasture for the cattle, horses, and mules. Still another portion was for fruit trees and cabins for the slaves. Approximately four hundred acres were left as woodland for the hogs to root in. The immediate three acres running down to the river, on which the house sat, were Miss Lottie's to do with as she wished.

We had only fifty-five slaves—not many, compared to other plantations in our area. Grandfather had always found the "peculiar institution" rather puzzling. Truth be told, it was convenient, but the ownership of slaves was always for him more of a way to fit in. People made such a fuss about the issue. He saw little difference between slavery and the poor, oppressed workers in the factories in England and the North.

In addition to the slaves, we had seven servants who were white. These included the overseer, the stable master, one of the grooms who saw to the horses, Grandfather's valet, Miss Lottie's maid, two other maids, and our governess.

The governess, overseer, and valet were paid. Grandfather had paid the passage of the other four servants who came from England to America looking for a better life. In exchange, they worked for him until their passage and expenses were paid off. In later years, the white servants would leave to make a life of their own. They would be replaced by slaves.

Looking back, I now realize that life for our slaves, although not as difficult on our plantation as others, must have been very harsh. Most of the slaves labored in the fields under the watchful eyes of the foreman. The foreman was usually one of the field hands who had performed some task to set himself apart from the others or had distinguished himself by commanding the respect of the other hands. The foreman answered to the overseer. The overseer would be white and would have been hired by the plantation owner. He would live on the estate when the owner was absent and make sure that things ran smoothly and that the slaves stayed busy.

Of the fifty-five slaves we owned, on average, forty or so would have been considered "full hands," that is to say, fully grown but not elderly. Each had his or her specialty. The slaves who knew a trade were the most valuable and accorded the most privilege. These would be the cooper, the blacksmith, carpenters, and those who could repair a wagon or wheels and so on. Occasionally, as an additional source of income for their owners, these slaves would be rented to other plantations. On some plantations, including ours, the slaves were allowed to keep a portion of the money they earned. A slave who was lucky and very resourceful could sometimes make enough money to buy his freedom. If a slave showed no aptitude or skills and could not be trained, he became a field hand or was sold.

Several female slaves worked in the fields with the men; others did laundry, cooked, or worked in the garden that fed the family. The female slaves, when not involved in these tasks, wove sweet grass baskets or made clothing for their families. On some plantations, women also served as maids in the big house. The youngest children helped as best as they were able or they might be made to help with the livestock. Occasionally, a Negro child might be "given" to one of us younger children as a companion. Often these same slaves were trained as a valet or ladies' maid. Only the smallest offspring were excused from work. They were attended to usually by an older slave woman who was too old to work in the fields. The cooks and house servants were, of course, in another class again and frequently enjoyed many special privileges.

As spring turned into summer, we averaged thirteen hours of daylight in South Carolina. The field hands would work six days a week. They toiled under the relentless South Carolina sun from dawn till dusk. On the Sabbath, they would rest. Each morning, the workers would head out across the freshly plowed and greening fields, often without breakfast. They would carry with them a bit of food left over from the previous night's meal. This would be eaten on a brief break during mid-morning. At noon, one of the female slaves would bring dinner to the hungry workers. They would eat, drink, and perhaps rest for a short time until returning to their tasks. The slaves would break for the day, just before dusk, when the foreman rang the bell, telling them it was time to return home.

Exhausted and soaked with perspiration, the slaves would wipe the sweat from their brows and fall in line. Trudging wearily, they would form a single column, one behind the other. Sometimes, as they made their way home along the edges of the fields, they would sing as they walked.

They sang songs in Gullah, tunes so old that no one could remember their origins. The slaves would return, their bodies heavy with fatigue, to the oak-shaded alley where their six small brick cabins lined up in two neat rows. The chickens would squawk, the dogs would bark, and wives would call to husbands and children to fathers. Together, they would eat their evening meal, which would have been prepared by one of the cooks. After eating, they would gather for a while and tell stories or play a little music before turning in for the night.

Finally, the voices would grow silent. The dancing red and orange flames would fade to crackling amber and sienna embers. The breeze would rustle the leaves of the live oaks, and a chorus of night insects and frogs would lull to sleep, in the sultry spring air, both master and slave. Here in the dark, each in their own place, united by their need for rest and sleep, all were equal for a few brief hours.

In the fragile light of the dawning day, the rhythm would begin anew. We would return, each to his station and his place in our neatly ordered world. Every one of us knew exactly what the world and the coming day expected from us.

Inside the big house, each day began at seven o'clock sharp in the dining room. We would wake each morning to the smell of fresh coffee brewing. The aroma of bacon and ham would mingle with the scent of jasmine, making the air a feast for the senses. Sometimes we could hear the cook arguing with the kitchen help, their voices canceling the chatter of the birds, mingling with the tinkle of the silver and the clatter of china as the table was set.

Everyone present at Grand Oak House was expected to be at his or her place, dressed and groomed, promptly for each meal. Nobody picked up a fork or spoon until everyone had been seated. This was Grandfather's rule. If any one of us arrived late, we could expect to see Grandfather sitting at the head of the long mahogany table with his pocket watch in his hand. Grandfather's head would be bowed. He would appear to be studying his gold watch as if he expected it to speak. The family, already seated, would listen as his foot impatiently tapped the carpet beneath his chair. As we made our way to our place late, the tapping would stop. Grandfather would not raise his head from his watch, but his steel blue eyes would look up and follow us to our chairs. Once we had taken our seats, Grandfather would close his watch with a sharp click and return it to his pocket. Not a word was spoken. We knew better than to offer an explanation for our tardiness. We would be dealt with later.

Promptly, at eight fifteen, the breakfast dishes were cleared, and Grandfather would walk to the back courtyard where the groom would be standing with his favorite mount. Accompanied by my father and Hawkins, the overseer, he would tour the plantation. Grandfather would dole out advice, comment on the livestock, and make suggestions to increase the farm's productivity.

While the men were attending to the details of running the plantation, Grandmother would tend to the details of the running of the house. She would plan menus, inventory food, and delegate household tasks to the servants. Grandmother might also supervise the maintenance of the gardens and entertain any guests who might be staying at the house. The other ladies staying at the house would sew, read, or amuse themselves with a fashionable card game.

As children, our mornings were taken up with lessons. We were taught to read and write with due attention paid to arithmetic and geography. Some mornings, we were taught to dance or we acted out little plays, plays meant to teach us proper manners and conduct.

Once a month, the music teacher came from town to give us lessons. Ethne was on Grandmother's pianoforte, our brother, James, played the flute, and I studied the fiddle.

At exactly twelve noon, the plantation bell would ring. The slaves would break for an hour or so to eat and rest. Once again, we would return to the dining room, this time for dinner. Dinner would be a lighter meal than supper. Depending on the season, we might have chicken and potatoes with a rich gravy or maybe pork with yams. There would be vegetables too—okra, beans, beets, or greens. After dinner, there would be a nice pie or cake or maybe a fresh, warm cobbler.

After dinner, Grandfather would retire to his office to go over the plantation accounts or handle correspondence from the mills in England. If we were in the city, the afternoons for the ladies would be taken up by calling. In the country, one might call at the neighbors, but traditionally Grandmother caught up on the mountain of correspondence she always seemed to have.

The afternoons were ours to do with as we wished. Ethne would play with her dolls, practice her music, or learn sewing from Mother. As boys, we were always about whatever mischief we could find.

When I was ten, Grandfather gave me a Negro boy name Jawn. Jawn, two years my senior, was big for his age and showed no signs of slowing his growth any time soon. Grandfather's reason for this gift was to teach me how to manage people, but Jawn's being older meant that he could look out for me as well.

Sometimes my brother and I would play with the Murphy boys next door. We would spend hours pretending to be pirates, occasionally storming one of Ethne's tea parties and kidnapping one of her dolls for ransom. She would cry and run to Grandmother, and we would be forced to return our prisoner.

At five o'clock sharp, the bell would ring again, summoning us home to get ready for supper. We had exactly one hour to get cleaned up and changed for the evening meal, which was served promptly at six o'clock. Supper would be a much bigger meal than dinner, wine would be served, and there might be two kinds of meat, three or four vegetables, and there was always rice and at least three kinds of dessert. As young children, we did not usually eat with the adults. Sometimes, if there were no guests at the house, we were allowed to dine with the grownups. This was done to allow us the opportunity to exercise our table manners. These nights were always special. I looked forward to the day I turned thirteen and could join the adults at the table for every meal.

After the evening meal, the children usually went off to bed. The ladies would gather in Grandmother's sitting room to gossip. The men would retire to the library to enjoy their cigars and brandy. As we got older, on special nights, we might be allowed to stay up a little later. Occasionally on these nights, we would adjourn to the ballroom. Grandmother would have rows of chairs set up around the pianoforte, and Ethne would play for the adults. Often I would accompany her on the fiddle. If there were guests staying at the house who possessed musical abilities, they might also volunteer to join the entertainment.

On Sunday, the family and house servants were loaded into two carriages to travel to church. As I look back now, I think this was done more to please Grandmother, who was a devout Episcopalian, than because of Grandfather's belief in the Almighty. Grandfather believed that a man made his own destiny. Grandmother believed that grace and happiness were granted by God. She wanted to make sure that Jesus and the Reverend Goodwin knew us all by name. Once a month, on Sunday evening, after the good Reverend had made his calls, he would arrive at Grand Oak. Once there, he would walk down to the slaves' quarters and offer a brief service before returning to the big house for supper with our family.

The most memorable event of my young life was the loss of my mother. My younger brother, John, had died when I was three. I could not remember him. Mother was different. I was seven when she died, and I remember her to this day.

My mother's family hailed from Fayetteville, North Carolina. Her Scottish ancestors had settled there about the same time my great-grandfather arrived in Charleston. My maternal grandfather, Morris Everson, moved his young family to Goose Creek, South Carolina, in 1802. There he established a peach plantation known as Sycamore hill.

Morris and Nancy Everson had four children. Euphemia was the oldest, followed by her sisters Rebecca Jane and my mother, Louisa Rose, then their brother, Andre Philippe.

As they grew to adulthood, the sisters came to be known as the three graces of Sycamore Hill. It was said that among them, the three young ladies possessed beauty, compassion, and intelligence.

Mother's brother, my Uncle Philippe, was another matter. Andre Philippe was called Philippe. He was the only male heir. He was the apple of his father's eye and the joy of his doting mother. By his twenty-first birthday Philippe stood exactly six feet tall. He was well-built and, like his siblings, had thick, wavy black hair. Aunt Effie would tell my siblings and me how she and her sisters would tease him and say it was a shame to waste those indigo blue eyes and those thick, black eyelashes on a boy.

By the time I was old enough to remember anything about him, Uncle Philippe had been killed in a duel. I never knew the truth, but the people in town had gossiped for years that he had run off to Paris with a female slave of Etienne De La Croix, who was Aunt Effie's neighbor in Charleston. After his mistress died, Philippe returned to Charleston. He had with him a young girl. Before anyone learned the truth about her parentage, Philippe was dead. Aunt Effie took the girl, whom she called Lizzie, and raised her as a personal maid. They became constant companions after Uncle Henry was killed by a runaway buggy. As the girl grew to maturity our whole family couldn't help but notice the resemblance she bore to the De La Croix's former slave. This fact didn't escape the notice of the people in town for they gossiped about it for years.

On May 17, 1822, at seventeen years of age, my mother, Louisa, married into the McGuire clan of Grand Oak Plantation. My mother's sister Rebecca had married into a family named Jackson, from Savannah in the year previous. In March of 1823, Aunt Effie married Colonel Henry Albert Scott at the family estate in Goose Creek.

As I remember him, Uncle Henry was a stout, solidly built man with magnificent mutton chop whiskers and impeccable taste in suits. He always smelled of leather and peppermint. The peppermints were kept in his pockets because Euphemia didn't like the smell of the cigars of which he was so fond. Uncle Henry had fought in the War of 1812 and retired a colonel. He insisted that everyone call him Colonel until the day he died.

Because she lived so far away, mother's sister, our Aunt Rebecca, did not get the chance to visit often. Since Aunt Effie and Mother both lived in the Charleston area, they remained very close. When Aunt Effie and Uncle Henry learned that they would have no children, Aunt Effie began to spend as much time as possible with us. When my family was at the house in town, Mother and Aunt Effie would sit together in the loft and sing in the choir at Saint Michael's. Uncle Henry would sit with my grandparents, my brother James, and me in the family pew.

In November of 1829, James and I would have a new little sister. One day there was a great deal of commotion at Grand Oak. Grandmother instructed Father to take James and me out of the house and not come back until evening. As we left, the women were running around excitedly. I wanted to stay to see what was happening, but father said that the goings-on were women's business and that we must leave. "But," he promised, "when we come back, there will be a surprise for you and James."

Ethne Rebecca McGuire arrived unremarkably, as babies often do. That evening, Father bought James and me into the room where Mother lay, propped up on pillows, in the same Charleston rice bed in which we all had been born. She held in her arms a crying, red-faced, bundle of pink. We looked at Mother from across the room.

"Boys," she said, "come here and meet your new little sister."

We walked closer to the bed. The child began to cry louder.

"Are we going to keep her?" I asked.

Father laughed. "Yes, of course we are, and you and James are going to help take care of her."

James made a face. "Is she always gonna make so much noise?" he asked.

Father smiled at him. "No, son. She's just hungry, that's all. Why don't we leave your mother alone so she can feed her?"

After our sister was born, Mother was never quite herself again. She always seemed to be tired, and she didn't laugh as much. By April, she seldom left her room.

One afternoon, Father sent one of the Negroes to fetch the doctor. He came quickly. All morning, the adults kept going in and out of Mother's room. We wanted to see Mother too, but they would not let us in. Then, late in the afternoon, Aunt Effie came from her sister's room. She was crying. We could hear father shouting, "No! No!" over and over again. Aunt Effie gathered James and me close and hugged us.

"We want to see Mother, please," I requested.

"Your Mother isn't here anymore, Charles. She has gone to see the angels."

"Why didn't we see her leave?"

"Because God came, and her spirit left with him. We need you both to be big boys now. I want you to take your brother and go sit in the parlor. Your father and the rest of us will be along in just a few minutes."

Mammy appeared in the hall.

"Mammy, would you take the boys to the parlor?" she asked.

For the next three days, the adults were quiet and hushed. Mother's sisters dressed her to go away. I can still see her wearing a gown of pale lavender. Her face looked so calm and peaceful as she lay across her bed. Her hands were folded at her waist, and she held a bouquet of roses from the garden. I remember thinking that she looked as though she was only sleeping, but try as I might, I could not wake her. For three days, the neighbors and the family came to visit. As was customary in those days, they would sit with Mother in her room all through the night.

I remember thinking that if Jesus rose on the third day, perhaps Mother would too. But it was not to be. On the third day, some men arrived in the longest, fanciest coach I had ever seen.

The coach had glass sides with velvet curtains, and it was pulled by six white horses, each with white feathers on their heads. In the carriage was a long, black box that the men carried into the house and up to Mother's room.

Suddenly there was a lot of wailing and crying coming from upstairs. Our mammy took us children outside to the garden. After a while, the men came back downstairs with the box. They put it in the back of the long, black carriage. By now, the family and guest carriages had been lined up on the street behind the fancy coach. My brother, sister, and I rode in Aunt Effie and Uncle Henry's carriage. The others followed behind us. We took Mother to church for the last time.

I can still see the procession in slow motion from the church to the little stone house at the rear of the churchyard. Aunt Effie said that the angels lived there. I remember saying that it didn't seem big enough for very many angels to live in. Aunt Effie smiled and said they just stayed there when they were visiting earth; the rest of the time, they lived in heaven.

Even as I write this, I can smell the flowers that were placed all around the doors of the little stone house. I can see the long, black box sitting on a marble table at the back of the inside wall. There was a window of brightly colored glass over the table. The design had clouds parting, revealing a blue sky. A hand reached through the clouds to pick an elegant stem of white lilies. The afternoon sunlight poured through the window, illuminating the flowers in the glass and etching their image on the shiny black box beneath the window.

The smell of magnolia floated down from the branches of the trees that towered overhead. A soft muffled sobbing could be heard on the breeze. From somewhere, a mocking bird sounded a rude alarm, which seemed out of place at this somber scene. Father Goodwin was standing in the door of the angel's house. On either side of him stood two men. Father Goodwin talked for a while and ended with some kind words about Mother. He sprinkled water on the box and walked out of the little house. The two men swung shut the great iron gates, which served as doors to the mausoleum. The clang of the metal echoed through the churchyard, and everything faded to black.

That September at Grand Oak, the world seemed so different. Mother was gone. Father had no time for us. Aunt Effie was busy taking care of her sister's estate, and we just seemed to be in the way no matter what we did. The only thing that never changed was the oak on the front lawn of the big house. As children, we spent hours playing in its shade and climbing in its branches. One warm afternoon, we sat beneath the tree with Jawn and Billy and Jimmy Murphy.

"I miss Mother," said James.

"So do I," I said.

"Where is heaven, anyway?" he asked.

Billy answered him. "My mammy says it's above the clouds. She says that we hafta be good cause the people who have gone there can stand on the edges and look down at us."

"Can they see us now?" questioned James.

"I suppose they could if they were looking at us," he said.

James looked skyward; he smiled and waved. "Do you think that this tree reaches all the way to the clouds?" he asked.

"My Pa he says that the roots, they reach all the way down to the devil, and the top, it reaches way up to God and well, we is just all leaves in between. Maybe if you climb up high enough you can see them people on the clouds."

James's eyes opened wide. "Do you really think so?"

"There's only one way to find out. I'll race ya," said Jimmy.

With that, we jumped to our feet and began to climb the old oak. A little voice in the back of my head told me that this was not a good idea. We had been warned many times not to climb in the tree. That had never stopped us before, but today something seemed different. Jimmy went first, followed by James, then Billy and myself.

"Are you comin'?" called Jimmy to Jawn on the ground.

"No, sir. I is scared of heights an' besides you know you ain't s'posed to be climbin' in that there tree."

"Fraidy cat," teased Jimmy.

"I ain't no fraidy cat. I just got better sense that's all." Jawn crossed his arms and stuck out his lip. "You go on an' climb up an' tell me what you sees."

Jimmy scaled the trunk like a squirrel being chased by a hound dog. The rest of the children being smaller had a little more difficulty.

"I see somethin'," called Jimmy.

"What...what do you see?" called a chorus of voices from below.

"I don't know. I think it's a face in the clouds."

The rest of us below, myself included, accelerated their efforts to scale the tree.

That's when it happened. James, who was a few feet further up the tree than me, slipped on a clump of Spanish moss and lost his footing. He screamed as he plummeted from the tree.

As he passed me, I tried in vain to grab him. When I reached for him, I lost my balance and fell from the tree as well. We both fell to the ground.

As I fell, I hit my head hard on a branch. I saw stars, and then I seemed to be floating in slow motion through the limbs of the tree. Just for a moment, I saw Mother's face in the clouds; she was dressed all in white. She smiled at me. Then she was gone.

Jawn scooped James up and ran, carrying him like a rag doll, back to the gallery of the big house. He took the steps two at a time as he screamed for the adults. Father came running, followed by Grandfather, Grandmother, and the house servants. Jawn told our Grandfather what had happened.

The next thing I remember I was laying on my back on the floor of the veranda. I could see blurry faces all looking down at me as if from a great distance, and there were voices. They seemed to be calling words I could not understand. My head hurt. There was something cool and wet on my forehead. Slowly, I realized that the voices were calling my name. I began to recognize the faces of my family. I blinked and coughed. Grandmother was sitting on the veranda floor, holding my head in her lap. She grabbed me and hugged me to her. She rocked back and forth. "He's okay. He's okay," she kept repeating.

As I returned to consciousness, the focus shifted from me to James. Grandmother's maid had come running to help when she heard the commotion. "He's still not moving, and he is awfully pale," she said.

Father yelled at one of the slaves who had come to the edge of the porch, "Run, boy, run. Go hook up one of the wagons. We'll take him back to town."

Grandfather grabbed Father by the arm, "Use your head, son. We can't bump the boy all over the countryside in a wagon. His bones got enough of a rattling falling out of that tree. Saddle up a horse and get to Doc Taylor's as fast as you can. Bring him back here."

Within minutes, with pounding hoofs and a cloud of dust, Father was off down the long tree-lined drive. He returned that night, well after dark, with the doctor. I still could not sit upright without feeling nauseous, but the doctor said this would pass. I just had a mild concussion. The family watched all night and into the morning over my brother, James. It looked for a time as if he would rally, but in midmorning, the doctor walked out onto the gallery. His weather-lined face was tired; his shirt sleeves were rolled up to his elbows. He shook his head slowly and ran his fingers through his shock of gray hair. He said, "I'm sorry."

Grandmother began to cry and buried her face in the folds of her husband's jacket. He stroked her head absently, and his eyes welled with tears. Father ran into the house and up the stairs; his boots sounded like thunder on the steps as he took them two at a time. After about twenty minutes, he emerged from upstairs. He violently stormed from the house, shoving anyone or anything in his way. With broad, purposeful steps, he headed in the direction of the tool shed. Emerging moments later, he held in his hand an axe. He headed for the old oak. The tree had taken his son; Father would have his revenge. On the porch, the adults watched, transfixed, as he began to swing at the tree like a mad man. With deft strong strokes, he hit the tree again and again. Chunks of wood and bark began to fly. For a moment, it looked as though he would actually succeed in cutting down the ancient tree.

"Charles, do something," begged Grandmother.

"Leave him be, Lottie," said Grandfather. "He can't hurt that tree. He needs to get the poison from his system. He'll tire soon enough."

With Herculean strength, Father hit the tree several more times. The mighty oak stood, unaffected by the assault. Father stepped back, wobbled a little, then, with a violence that surprised us all, threw the axe toward the river. He staggered a few steps in the direction it had flown. He turned around and dropped to his knees at the foot of the tree. He buried his face in his hands. His chest heaved, his shoulders started to shake, and he began to cry. Grandfather turned and went into the house.

We returned to Charleston. For the second time that year, we visited the stone house where the angels lived. Unable to cope with the loss of his wife and two of his sons, one week later, Father left alone for England. We wouldn't see him again until Grandfather died.

On my eighteenth birthday, Grandfather decided that I had learned everything I needed to know from the schools available in Charleston. I was sent off to England to finish my education.

Grandfather made the voyage with me. He spent the first year showing me around London and introducing me to people I would need to know. The chain of command was similar to that of the plantation. There were managers, overseers, and foremen. There was an assortment of people whose job it was to keep the management abreast of all that was happening, and then there were the workers. Grandfather taught me himself all that I would need to know to run the mills. After two years, confident that I could handle production, Grandfather began to leave me in charge when he returned to Charleston to see to affairs there.

The years I spent in England were some of the most challenging years of my life, but they were also among the most rewarding. My days were filled with studies at school, and my nights, I spent reading anything and everything I could. When I was not involved with classes, I was working at the family textile mills. I didn't realize it at the time, but I was making connections and meeting people with whom I would be involved for a lifetime.

I really came to enjoy the company of the gentlemen I was meeting in London. I knew that the ladies at home would never approve of my new acquaintances, who introduced me to fine Scotch whiskeys and good cigars. They took me to salons where folks gambled in smoke-filled backrooms till the wee hours of the morning, and women of questionable virtue entertained gentleman callers in private rooms.

My taste for good Scotch and cigars lasted me a lifetime, but I soon grew tired of the empty, meaningless dalliances in the salons. I remembered how they contributed to my Father's downfall, and I had no desire to follow in his footsteps. When I got an occasional weekend free, there were invitations to the country to take advantage of. There was always a good horse race or a hunt on the agenda.

I would often run into an old acquaintance, Josephine St. John, who was now living in London. I would frequently accompany her to events both in the city and country. Josephine was not the little boy I had met that first day at Grand Oak. She had grown into a beautiful woman. Gone were the boyish affectations of her youth. They were replaced by grace, intelligence, and a marvelous curiosity about life.

I first met Josephine Abigail St. John on a warm April afternoon when I was eleven years old. Jimmy Murphy, who was ten, and Billy his brother, who was eight, lived on the property next to ours. We were best friends. We had decided it would be a good idea to build a boat and sail from the plantation to Charleston to visit Aunt Effie. We had spent three days building our boat and believed it to be a thing of great beauty. We were extolling its virtues when a curious-looking redheaded boy appeared to tell us we had gone about the process all wrong. After a passionate exchange, we realized that he was right. Then came the real surprise: he was actually not a boy at all! He was a girl dressed as a boy. I can still see the look of shock and surprise on the faces of Billy and Jimmy as Jo took off her hat and shook out her mane of red hair.

The reason for the masquerade was simple. Josephine's father was in the import-export business. Her mother ran the family store in Charleston known as the Abby. As a child Josephine traveled with her father all over the world. One day when visiting China, a pair of superstitious brothers spied her on her father's ship. Red is the Chinese color for good luck. When the brothers saw Josephine's red hair, they thought her to be an angel. They reasoned that if they had her they would always have fair sailing, so they kidnapped her. After a frantic search and battle to get his daughter back, Josephine's father sailed straight for Charleston, where he placed his daughter in the care of her mother and returned to sea.

Josephine was willful and headstrong. She wanted no part of life on land, so she cut her hair, dressed as a boy, and stowed away on her father's ship. The ruse wasn't discovered until it was too late. Josephine's father eventually forgave her. The disguise worked, and until she was thirteen, Josephine was known by one and all as Jo.

Due to her unusual education, Josephine was different from our typical Southern women—no batting of eyes or bashful downcast glances for her. She always looked people straight in the eyes and made her feelings and opinions known.

In the drawing rooms of London, women were allowed to speak their minds. The qualities that frustrated the ladies of Charleston society made Josephine a much sought-after guest at the gathering places of the elite in London. Josephine was well traveled and always aware of the latest news and politics from both sides of the ocean. In short, Josephine was every inch a lady, but she thought like a man. When the situation called for it, she could outshoot, out-drink, and out-swear any man in Charleston or London. She was the best of both worlds. She was one of the boys but different. She was a lady. That was why I enjoyed her company so much.

Time has a way of passing much too quickly; and before I knew it, I found that I was celebrating my thirtieth birthday. I was saddled with the responsibilities of my caste and embroiled with the politics of the time. The running of the mills was easy politics were, however, a tricky river to navigate. Politics were everywhere, and everybody had an opinion. Grandmother did not allow political discussions at the supper table. She said that the arguments they caused were bad for digestion. I tried to stay out of this arena and was successful for the most part, but I would eventually get swept away in the tide of events that would necessitate my return to Charleston.

It was during a weekend outing at the country home of Lord and Lady Conway that I realized that the time was coming when I would have to return home and face changing political issues head on. The evening had started pleasantly enough. The ladies looked lovely, and the gentlemen were handsome. The dinner conversation was agreeable. The feast that had been set before us was fit for a king.

The conversation began with economics, led into the issue of slavery, and then turned to the burning question of the day: would there be war in the States, and if so, would England step in to help the South? We were all well aware of the high tariffs the Northern state legislators were placing on goods imported from Europe. The North had realized that we, in the South, were selling most of our cotton to European mills—my own family's mill included—and that in exchange, we were buying most of our goods from European manufacturers, thus ensuring a healthy commerce between us. Unfortunately, this effectively cut the Northern states out of the financial loop. In the South, our economy was prospering like never before; our cotton accounted for 57 percent of all American exports.

It was obvious to me to that the issues clouding the American political scene were a conflict of economics and individual and states' rights.

"Mr. McGuire, you are an American. Have you read Miss Stowe's book? The one about slavery in the South?" The question came from Lady Agnes. A look of expectation in shone in her large fish eyes.

"Lady Agnes, I really don't have much time to read. Running the mills keeps me quite busy," I lied.

The truth was I had read the damned little book. I realized that as a gentleman, it would not be appropriate to voice my true feelings about this obvious assassination of our Southern culture at the dinner table. I may have spent the last twelve years in England, but I was still a Southerner at heart. No slave at Grand Oak had ever been beaten, tortured, or chased by dogs, and I was not aware of any of our neighbors exercising excessive cruelty either.

The other guests would not let the matter drop. They kept up their line of questioning.

"Well, do you find that it is true? Do the slave owners really beat their slaves and chase them with dogs?" asked one of the gentlemen at the table.

"A man who would beat his slaves would be just as likely to beat his white wife and children," I said.

Everyone at the table sat back in astonishment. Surprise was written on their faces. "What do you mean, Mr. McGuire?" asked one of the dinner guests.

"All I am saying is that there are sadistic people in all walks of life. There will always be people who enjoy bullying someone who is weaker or in a position of servitude. The truth of the matter is that slaves are much too valuable to mistreat."

"I have read the book." The voice belonged to a popish little man named Harrison. His glowing red cheeks, round eyes, and voluminous whiskers made him look like a gibbon.

"I have read it also." Another guest joined the chorus. "Whether or not they are mistreated, I feel that it is despicable how Americans view their slaves as property."

More comments followed, and I listened as long as I could. Suddenly, I heard a voice say, "It is unfair to judge a people and culture after reading one book. The author clearly has her own prejudges and politics in mind. Had she bothered to spend any time among decent, God-fearing people in the South, she would have found a very different reality. Instead, she chose to write a vituperative essay filled with stereotypes and half truths."

I glanced around the supper table. All eyes had turned to me. Suddenly, I realized that the voice was mine. It was too late now to take back my words. I had lifted the lid from Pandora's Box, and the demons were flying free. I realized it didn't matter; my words were the truth. I was, after all, a South Carolinian, and these were my people who were being so harshly judged. Lady Agnes's fish eyes were blinking expectantly, and Mr. Harrison was making an odd sputtering movement with his mouth that set his simian whiskers in motion.

"I thought you had not read the book, Mr. McGuire," said Lady Agnes calmly.

"I haven't." I denied Miss Stowe a second time. I regretted the lie, but I could not legitimize this woman or her book.

"For not having read the book, you seem very well acquainted with it."

"After having read opinions in the papers and listening to the conversation here at the table, I find it is easy enough to guess at the nature of the book. Miss Stowe didn't bother to mention the living conditions of the white factory workers in New York and other Northern cities. Make no mistake, the factory owners did not give up their slaves out of virtue or a desire to give them equal rights. They were motivated by one thing—greed. They gave up their slaves because they found a constant steam of immigrants who would work twelve hours a day, six days a week, for next to nothing. If the workers complained, there was an endless line of people waiting to take their job. Slaves cost money to house, clothe, and feed. By contrast, immigrants are paid a measly wage. At the end of the day, they go home and are no longer the problem of the factory owners. With the pennies they earn, the refugees are expected to provide clothes and food for their families. They are expected to find decent housing and care for their sick and elderly. They live in the most terrible crowded slums and work from sunup till sundown six days a week. Those workers are just as bound to those menial jobs as our slaves may be to us. By contrast, our slaves are fed and clothed. We care for the old and the young alike. We give them housing and education for a trade if they show an aptitude for it."

"Well, Mr. McGuire, what reason would Ms. Stowe have to make up such a distasteful story?" questioned Lady Agnes. "Surly there must be some truth to it."

"Perhaps, Mr. McGuire, you have been away from home too long. Conceivably, things have changed in your absence," said Mr. Harrison, looking pleased with himself.

I felt my face flush. I had never had any great love for slavery. I had just always considered it a fact of life, and now here I sat, defending it. It was at this moment I began to understand the complexity of the whole issue. The constitution guaranteed us the right to decide this issue for ourselves. That damned little piece of fiction was just that! It was nothing more than an incendiary to fan the flames of war. Given time, I believe that most of us would have freed our slaves. I realized that it was time for me to return to my home and my people.

A Memorable Passage

The golden South Carolina sunshine spilled over the deck of the ship, warming my body and soul to the very core. I was home. I was suddenly overcome by the realization of how much I had missed Charleston. My native land held in her bosom the passions and secrets of all who loved her. She was a beautiful woman, dressed and corseted; she appeared unattainable. But like all women, once beyond the exterior, there was much more to be discovered. She could be charming and gracious. She could seduce a man with exotic perfumes or romance him in any tongue. She was alive with mystery and excitement, but in a moment's notice she could turn, consuming a man, using him, and discarding him.

As I stood on the bow of the ship, looking across the bustling harbor, I realized Charleston's heartbeat was my heartbeat. Her balmy morning breezes, her languid humid afternoons, and her sultry moonlit evenings ran deep within my blood. For better or worse, I shared her dreams, her secrets, her pride, and her shortcomings. I felt guilty at having left her so long; I was grateful to be home.

I shielded my eyes with my hand from the bright afternoon sun. I searched the crowd for a familiar face. During my twelve years in England, I had returned home to Charleston only once, the last time being six years ago for my sister's wedding. I was surprised to see how the city had grown during my absence. Charleston seemed to be bursting at the seams that spring of 1853. The planting was over, and my family was in town, enjoying the balmy late spring weather. I spied in the crowd a shiny, black phaeton pulled by a handsome bay. A very large Negro sat at the reigns. The driver spotted me; eagerly he snatched his hat from his head and waved it in the air excitedly.

He called out to me. "Masta Charles! Masta Charles!" It was Jawn.

I walked toward the carriage, smiling at seeing a familiar face. With one jump, Jawn was out of the coach, running eagerly in my direction.

"Jawn, good heavens, what are they feeding you? You've gotten as big as a cedar tree," I said.

He grabbed my hand and shook it enthusiastically. Jawn ginned from ear to ear.

"Yes, sir. I guess I growed a bit since you last seen me. They calls me Big Jawn now."

He grinned with pride.

"It sure is good to have you home. They is all getting ready for you back at the house. Does you need me to get your trunks?"

"No, Jawn. The ship will have them sent up to the house."

"Yes, sir, Masta Charles."

We climbed into the phaeton for the drive to Grandfather's townhouse. I glanced at the man in the seat beside me. He stood at six foot three in his bare feet, and his shoulders were as broad as a barn. His immense hands held the reigns with a surprising delicateness. He stared directly forward as he drove. After the accident with my brother, Grandfather had been impressed by the way that Jawn had conducted himself. Grandfather knew that Jawn had tried to talk us out climbing the tree, and he knew that Jawn had raced to the house with my brother in his arms to tell us what had happened. After that day, it was decided that

Jawn would be trained to serve the family in the house. Jawn took to his education seriously. I was impressed by the change in his speech. He chose his words more carefully, and his child-like enthusiasm was more controlled. There seemed to be a quiet dignity about him.

During the twenty-minute drive home, Jawn caught me up on all of the gossip in town. "Old Masta, he's been feeling kinda tired lately. The doctor, he say old Masta got to watch out for his heart. Your Gram'ma, she's been clucking at him like a mother hen. Miss Euphemia and Miss Ethne, they is all doin' well. Miss Ethne and Masta Matthew has a new baby. She was right disappointed when your pa didn't come home for the weddin'. The house has been in a state since they heard you was comin' home. Miss Euphemia, she was wantin' to throw a big party, but your Gram'ma, she said, 'No, sir. You let young Masta Charles get rested up from his trip first. And all the single ladies in town, they've been callin' on your gram'ma. I s'pose they heard you still don't got a missus yet. Miss Josephine she come home 'bout four weeks ago. She's staying with her folks here in town."

At the mention of Josephine's name, my interest piqued. So this was where she had disappeared to. I had not seen her in London for a while. I found it odd when she just disappeared without saying good-bye; I had missed her. I had called at her family's townhouse but been told she had left for a spell. No other information had been given to me. I had felt quite jilted by her unannounced departure. We arrived at our destination before I had the opportunity to question Jawn more about Josephine. He pulled back on the reigns, stopping the carriage in front of Grandfather's house. Jumping out of the phaeton, I grabbed my bag from the seat.

"Take her around back to the carriage house," I said. "I want to surprise everyone and go in through the front door."

"Yes, sir," said John. He flicked the reigns, and the phaeton disappeared down the street.

I walked up the steps and opened the old cypress door with the glass fanlight above. I stepped through the portal onto the polished wooden floor of the first level of the piazza. I stopped to look around at the sights and sounds I had missed so. Tiny Carolina wrens twittered gaily as they played hide and seek amongst the shiny emerald leaves of the gardenias planted along the railings. Grandmother's wedding vine twined gracefully up the columns of the veranda. The slightest breeze would set the dainty leaves dancing in the afternoon sunlight. They created shifting lacelike patterns on the soft coral walls of the house. The scent of gardenia mixed with magnolia and freshly cut grass as it drifted onto the piazza. A soft wind set the stiff glossy leaves of the magnolia clacking together; the sound was like a dozen tiny, leather-gloved hands clapping to welcome me home. From somewhere inside the house I heard someone playing the piano.

I opened the hallway door and made my way toward the music. I walked up the staircase to the upstairs family rooms. A loose floorboard creaked under my foot. I thought I heard a voice whisper, "Quiet." Someone giggled, and the piano stopped abruptly. I walked into the coolness of the broad hallway at the top of the stairs. I set my bag down on the carpet. Faces long forgotten stared down haughtily at me from their gold-gilt frames. Everywhere around me, polished mahogany gleamed, crystal and silver sparkled. The whole hallway was filled with fresh cut flowers. However, not a soul was on hand to greet me.

"Hello! Hello! Is anybody here?" I called out. "That's strange," I said to myself. "I thought everyone was expecting me."

I took two steps forward in the direction of the open drawing room door. Suddenly, people started popping out of doors from both sides of the hallway shouting, "Surprise!" I jumped backward. As my heart almost stopped, I uttered a phrase that a gentleman should not repeat. The piano started again, this time joined by a chorus of voices singing "For He's a Jolly Good Fellow." I turned the color of the roses on the table and hoped that my oath had been obscured by the shouts of surprise and the music in the room.

"Welcome home, Charles. We've all missed you so." It was Aunt Effie. With a rustle of silk, she was at my side, followed by Ethne and Josephine.

I wanted to ask Josephine why she had departed so hastily from London, but now was not the time.

I bent to kiss her outstretched hand.

She smiled and said, "I see you finally found me."

Before I could answer, Grandmother made herself heard above the din.

"Let me through. Let me through." Grandmother pushed through the crowd, using her walking stick. "Let me get a good look at you, Charles. I thought we had lost you to England for good."

Grandmother's hair had turned completely white, but she still had that mischievous twinkle in her blue eyes. Charlotte Rutledge seemed shorter than I remembered, perhaps because I had grown since I had last seen her. I now stood exactly six feet tall in my bare feet. I had inherited my father's height and broad shoulders. My strawberry hair and red beard came from my grandfather, but my eyes were Rutledge blue.

"It would appear that England has agreed with you," said Grandmother, nodding her approval. "How handsome and tall you have become. I like the beard; it makes you look distinguished."

I felt a little embarrassed by all of the attention, but the feeling faded as I looked around the hallway at the smiling faces of all of the people I loved assembled in one room. They had come to welcome me home.

I bent and kissed my Grandmother. "Where is the captain?" I asked. The family had taken to calling grandfather Captain ever since he took over running the fleet of ships that he owned.

"He is waiting for you in the parlor," answered Grandmother "He doesn't get around as well these days. We try not to excite him."

Grandmother handed her cane to Ethne and took me by the arm. Together we walked into the parlor. I looked around the room, remembering all of the moments we had shared here. Things had not changed in my absence. The royal blue rugs with their circles of gold stars that I had played on as a child still looked plush and welcoming. The windows with their white casements were crowned with blue damask drapes, lined in gold chintz, and decorated with gold silk tassels. They stood open to welcome the afternoon breeze. Grandmother's French Empire furniture, upholstered in azure damask with gold bees, was tastefully arranged about the room. Bouquets of Mother's famous roses had been brought from Grand Oak for the occasion; the fragrant blossoms spilled over the tops of porcelain bowls and vases, melting into pools of rich color as they flowed over rosewood tabletops. The late afternoon sun shone through the high, open windows and caught the prisms of the chandelier. The effect of the sunlight in the crystal was pleasing; it set little rainbows dancing around the room.

Grandfather sat in a chair in front of the open window at the end of the room. With a great deal of effort and the assistance of his valet, Cuff, he stood as Grandmother and I walked across the room to him. He was, as always, meticulously dressed. His hair and beard, now the color of an angry November sky, were neatly groomed. His green frockcoat with its black velvet collar seemed out of place with all of the blue surrounding him. Grandfather, too, seemed shorter than I remembered. He had once seemed to me as tall and as straight as a Palmetto tree. His posture was not quite so erect, and the fire seemed gone from his eyes, but he was still an impressive man. Grandfather had never been one to show his emotions, but he smiled as I walked over to him. I could see the pride shine in his eyes as he squared his shoulders and set his jaw to greet me.

"Charles, our prodigal son has returned to us," said Grandmother.

I extended my hand to my grandfather. The room behind me began to fill with people spilling in from the hallway. Grandfather reached out both of his weathered hands and took my hand in his. He looked me in the eyes and said, "Welcome home, son. Welcome home." He pulled me close and patted my back. Had it been any other man in the world, I would have thought that the little flash of light I saw in his eye was a tear, but knowing my grandfather's pride, I was sure that it was just one of the little dancing rainbows from the sunlight in the chandelier.

I spent the next few weeks visiting and catching up on all of the things I had missed during my absence.

With the admission of California, our newest state to the Union, our country now stretched from the Atlantic to the Pacific.

Franklin Pierce was our president. When he took the oath of office, he promised a new era of peace and prosperity.

I became fast friends with Ethne's husband. He was a gentleman from a good family. He owned a successful law practice in town.

Aunt Effie and Lizzie were still battling. They argued like an old married couple. Lizzie had grown into a striking woman. If her parentage was to be believed, she had inherited her mother's high cheekbones and black curly hair. She was high-spirited and somewhat flighty, but she was good company for Aunt Effie.

The Abby, the St. John's family store, was doing well. Captain St. John no longer traveled. He spent his mornings at the store, spinning yarns about his travels to anyone who would listen. Mrs. St. John would tire of him underfoot; she felt he was annoying the customers. She would often send him on some manufactured errand in the afternoons just so that she could enjoy a little peace and quiet.

Bashiere, the loyal St. John family slave, was still at his post in the shop, a little grayer, a little slower, and maybe a little hard of hearing, but he still stood guard over the St. John domain.

I paid a call on Miss Josephine and her parents. Josephine and I renewed our friendship and soon set tongues wagging as we began the round of parties, teas, and social events that occupied those last happy days of peace and plenty that President Pierce had promised.

As the oppressive humid summer melted on, the city, although at a slower pace, went about business as usual. Grandfather's health did not allow him to travel, so we stayed at the house in town. Aunt Effie and Lizzie had gone north to escape the heat. Ethne and her new husband were in Virginia, visiting her husband's relatives and enjoying the cooler inland air. Josephine had stayed in town with her parents, and many of the neighbors were off to parts cooler then the steamy city.

One particularly hot August afternoon, Grandmother and I sat on the piazza, hoping for a breeze from the river. Except for the ever-present servants and slaves, we were alone at the house with Grandfather.

Grandmother sat slowly rocking in her chair. Dressed only in a simple cotton wrapper, she had worn little velvet slippers out onto the piazza. She had taken them off, and they now rested on the floor beside her chair. She wore no stays under her wrapper or no stockings on her now bare feet. I too had cast off my shoes. I kept her company, wearing only my trousers and shirtsleeves. It was too hot for a tie and vest. This degree of informality would have been unthinkable during the season or in front of anyone not family, but in the heat of the summer, behind closed veranda doors, the neighbors, who had not left the city for cooler climates minded their "South side" manners and pretended not to notice.

Grandmother sat languidly fanning herself with a palmetto leaf fan one of the Negroes had woven. "I do believe it is hotter then the door hinges of hell," she drawled.

I chuckled and dabbed the perspiration from my forehead with my handkerchief. "I think I had forgotten just how hot it can get here in the summer," I agreed.

"You have been spoiled by those mild English summers, Charles," scolded Grandmother. "You must remember you are a Southerner. This humid weather puts fire in our blood. It is what makes us passionate and strong. The English are mild and complacent like their weather."

Before I could respond, a young Negro girl stepped onto the veranda. She carried a silver tray on which sat a pitcher of lemon water and two crystal glasses. She sat the tray down on the table between the wicker chairs in which we sat.

"Does you want anythin' else, ma'am?" she asked.

"No, Hannah," said Grandmother.

The girl bowed and retreated into the house.

"There is a good example of a people made stronger by the heat. It doesn't seem to bother them at all. They just keep right on going, no matter how hot it gets. Why they even—"

Suddenly, from inside the house, the sound of breaking glass and a dull thud interrupted Grandmother. I heard poor Hannah, who had only moments before brought us the lemon water, scream. I sprang from my chair and ran toward the sound, which had come from the library.

I pushed the girl aside and ran into the room. There, face down on the polished cypress floor, lay Grandfather. On one side of him, now in pieces, lay one of grandmother's French ceramic urns. At his head lay two shattered glasses and a decanter of Bourbon that had come to rest on its side. The open decanter lay bleeding its contents onto the floor. I rushed to Grandfather's side and turned him over. His face was deathly white, and his eyes looked empty.

I shook him slightly. "Grandpa, Grandpa, are you all right?" I cried. No response. I looked up to see Grandmother standing in the door, her hand over her mouth, Hannah stood beside her with her face buried in Grandmother's shoulder.

"Hannah!" My voice cracked like a whip. The girl looked as though she had been hit. She stared at me with startled eyes. "Run, quickly! Find Cuff," I ordered. "Tell him to fetch Dr. Hitchens as quickly as possible. Tell him to tell the doctor I think its Grandfather's heart. Hurry!" She disappeared into the hallway.

Grandmother rushed over to where I sat on the floor with Grandfather's head in my lap. She sat on the floor beside me and stroked his head, "Charles…Charles," she cried. "Come back to me, Charles."

Grandfather seemed to rally at the sound of his wife's voice. He smiled at her and muttered something unintelligible. The smile left his face, and his expression turned to one of pain.

I have no idea how long we sat on the floor there in the library. It seemed like an eternity until Cuff brought Dr. Hitchens up the stairs to where we sat keeping Grandfather company.

"I'm sorry, Mrs. McGuire. Don't worry. I'm here," he said to Grandmother.

To me, he said, "Why don't you take your grandmother into the next room while I examine the captain?"

When Dr. Hitchens finally joined us in the parlor, the news was not good.

Since I was the only male in the room, the doctor addressed me first. "Mr. McGuire," he said, "may I see you in the hall?"

Grandmother stood up. She drew her five-foot-three frame to its full height. Looking up to the doctor's spectacled eyes, she said, "Whatever you have to say about my husband, Dr. Hitchens, you may say in front of me."

"I beg your pardon," said the doctor. He paused. "I am afraid you were right. It is the captain's heart."

Grandmother dropped into the chair beside her.

"Are you all right?" I asked.

Grandmother nodded yes. To the doctor, she said, "Pray continue."

"The captain has had a stroke. I cannot tell how bad it is. Considering his age and his health, there is not much we can do but wait and see. I am afraid all we can do is take him to his room and put him in his bed. I would not want to move him any farther. The first few hours after a stroke are critical."

Grandmother sat nervously playing with her hands as we listened to the doctor. I wasn't sure if she was hearing what Dr. Hitchens was saying. The doctor stopped talking, and for a moment, the room was eerily silent. Then Grandmother looked up at me and said, "You know, those urns were a wedding gift from my mother and father. I don't know how I will explain that we broke one." The doctor and I looked at each other.

"Mrs. McGuire," he said. "Do you understand? The captain may not recover."

"Of course I understand you." Grandmother snapped. "The captain will be fine. He has been through tougher things than this. He just needs rest, that's all."

Not wanting to upset her with the seriousness of Grandfather's condition, the doctor said, "Perhaps you are right, Mrs.

McGuire. Rest would be beneficial right now. Why don't you let Charles and me see to the captain? I assure you that we will do all that we can. It has been a difficult morning for both of you, and this heat certainly takes its toll. Perhaps you should rest as well."

Grandmother's tone softened. "Yes, I am feeling tired. Charles, will you find Hannah, please? I think I will to go to my room and lie down."

"Certainly," I said. I went into the hallway. I called to Hannah. She came and took Grandmother by the hand and led her to her room.

Once they had left the parlor, the doctor turned to me and said, "I will leave a little laudanum for Mrs. McGuire; it will calm her nerves. But there is not much I can do for the captain. Keep him as cool as you are able, give him lots of liquids, and watch him day and night. We will have to wait and see. I am afraid he is in God's hands." I thanked the doctor and showed him to the door.

That evening, a powerful summer thunderstorm brought relief from the oppressive heat. Grandfather survived the night. The next day, I sent word to my sister and her husband and to Aunt Effie. I suggested that they might wish to come home. I also wrote to my father in England, though I had no idea if he would return; he had not spoken to his father since he had cut him from the family business. That had been over twenty years.

Over the next few weeks, Grandmother never left the captain's side. She made sure that the servants constantly brought cool towels for his forehead and water to fill the pitcher by his bed. She would hold his hand as Cuff trimmed his beard and combed his hair. She would whisper to him, asking if he remembered secrets from their past. After about a week, Grandfather seemed to improve a little. He could sit up in bed, and he recognized the voices of people who were speaking to him. He could eat if fed, but he had trouble holding a fork by himself. By mid-September, his speech could be understood by a few close family members, and he was able to sit by himself in a chair on the piazza.

He kept repeating, "Take me home, Lottie. I want to go home."

Grandmother would hold his hand and stroke his wavy hair. She would tell him, "Charles, you are home."

The captain would look around a little confused and say, "No, I want to go to our home."

We soon came to realize that he meant Grand Oak. The doctor said that we should not move him, but the captain grew more and more insistent with each passing day.

We decided that it was probably best for his soul to take him back to his beloved home in the country. It would be better not to bounce him over the rough roads to Grand Oak, so we loaded him and the family onto a barge and sailed up the Ashley to the plantation.

Our trip was uneventful. For three weeks, Grandfather seemed as happy as his health would permit, but on October 21, 1853, at four o'clock in the afternoon, we lost him.

Grandfather had built a beautiful mausoleum in the churchyard at Saint Michael's. He had intended to have the entire family buried there when their time came. My mother and brother were already entombed there. A few days before his death, he had made Grandmother promise not to take him from Grand Oak when he died.

"Do you remember the day under the oak that you said you could spend forever here?" he whispered in a soft voice.

Grandmother held his hand. She pressed it to her lips and kissed it gently.

"Yes, Charles. I remember," she smiled.

Grandfather smiled back. He squeezed his wife's hand.

"I know how much you wanted to be in town with the family, but I can't leave here. Couldn't we be here together forever?" he begged.

Grandmother smiled. She didn't even have to think about her reply. "Of course, Charles. Anything your heart desires."

One week later, we laid Grandfather to rest at Grand Oak in the cedar grove by a shallow, peaceful stream that flowed to the Ashley.

Father arrived at the great house two days after we buried Grandfather. I must admit I was surprised to see him. He looked sober and clean, but he was painfully thin. His hair had receded, and his gray eyes wore a look as though there was nothing left for the world to show him. Grandmother wept when she saw him. I think that she thought he would stay, but even after all of the years since the death of my mother and brother, the memories were still too much for him to bear.

Even if he had considered staying, the reading of the will crushed any hope of his remaining in Charleston. When Grandfather had cut him from his life, he made the break clean and permanent. Grandfather left everything to me, everything except the townhouse in Charleston, which he left to Grandmother. I found his choice curious, for Grand Oak had been built for Grandmother. Perhaps he felt that the overseeing of the plantation would be too much of a burden to her. In any case, Grand Oak, the slaves, the mills in England, and the other family holdings were now my responsibility.

A Hasty Departure

Now that the future on Grand Oak was in my hands, I would need to inventory the condition of the house, outbuildings, barns, and the slave quarters to decide what they needed to bring them up to date

The barn and stables were in good hands, as were Grandfather's prized horses. I knew the stable master from my days in England. He had come to work for Grandfather ten years ago. His knowledge and experience proved very valuable to me.

The overseer, who would have been in charge of the slaves and the general running of the property, I knew very little about. I did know that he was an Irish Yankee named Clarence Henderson. Henderson had come to New York City as a small child from County Cork, Ireland. He was a smallish simian man, bowl legged and hirsute. His grammar betrayed him as working class, and he spoke with an annoying accent that was a mixture of lower class Irish and New York slang. He was the result of the union of an Irish Catholic mother who had little time for him and a Protestant father who used the boy as his personal punching bag. Like his constantly battling parents, he was always at war with himself, struggling with self-respect issues and a good man's ruination—in his case, whiskey. He had only been the overseer at Grand Oak for five years.

I suppose Grandfather had hired him out of pity, probably planning on trying to help him become a better person through constant supervision and honest labor. The plan was destined to fail. As Grandfather had gotten more and more ill, he had made fewer trips to the plantation, leaving Henderson to run things as he pleased.

I knew that Henderson was not well liked in town. Rumor had it that he had a cruel, sadistic streak, especially when he drank, which apparently was often. I had heard that he was not above taking a strap to anyone man, woman, or child who had displeased him. During these punishments, he would make the other slaves stand and watch as a deterrent to any future acts of disobedience. He also had a habit of entering the price of the crop he delivered to market incorrectly into the books and pocketing the difference.

I could not turn to the ladies for an accurate opinion of the man, as they would not have bothered with business matters. With the exception of Big Jawn, I could not talk to the house servants; they looked down on the field-hand class and did not interact with them. I was sure that they knew all of the plantation gossip, but they were too proud to admit it. I could not turn to the field hands because they were too afraid to talk honestly to me for fear of reprisals in my absence. I needed to find out for myself what kind of man Henderson was and if I could trust him when I was away from the plantation.

Henderson arrived at the back door of the house on a lazy Sunday autumn afternoon. Together we rode down to the slave village. The slave's cabins sat a good piece downwind from the main house. I had been discouraged from visiting the cabins when I was a child, but that had never stopped me or my siblings.

Under the paternal embrace of an ancient live oak sat the first of a dozen or so buildings that made up the slave village.

The first building we passed was one story high and made of brick. It had an A-frame tile roof and measured approximately twenty-five feet by twenty-six feet. The building was used by the blacksmith and his family. Another building of similar size and construction stood across from it. That building was home to the cooper, who also repaired the wooden carts and such. Nearby stood a smaller structure, also of brick, for storage.

The six brick and timber cabins that were home to the field hands squatted on the crude ground beneath heavy tiled roofs. There was no grass around the cabins; the grass had been worn away long ago by the trampling of many feet scurrying from here to there.

Every night before the slaves retired, they would sweep the cabins clean and then sweep the yard around the cabins. The women would make neat, straight lines in the sandy dust surrounding the cabins. This was an old African custom. It was traditional to sweep away the evil spirits and bad luck so that slaves wouldn't be bothered as they slept. I suspect the real reason for doing this came with them from Africa. It was so that they could tell if there had been any visitors during the night. Visitors weren't always human. Sometimes snakes or alligators would search for food around the cabins or chicken coops.

The cabins appeared to be anchored to the dry, dusty dirt by tall chimneys that spewed plumes of slate colored smoke. The smoke rose skyward. It danced among great columns of Spanish moss and oak leaves before unraveling into the afternoon haze. Just behind or to the side of each cabin was a garden where the slaves grew vegetables and herbs for their medicines.

A whirring dervish of laughing children, squawking chickens, and barking dogs swirled about the dwellings like leaves spun by a wind-devil. In the shade of one of the great oaks, a group of older women sat in a circle weaving baskets of sweet grass and pine needles. In front of two of the cabins, the male slaves, dressed in their Sunday clothes, sat at small tables as their women attended to them. Most of the men wore homespun shirts buttoned to the neck. A few wore shirts of calico or prints. Some of the older men wore sack coats over their shirts. They also wore heavy cloth trousers of dull brown; most were without belts or shoes.

A pair of bright carmine-red suspenders held up the pants of one man, a slave known as Eustis. The suspenders had been a gift from Old Master one Christmas. They were a reward to Eustis, whose keen eyesight and quick thinking saved one of the other slaves from being attacked by an alligator in one of the irrigation ditches where he had been working. Any item colored red was especially valuable to the slaves. Red was a sign of wealth, importance, or both.

The women wore brightly colored cotton fabric on their heads wrapped like burnooses. Their dresses were made of calico or stripes and checks. I suspected some of them had been made from old dresses the ladies in the big house had discarded and given to them to remake for their use.

The children were dressed in an assortment of ill-fitting garments the same color as the sepia dust that surrounded the cabins.

We dismounted our horses and walked toward the dwellings. The men stood, and the women who were not already outside came to the doors of the cabins. The children ran to their parents' sides. They blinked at us with owl-like eyes from behind their mother's skirts.

Without the agitation of the children, the dust cloud, with its chickens and dogs, ballooned slowly to the ground. A warm breeze stirred the leaves in the trees. The moss-laden branches waved us closer. After years of seeing the milk-white complexions of the factory workers in England looking up to me as I inspected the daily progress in the mills, I was struck by the contrast of these ebony faces with their dark eyes and rows of perfect ivory teeth. I will never forget the look in their eyes as they stared expectantly at me.

I was the third generation of owners of Grand Oak. I recognized many of the men and women; they were older and weathered from years of working in the fields. I was looking at the faces of four generations of Africans, many of whom had been born on the plantation. I felt a little guilty that I could not recall most of their names. There was fear, but there was also uncertainty mixed with hope and just a little bit of defiance in their eyes. The slaves lived with the constant fear that after the death of their master, the new master may not be able to afford to keep them all or may simply not like a slave, and they would be sold away from their families.

Suddenly there was recognition. A murmur went through the crowd, "It's L'il Massa. It's L'il Massa."

At first, I did not understand what they meant. Then it dawned on me. I had to chuckle to myself. The slaves had always referred to Grandfather as Old Master and to my father as Young Master. I was, therefore, by default, called Little Master.

"You all quiet down now. Show some respect," barked Henderson. He had been in the South for nearly nine years, but he still had no knowledge of our idioms. He did not see the name they called me for the term of affection and recognition that it was.

I walked into the midst of the crowd assembled. I said, "I am sure that by now you are aware that Old Master is gone. I will be taking over the running of the plantation. I would like you to address me in the future as Master Charles. I want to assure you that all of you have a home here at Grand Oak; none of you will be sold. I have come this afternoon to inspect your cabins and to make sure that they are in good repair. If any of you are being mistreated or have any problems, I want to give you a chance to address them now."

The assembled slaves remained quiet, some of them meeting my gaze, others looking at the dry, dusty earth beneath their feet.

"They don't got nothin' to say. They ain't no problems here," said Henderson as he scowled at them from beneath bushy brown eyebrows that grew together in the center, giving the appearance of a furry caterpillar resting on his brow. He spat at the ground. "Ain't that right?"

There came no response from the slaves. "I said ain't that right?" repeated Henderson.

A few mumbled "Yes, sirs," came from the slaves. I realized that it was pointless to question them in front of Henderson.

"I want to see the inside of the cabins," I said to the overseer.

"Don't know why you'd wanna see 'em. Ain't much to see," he replied.

"Nevertheless, I want to see them," I said.

We walked to the cabin closest to us followed by the slaves who lived there. The women in the doorway parted to let us enter.

As many as ten or as few as seven people lived in one cabin. Each dwelling consisted of one large room measuring twenty-one feet by eighteen feet.

One entered the cabin by a wooden door flanked by a window on either side. In addition, there were two windows on the right side but none on the rear or the left side of the cabin. There was no glass at the windows. They closed with wooden shutters painted with the same brick red as the doors.

The floor was wood laid over hard packed dirt. On the floor was a rug woven out of marsh grass and reeds. The simple design in the weaving was surprisingly beautiful.

In the center of the back wall was a large brick fireplace used for heat in the winter and cooking all year round. A large iron skillet and a couple of rusty pans for fixing food hung from iron hooks beside the hearth. Nearby stood a broom made of sticks and grass with a handle so crooked I couldn't see how it could work.

To the right of the fireplace was a sturdy wooden ladder that gave access to a loft where the children slept. I climbed the ladder and peered into the loft. There were no feather ticks or woolen blankets to sleep on, only crude bags of cloth filled with straw and heavy burlap bags opened to make a crude kind of blanket.

My curiosity sated, I descended the ladder and continued my inspection of the main level. In the center of the room sat a square wooden table and six unmatched chairs; these could be moved outside in nice weather. On the left side was an old wooden bed with a straw tick. A surprisingly beautiful quilt covered the bed. I walked over and examined it more closely.

An elderly woman at the door called out to me, "I made that there quilt out of old clothes that the missus sends out from the big house," she said.

I could tell by the concern in her voice that she was afraid that I might accuse her of stealing the fabric. I wondered how often these people might have been falsely accused of taking things. "It's beautiful," I said. "What is your name?"

"Sarah." answered the woman.

"Sarah, like in the Bible?" I asked.

"Yes, sir." She grinned at me.

"Where did you learn to sew like this?"

"My momma. She done teached me. When the missus from the big house, she see how I sews she teach me some more. After a spell, I do sewin' for the whole family. They lets me keep the fabric what's left over."

"Well, it's very beautiful. You should be very proud of yourself," I said.

I continued my inspection of the cabin. I found an old barrel in the front corner. A pipe ran into it from the roof, providing fresh water inside. I smiled to myself at their industriousness. There was also a loom and an ancient spinning wheel.

I inspected each of the other cabins. Except for the loom and the spinning wheel, their contents varied little from cabin to cabin. I questioned the slaves about what they ate. I was told that they fed themselves from their garden in season, and they had fish from the river and whatever game they could hunt out on the estate.

When I asked about rice and flour, I was met with silence. I knew that a quantity of these materials was set aside to be distributed to the slaves, and, as I suspected, apparently Henderson was not giving it to them. This I resolved to deal with later.

With my tour of the slave quarters complete, I dismissed Henderson and rode back to the big house by myself.

I spent the next few days thinking about the slaves. They seemed to be neither happy nor unhappy, only resigned to their place. Surely there were many white men, women, and children in the cities who lived in overcrowded slums enduring conditions far worse than our slaves. The factory workers were just as much slaves to their menial tasks, working as many, if not more, hours than our Negroes. They could no more escape their circumstance than could these people here at Grand Oak.

Grandfather's words suddenly rang very true to me. "Whether slave or free, black or white, there will always be poor among us. To those of us who are born with much falls the responsibility for the care of those who do not have our advantages." The care of these people had been entrusted to me. I was responsible for their health and welfare.

I thought for a time perhaps I should free the slaves, but it was now illegal to free Negroes in South Carolina. They outnumbered whites two to one. There was a great fear of them rising up and attacking their former masters.

If I did release them, there was always the danger that they would be conscripted and resold into slavery. The abolitionists were crying out to free the Negroes, but no one bothered to ask the question, "What would become of them if they were suddenly freed?" We fed them, clothed them, and took care of them. They were like children. How would they take care of themselves if we suddenly turned them out on their own? No, it was better for them to remain in my care at Grand Oak.

There was also the religious issue. Many of us believed that God himself had sent the Negroes to us so that we could civilize them and introduce them to Christianity. The last issue had always made me a little uncertain; after all, that was the same as saying that God approved of slavery. Who knows? Perhaps he did. We had always treated our slaves humanely, but I was sure now that Henderson was abusing them. That was within my power to change.

I sat one evening in the library of Grand Oak. I was feeling confident that I had made the right decision about the slaves. Big Jawn came into the room to see if I needed anything.

"Evenin', Masta Charles. Would you like me to get you anythin' before you go to bed?" he asked.

"No, thank you, Big Jawn," I answered. "Jawn, I want to ask you a question."

"Yes, sir."

"Jawn, would you want to be free?"

"Free," repeated Jawn, his eyes widening.

"Yes. Would you like to be free?"

He hesitated before answering me. He scratched his head and slowly began, "Well, the way I sees it, I is already free."

"I don't understand," I said.

"Well, Masta Charles, you may own my body, but you can't never own my spirit or my heart. Can't nobody take them from me. I was borned here an' I reckons I'll die here. This here is my home, an' Old Masta, he like family to me. They ain't nowhere I'd rather be, so the way I sees it, I is already free."

"Do any of the other slaves feel this way?"

"Well, Masta Charles, I can't speak for all of 'em. But there be good and bad in all peoples. Some of them hands, they is a whole heap of worthless. You can't trust 'em outta your sight, and some of 'em, you ain't never gonna make happy. They most likely run off the first chance they gets. But most of 'em, they is proud to be here. Everybody in Charleston knows Grand Oak; she's one of the best plantations on the river, and we all owned by one of the finest families in the South." With this, Big Jawn puffed his out chest. "I expects most of us would just as soon stay here."

I was touched by the simple loyalty of this man. His logic was correct. He was just as much a part of the plantation as I was. At the end of the day, I was as bound to this place and these people as he. One day all of us, black and white, would be equal in the deep, loamy earth of the cedar grove at Grand Oak. I bid Big Jawn good night, and the next day I fired Henderson.

"After all I've done for your granddaddy, how can you treat me this way?" he whined.

"Mr. Henderson, I cannot see that you have done well by this family at all. You have mistreated the slaves. You have taken food meant to feed them, and you have sold supplies that didn't belong to you to make more money for yourself. As I see it, the plantation is better off without you."

Henderson's monkey face twisted into an expression of contempt. "Them's all lies. You can't believe them lying darkies," he said.

I felt my face redden and my fists clench, "I want you and all of your belongings off this property in two hours! Do I make myself clear?" I ordered.

"I'll be gone just as soon as I get this month's wages. I ain't leavin' till I get what's owed me," said Henderson.

"You expect money from me? You're lucky I don't have you horsewhipped like you did my slaves, or at the very least have you arrested for thievery."

"That ain't right. I told you, them's all lies."

I felt myself getting angrier by the minute. I wanted this man off my property.

"One hour…I want you out of here in one hour. Do you want to try for fifteen minutes?" I asked.

"This just ain't fair. You ain't heard the last of Clarence Henderson," he threatened.

"I'm going for my gun! If you're smart, you won't be here when I get back."

Henderson turned and mumbled something to himself. He began throwing things from the chest of drawers onto the rumpled bed in the overseer's cottage. I left him to his task. I went to the big house to get my gun. Henderson must have made a hasty departure, for when I returned one hour later, there was no sign of the disgruntled little man.

I kept watch for a few days. I expected Henderson to return and stir up mischief, but the next week stayed quiet. Confident that Henderson's threats had been empty, I went into town to find a new overseer. I stayed at Grandmother's townhouse for a fortnight. I interviewed several men to oversee the running of Grand Oak. I found one agreeable candidate, a man from Tennessee whom I felt I could trust. He was a Southerner. His father had been a slave owner. His mother was a Quaker. I felt he would be less apt to mistreat the Negroes.

Three weeks after firing Henderson, I returned to the plantation to check on things and make ready for the new overseer. He
was to meet me at the house at the start of the new week. Late
on the night I returned, I was awakened by an urgent pounding on the front door. I jumped out of bed into my trousers and
shirt and ran through the hall and down the stairs. I reached the
front door just as Big Jawn came running from the first floor of
the back of the house where he slept. He was struggling into his
shirt as he ran.

"Masta Charles, what's all the commotion?" he shouted over
the screaming and pounding.

Ignoring him, I opened the heavy oak door. One of the slave
women was crying and hollering. She fell, screaming, at my feet.

"Masta Charles! Masta Charles! He done come back he say
he goin' to kill us all. He tryin' to set the cabins on fire. He goin'
to burn them to de ground with us inside. You got to do somethin, Masta Charles."

"Who's come back?" I asked.

"The overseer…he's all liquored up, an' I ain't never seed him
so mad. He got the devil himself in him," cried the girl.

"Big Jawn, get a couple of guns from the cabinet. Hurry!" I
ordered.

In a minute, we were out the front door and running across
the lawn. As we ran in the direction of the slave quarters, I
could smell acrid smoke and see an orange glow coming from
the cabins. We reached the cooper's building to see a wagon, a
stack of barrels, and a pile of wood blazing brightly. Henderson
and his accomplice, trying to start fires, had piled hay and wood
around some of the buildings and lit them on fire. Columns of
flame sent sparks popping out in all directions as they lit the
night sky. Thick, black smoke billowed heavenward. The cabins
and outbuildings would not be easy to burn. They had been
made from brick to keep them safe from cooking fires, but the

meager furnishings and things stored in them would be easily destroyed by fire.

We found Henderson mad with rage. His pale skin was aglow with the red light of the fire. He was trying to chop through the door of one of the cabins with an axe. He was wet with sweat; his eyes were bulging. He looked like Satan himself.

He was screaming, "I know you're in there! I'm gonna kill you, all you filthy, lying darkies. You can't hide from me. Get out here now."

"Henderson!" I yelled. "Get away from that door, or so help me, I'll shoot you where you stand."

He turned to look at me. "I ain't finished yet." He snarled.

"Oh yes, you are," I answered. I raised my rifle to fire. Someone hit me from behind just as I fired. It knocked me off balance. The bullet from my gun missed Henderson and ricocheted harmlessly off the brick wall of the cabin.

I staggered for a second and then regained my balance. From close behind me, I heard an odd noise, like the sound a knife makes when stuck into a watermelon. Someone cried out in pain, and something fell to the ground.

I saw Henderson throw the axe he held in my direction. Then he grabbed the pistol from his belt and fired just to my left. Out of the corner of my eye, I saw a flash of red as something beside me hit the ground hard. Still groggy, I raised my gun. Henderson was staring directly at me, his pistol in his outstretched hand. His face was twisted into a look of hate.

"I told you, don't mess with me. Now I'll get what I got coming to me," he said.

From somewhere behind Henderson came a flash of gunpowder. Henderson's head jerked a little to one side. His body seemed to shudder. In slow motion, he steadied himself. Still dazed, I struggled to aim my rifle before he could fire. He just stood there with a queer look on his face. The color drained from his skin, and he opened his mouth as if to speak. A stream of blood began to trickle from his lips. His cold, dead eyes met mine one last time, and he fell face first with a thud into the dirt. I dropped to my knees.

Standing there, behind where Henderson had stood, was Big Jawn. He held in his hands a smoking rifle. The doors to the cabins began to open, and one of the women ran to the ground behind me. She began to scream and wail. There on the ground behind me lay two bodies. One was a rough-looking white man I did not know. Henderson must have enlisted help in town.

By his side lay another body face down in the soil. The body was wearing a white shirt and carmine-red suspenders. A group of women was gathering to help the old woman who sat crying with his head in her lap.

The slaves were able to put the flames out with buckets of water from the river. Fortunately, there had been little damage to the buildings. Big Jawn helped me back to the big house. By now, the whole house was up. I sat in the parlor with a cold cloth on the back of my head where I had been hit.

Two people, both of them slaves, saved my life that night. As I prepared to fire at Henderson, his accomplice hit me from behind. Seeing what was about to happen, Eustis snuck up behind the man and stabbed him before he could hit me dead on. As the man was stabbed, he fell sideways, only grazing my head. Henderson saw Eustis stab his friend, and so he shot him.

Poor Eustis paid for saving my life with his own. Big Jawn had snuck around the side of the cabin where Henderson stood, hoping to catch the former overseer between himself and me. When he saw Henderson aim his gun at me, he shot him.

"Masta Charles, what we gonna do 'bout them dead folks?" asked Big Jawn.

I thought for a moment. It didn't matter that Henderson had shot and killed a black man; he was white, and a slave was only property. What did matter was that Eustis, a slave, had stabbed a white man. He was dead, so he was safe from the authorities. Big Jawn was another matter. He would be charged with murder. Nobody outside of Grand Oak could know what really happened. The slaves could be trusted with the secret.

Eustis was buried the next day with his red suspenders. We laid him to rest in one of my suits in the burying ground reserved for the slaves.

I did not want Henderson or his accomplice buried on the property. They would never be missed, and where Big Jawn and those who helped him took them, I do not know. They were gone. That was all that I cared about. No one black or white ever spoke about that night again.

A Most Thoughtful Gift

In January of 1857, as the nation continued to drift apart, James Buchanan became the fifteenth president of the United States. I poured myself into the renovation of the plantation house. My sister, Ethne, had her second child, and Josephine's father, Eugene St. John, died in Charleston. His funeral, or I should say his burial, was a most curious affair.

Eugene had always wanted to be buried at sea. Since he had always been intrigued by the legends of the Norse heroes, Mrs. St. John decided that he should have a Viking burial. No amount of pleading or begging could persuade her to change her mind. Fearing the townsfolk would think her mother mad, Josephine begged her not to let anyone know her plans. No one except for Josephine, her mother, Aunt Effie, me, and the few surviving members of Eugene's crew ever knew the truth.

There was a big service in town, with lots of wailing and weeping. Nobody at the funeral suspected that the box that was buried in the burying ground of the circular, congregational church was filled with bricks. No one saw the sailors load the plain pine box onto the *Valhalla* late that afternoon. The towns-folk didn't see the wood platform and the barrels of kindling that were bought aboard the boat.

Unobserved by anyone, a small group of people dressed in black boarded the ship in the gathering dusk.

It was not long after her husband's death that Mrs. St. John decided that she wanted to return to England and what was left of her family before she died. She missed the gentle English rains and the flowers that grew in profusion throughout the countryside. Mrs. St. John closed The Abby and the house in town; then, with Bashiere, she set sail for England. To my surprise and disappointment, Josephine accompanied her mother home. It never occurred to me that I was being selfish. Mrs. St. John needed her daughter to help her settle back into her life in England. The only thought that occurred to me was who would fill the hole in my life that Josephine's departure left?

As the world around us spun out of control, we did our best to go about our daily lives. It was difficult. The rumblings of secession and pending war were everywhere. They dominated not only the newspapers, but most dinner conversation as well.

It was the opinion of everyone living in the South that England would surely come to our aid. After all, their mills couldn't function without our cotton. Their economy would certainly suffer without the South. I hadn't the heart to tell them that I did not believe that England wanted any part in our fight.

To make matters worse, we were fighting amongst ourselves. The Democrats had split, and the Whigs were destroyed. A new threat to the South had risen—the Republicans. When Republicans lost their majority in the House in 1856, every significant bill they tried to pass fell before Southern votes in the Senate or a presidential veto. The federal government, it seemed, was at war with itself. Bitter hostility between Republicans and Southern Democrats prevailed on the floor of Congress.

Things came to a head when Congressman Brooks physically attacked Senator Sumner in the Senate chambers with his cane. The attack had been in retaliation for a speech Sumner made that criticized Southerners for proslavery violence in Kansas. Sumner received a severe beating, and enthusiastic Southerners sent Congressman Brooks canes by the dozens. The world seemed to be going mad.

One balmy spring day in 1859, after a little more then a two years absence from Charleston, Josephine, like the camellia blossoms, returned without warning. I was in town seeing to some financial affairs.

We were saddened to hear that Mrs. St. John had passed.

"Mother left with the last of the flowers and the autumn leaves," Josephine said, waxing poetic. The townsfolk were curious as to why Mrs. St. John had been buried so far from her husband, but we knew the truth. "Since Father is not in the churchyard, there was really no point in bringing her back to Charleston," Josephine told us. "We had her buried with her family in Sterling Shire."

Josephine opened her family's townhouse and set up residence there. Two weeks after her return, Josephine called on Grandmother, and two days later, giggling like schoolgirls, the pair left for Grand Oak.

"Charles, be a love and give us a day or two and then join us at Grand Oak. I have a surprise for you," Josephine said.

I didn't give the matter much thought. I finished my business in town. Three days later, I sailed up the river to the plantation. I arrived to find a small Negro boy who had been stationed there to keep watch for me. An older boy of about sixteen kept him company. He sat idly kicking his feet in the cool tourmaline water of the indolent river. As our boat edged toward the dock, the younger boy stood and ran swiftly to the house calling, "Masta Charles is come home. Masta Charles is come home!" The older boy stood, hitched up his dusty tattered trousers, and absentmindedly scratched his head.

"Masta Charles, the folks at the big house done sent me to fetch your things," he said.

Big Jawn had accompanied me from Charleston. He threw an indignant look at the boy.

"You run along, boy. I'll take Masta Charles's things. They shouldn't ought to send a boy to do a man's work."

The boy ran off in the direction of the slave cabins. Big Jawn and I walked up the paths of freshly raked oyster shells. The pristine gardens and grounds glistened like Eden in the afternoon sunlight.

It was a little late for the azaleas, but the perfume of the Cherokee roses drifted across the newly cut lawn. Josephine and Grandmother made a pretty picture as they sat on the new gallery of the house.

Josephine wore a blue watered silk gown that rippled like waves on the Aegean as it fluttered in the breeze.

Grandmother wore dark blue taffeta buttoned to the neck, and a large shell cameo brooch was fastened to the crisp white collar of her gown. Her hair was pulled neatly back, and she wore a little black lace cap on her head. The cap tied with satin ribbons beneath her chin.

I felt a great swell of pride as my eyes surveyed my home. Grand Oak looked like a Greek temple surrounded by a legion of live oaks. She set on a throne of lush, green, velvet grass. The sunlight turned the new columns to alabaster and the pediment, with its fanlight in the center, shone like a beacon in the harbor of Rhoads.

Josephine and Grandmother sat at a table the servants had brought from inside. The table was covered with a linen cloth embroidered with Grandmother's fancy work. In the center sat a bowl of roses cut from the garden, accompanied by a pitcher of lemon water and an assortment of biscuits in a silver and crystal biscuit box.

Isabelle stood as erect as a statue by the column closest to the steps. She wore a white cotton wrap around her head, and her calico dress and white cotton petticoat were finely pressed and starched. Her hands were folded in front of her. Isabelle was a handsome mulatto woman. Her mixed blood was obvious in her high cheekbones and thin lips. She ran the house when Grandmother was not in residence.

A small Negro girl sat petting the head of one of the hounds on the step below where Isabelle stood. As I started up the steps to the gallery, Grandmother and Josephine stood.

Isabelle spoke first. To me, she said, "Welcome home, Masta Charles." And to Big Jawn, she said, "You is needed around the back of the house."

Big Jawn bowed his head to me and then to the ladies on the porch and walked around to the back of the house.

"Charles, we thought that you had forgotten us out here in the country," said Grandmother.

"Now how could I forget my favorite ladies?" I asked as I bent and kissed Grandmother's hand. I turned and bowed to Josephine. "Miss Josephine."

Josephine bowed her head elegantly and curtsied. "Charles."

"Now, what is this surprise that you have for me?" I questioned, rubbing my hands together expectantly.

"Why don't you sit and have a glass of lemon water first? We are not quite ready to present it to you," answered Josephine.

"Not ready for me? What in heaven's name is it?" I asked.

"Charles, you have only just arrived. You have been impatient ever since you were a child. Sit and have a chat with us for a moment. Good things are worth waiting for," scolded Grandmother.

I sat as I was instructed, and we caught up on the news of the country. After about thirty minutes, Isabelle walked onto the porch from the hallway. She bent and whispered into Josephine's ear.

Josephine looked startled. "What do you mean two of them are missing? Who is supposed to be watching them?"

Again, Isabelle bent and whispered into Josephine's ear.

"Well, tell him to go look for them."

Isabelle shook her head. She answered, not bothering to whisper this time, "Well, lookin' ain't findin' an' he say he ain't wearin' those fancy blue clothes neither."

Josephine stood, turned to us, and said, "Excuse me." She left the gallery in a flurry of cotton petticoats and blue silk. Grandmother chuckled.

"Would you mind telling me what is going on?" I asked.

"Charles, let Josephine have her fun. She has worked really hard on this, and she wants it to be just right."

"You know how I feel about surprises," I said dryly.

Grandmother's expression turned from one of amusement to one of seriousness. "You know, Charles, if you are not careful, you are going to lose that girl."

"I don't know what you're talking about."

"Don't be curt with me, Charles," scolded Grandmother. "You know very well what I mean. It is high time you declared your intentions to Josephine. Neither of you is getting any younger. If you are not interested in marriage, you should tell her so she can find someone else. She would make a good wife for someone, and she deserves to be happy."

Grandmother's comments caught me off guard. I realized I had never really thought about getting married, and I never thought Josephine would want to be with anyone else either. Grandmother was correct; it was not fair. I would have to make a decision and soon.

Josephine bounced out onto the gallery. "We are ready," she called gaily. "Follow me."

Grandmother and I rose to follow her. The look that Grandmother gave me went unnoticed by Josephine, but it froze me to the core.

We followed Josephine through the hallway to the back of the house. She stopped at the door and produced a blindfold from the folds of her dress. "Here, Charles. Let me tie this on you."

I looked helplessly in Grandmother's direction. Her look said, "Do it or else!"

Josephine tied the blindfold over my eyes and led me through the door onto the portico. I stopped when I felt the railing in front of me. I put my hands on it to steady myself.

Once I was in place, Josephine counted to three and shouted, "Ready!"

She pulled the cloth from my eyes. I blinked for a moment in the late afternoon sunlight. There in the circular grass turnabout of the driveway stood Big Jawn, at least it looked like Big Jawn. In an effort to evoke a popular painting by Gainesboro she had seen in Paris, Josephine had dressed the gentle giant in a pair of blue satin breeches with matching stockings and blue slippers that looked two sizes too small. The ruffled white cotton shirt he wore looked a little too short at the sleeves, and his blue satin waistcoat was straining at the buttons. In his right hand, he held a shepherd's crook and a straw hat with blue ribbons.

He wore a look of utter humiliation on his face. Surrounding him, enjoying the fresh green grass, were a dozen Merino sheep. The rams had blue satin ribbons tied about their necks, and the ewes had pink satin ribbons tied on their tails.

"Surprise!" shouted Josephine.

"What in the name of…What is this?" I stammered.

"They are sheep," said Josephine.

"I can see that, but what are they doing here? And what have you done to Big Jawn?"

"I have bought them from England for you. And they are not just sheep; they are merino sheep," she said, ignoring my question about my manservant.

"Josephine, they are fine animals, but I'm a cotton planter. What am I going to do with sheep?" I asked.

"Well, if the war does come and your slaves are freed, you won't have anyone to pick cotton, so I thought you would be able to switch to raising sheep for wool. It could become a whole new industry here at Grand Oak." Josephine beamed, obviously pleased with herself. I looked helplessly at Grandmother.

Grandmother took Josephine by the arm and turned to the hallway door. "My, what a thoughtful child you are, my dear. What a most clever gift. Come, let's go back to the gallery and hear all about your idea."

I turned once more to view the tableaux on the lawn. I had to admit it was funny to see Big Jawn standing there helpless in his blue livery surrounded by a flock of ribbon-bedecked sheep.

Isabelle snickered from the doorway, and I waved Big Jawn off as I followed the ladies back through the house. Life around Josephine was never dull. Grandmother was right. Perhaps I should reevaluate our relationship.

THE HOURS BEFORE SUNSET

The "summer of the sheep," as it came to be known, was the next to the last of our summers of simple innocence. A little over a year later, on a mild November day in 1860, the family, Josephine, Mrs. Humphries, myself, and a couple of the neighbors were enjoying a luncheon hosted by Aunt Effie at her townhouse. Ethne was there, but her husband had been detained at his office.

The meal was pleasant, the conversation delightful (for once it did not revolve around the inevitability of war), and everyone seemed to be in a most gay mood. Suddenly there came from the entrance hall a great commotion. We heard someone running up the stairs and down the hall into the dining room where we sat. Ethne's husband, Matthew, quite out of breath and still wearing his hat, burst excitedly into the room.

He looked as though he had run all the way from his office. He was ringing his hands and shouting, "They've done it. They've actually gone and done it."

Aunt Effie rose from her seat at the head of the table, "Mr. Sullivan, there are ladies present. Please remove your hat and lower your voice."

Ethne's husband removed his hat; still excited he said, "But, Mrs. Scott, you don't understand they've gone and done it."

"Who has done what?"

"The ignorant Yankees and the Republicans, that's who; they've gone and elected Abe Lincoln president! This will mean war for sure."

Everyone at the table turned ashen as they looked to each other.

The national Democratic Party had split three ways in April. Northern Democrats had chosen Steven Douglass of Illinois as their candidate. The Constitutional Unionists ran John Bell of Tennessee, and the Southern Democrats had chosen John C. Breckenridge of Kentucky. The Republicans nominated Abraham Lincoln of Illinois. Lincoln had carried no Southern state but won the election in the Electoral College.

Aunt Effie sank back into her chair. She shook her head sadly. "Well, if you're going to stir the pot, you may as well use a big spoon!" she said.

"I suppose it is all right to use a big spoon, but couldn't they at least have found a more attractive one?" quipped Josephine.

The room broke into nervous laughter. Excited conversation followed as everyone shouted to make their questions to Matthew heard.

From there, our peaceful, graceful, sensible, world began to unravel. The die was cast on December 20, 1860, at Institute Hall in Charleston, just six weeks after the election of Lincoln to the presidency.

I will never forget the excitement and exhilaration on the day of the secession convention. The convention had begun on December 17 in the state capital in Columbia, but an outbreak of smallpox necessitated adjourning and relocating the convention to Charleston. The delegates arrived in Charleston at the Line Street station by train.

Everyone from the mayor to the heads of city government and members of the founding families (myself included) were on hand to greet them. A huge parade had been organized.

People came from everywhere. They lined the streets to watch the bands, militia companies, and volunteer fire brigades, and to cheer the delegates as they made their way to Institute Hall. Once inside the hall, speeches were made, opinions pro and con were heard, and committees were formed. Most important among these was the committee to which was entrusted drafting an ordinance of secession from the Federal Union. The committee was composed of the best-known and most passionate citizens of South Carolina.

Eventually the delegates retired to St. Andrew's Hall on Broad Street, where the resolution to secede passed unanimously 170 to 0.

Once the resolution passed, it was decided the signing should take place at a more grandiose location. Another parade accompanied the delegation back to Institute Hall for the actual signing. At 1:15 p.m., the first of 170 delegates signed the ordinance of secession. Two hours later, as the last of the delegates signed the paper, the deed was done.

As the ordinance was read, the crowd burst into pandemonium. Women cried and waved their handkerchiefs. Men slapped each other on their backs; some tossed their hats high into the air. It took several minutes for the din to wear down.

As I stood in the crowd and watched the maelstrom around me, I wondered if this was what that brave band of men had felt like so many years before when they had signed the Declaration of Independence, severing our ties to England. Somewhere in the back of my head, a small voice said, *What have we done?* All I could think of was the familiar quote: "We must all hang together (now) or we shall all hang separately."

By the time I walked outside, thousands of witnesses and the delegates were crowding the streets. *The Charleston Mercury* had already published its most famous headline ever: "The Union is dissolved!" Aunt Effie (and most of Charleston) kept that paper the rest of her life.

Two days later, Aunt Effie held the first "Secession Ball" in Charleston at her house in town.

One blustery February morning, there was a knock at the door of Grandmother's townhouse. A few moments later, Cuff came into the library where I sat reading the morning paper.

"Masta Charles, your Aunt Effie's man Isaac, he's downstairs. He said to give you this here letter from your Aunt Effie. He say your Aunt, she say to wait for your answer."

Cuff handed me the letter. I immediately recognized Aunt Effie's stationary and impeccable penmanship. I opened the envelope. It contained a request for me to join Aunt Effie at her house for supper that evening. She requested that I arrive an hour or so early so that she may seek my advice on a "most pressing matter." I smiled to myself as I wondered what issue might cause my dear aunt to seek out my advice so covertly. I crossed to my desk and penned my affirmative reply. I sealed the envelope and handed it to Cuff.

As I drove to Aunt Effie's, the damp, gray mist that had hung in the air most of the day seemed to be lifting. It looked like the sun might break through as I arrived at the townhouse that afternoon.

I handed my hat and coat to James and was told Aunt Effie was waiting for me in the upstairs drawing room.

Euphemia stood as I entered the room. She extended her hand to me and said, "Charles, how sweet you are to arrive early and visit with me."

I kissed the air above Aunt Effie's hand. "How kind of you to invite me. Whom are we expecting for supper?" I asked.

"Just the family—your sister, her husband, and your grandmother. Oh, and your cousin, Mary Alice, is here visiting from Savannah."

Mary Alice was actually my second cousin. She was the granddaughter of Aunt Effie's sister Rebecca. I had not seen her in some years. As I remembered her, she was a most beautiful child. She had inherited the Everson mane of dark mahogany hair and the blue eyes and pale skin. She was a little coltish, but time and age would round her figure. She was vain and disinterested in any subject that did not revolve around her.

She would chatter on for hours about things that were of no interest to anyone but herself.

"It's no wonder the poor girl can't find a husband," said Grandmother. "She opens her mouth, and whatever is inside her head just falls right out."

Mary Alice had been quite spoiled, and, like her great-uncle Philippe, she was well aware that her looks would open doors for her. When all else failed, a little pouting or an occasional tear would guarantee the desired results. Both Mary Alice's mother and Grandmother had passed. Her father eventually remarried a nice woman from Savannah, but Mary Alice, being so self-absorbed, had been slow to welcome her new stepmother. Mary Alice's four brothers were too busy with running the plantation to bother with a little sister. Her father was occupied with business and his new wife, so Mary Alice found herself alone in a household too busy to care about her.

"Since her mother's passing, I thought she might like to get out from under foot of all of those men at home," said Aunt Effie. "I thought Charleston might be a nice change of pace."

How much like Aunt Effie, I thought. *She raised us, and now she is shaping the values of another generation.*

"What was the most pressing matter you wanted to discuss? It sounded so serious."

"Oh, did I say I wanted to discuss something? Silly me, I meant I had something for you."

From the folds of her dress she produced a small, black, velvet pouch with a gold cord tying the top closed.

"I was going through some things, and I found this. I thought that you might like to have it." She smiled.

I took the pouch from Aunt Effie and opened it. Inside was a ring, a remarkable, two-carat rectangular-cut emerald surrounded by diamonds.

"It was your mother's engagement ring."

"Yes, I remember. But why are you giving it to me now?" I asked.

"I just thought you might like to have it, that's all. And besides, you never know when it may come in handy," said Aunt Effie.

I looked at the ring in my palm. It glittered brilliantly in the light. I thought of the times I had seen it on my mother's hand, and I thought about the last time I had seen her all dressed up to go away.

Aunt Effie must have read my mind. She squeezed my hand and said, "I miss her too. We all do. She was taken from us much too soon."

A knock at the door rescued us from our moment of sadness. I returned the emerald to its pouch and dropped the ring into my pocket. I heard James greet Grandmother and another guest whom I could not hear. After a moment, Grandmother entered the room, followed by, to my surprise, Josephine.

Grandmother greeted Aunt Effie.

"Euphemia, you know Miss St. John," said Grandmother.

"Good afternoon, Lottie; of course I know Miss St. John. My dear Josephine, how are you?" Euphemia kissed Josephine on both cheeks.

"I hope you don't mind my bringing this dear child, Euphemia. She was kind enough to call on me, and I invited her to join us for supper," said Grandmother.

"Certainly not. Miss St. John is welcome in my home anytime." To James, who was still standing at the door, she said, "Tell Belana we will be seven for dinner." I could have sworn I saw Aunt Effie wink at Grandmother.

"Here, Lottie, come and sit by the fire. It is still a little damp outside. Josephine, you may sit here on the divan." The ladies sat, and I remained standing by the fireplace.

"Would anyone like a tea or brandy?" asked Aunt Effie.

Grandmother and Josephine looked at each other and smiled. "Tea, thank you," they replied in unison.

"I'll take a scotch." I said.

Aunt Effie crossed the room and poured me a glass of liquor from the decanter on the table. She handed me my drink and sent Belana for the tea. She crossed and sat near Josephine.

"My, how fetching you look. Josephine, is that a new outfit?" asked Aunt Effie.

Josephine did look as beautiful as I had ever seen her; her dress was made from silk moiré. It was an ecru color with yards and yards of black soutache appliquéd in a fancy pattern around the hem and bodice.

She wore a saucy black hat with ostrich plumes and black tulle. The hat was perched at a rakish angle over her hair, which was pulled back at the sides and fell in sausage curls behind her. I liked the hat. It was typical of Josephine.

Most ladies of a certain age still wore bonnets in the states. Hats, especially one such as this, were reserved for younger girls. I could hear Mrs. Humphries now, accusing Josephine of trying to "dress mutton as lamb."

Josephine was unbuttoning the tiny black kid gloves she was wearing. I caught a glimpse of her diminutive wrists, they were as white and as smooth as satin.

"Why, yes it is. How kind you are to notice. I bought it on my last visit to London," she said, as she removed her gloves one finger at a time.

"Well, you look lovely, my dear," complimented Aunt Effie.

As I sipped my scotch, the sun broke through the last of the clouds and shone through the window behind Josephine. The sunlight set her auburn hair ablaze with a halo of light, and her skin looked as white as magnolia.

"Josephine, have you told Mrs. Scott and Charles your news?" Grandmother asked.

"No, I have not." she said.

"I hope it is good news, dear," said Aunt Effie.

Josephine smiled. She looked radiant. I could smell her rose-water perfume. I took a sip of my scotch.

"Why, yes, it is. I have sold The Abby, and I have put the house here up for sale. I am planning on moving back to London."

The sun retreated behind the clouds. The room darkened, taking Josephine's halo from her. I choked on the scotch and coughed violently as I sat the glass on the mantle.

"Are you all right, Charles?" asked Aunt Effie.

Unable to speak, I put my hand around my throat and nodded my head yes.

Unaffected by my outburst, Josephine continued calmly. "Yes, with Mother and Father gone and the probability of war coming, it just didn't make sense to stay here any longer. I do not want to get caught in the middle of this fight. And besides, sometimes we don't realize how much we miss something until it's gone. I never really realized how much England meant to me until I took Mother home." She looked at me and smiled innocently.

My mind raced. "But…but you can't go…who will I…I mean what…" I couldn't find my tongue.

Grandmother gave me that look. From her chair, she said, "Charles, if you have something to say, now might be the time."

"You…you can't go," I stammered.

"How sweet to know you will miss me. But my mind is made up. I am leaving tomorrow. The arrangements have been made," said Josephine.

"But you can't go."

"Why not?" asked Josephine.

"I…I…I love you!" I said at last.

Josephine smiled. I had never seen that smile before. The smile was not triumphant or victorious, such as I had seen on other girls at a moment like this, but rather a smile that said, "I have always known that you loved me, and I love you too."

Grandmother and Aunt Effie looked at each other and exchanged knowing glances. I was not sure if I had been set up or not. It didn't matter now. I rushed across the room. I sat beside her and took her hand in mine. Belana entered the room, bearing the silver tea service. She sat the tea service down and disappeared from the room.

"Josephine, I love you. I have always loved you. I never really realized how much until this moment. I can't bear the thought of you running off to England and leaving again. There is nothing for you there."

"Well, what reason is there to stay here?"

"Why, there's my family. They all love you. And then there's all of your friends. And there's me."

I dropped to my knees in front of her. "I want you to stay. I've made up my mind. I want you to be my wife. I want you to stay here in Charleston with me."

"Oh, Charles, you look like a fool. Get off you knees, you silly."

"I am a fool. I should have realized sooner how much I needed you. I won't let you go!"

Aunt Effie put her hand to her mouth. "Ahem," she whispered.

I remembered the ring in my pocket. I fumbled for the little pouch containing the ring. I found it and removed the emerald. I took Josephine's hand in mine again. I slipped the ring on her finger. I looked up at Josephine. At that moment, I couldn't tell which was greener, the emerald or her eyes.

Josephine lifted the ring close to her. "Oh, Charles, it's beautiful. But I can't stay; the arrangements have all been made."

"Josephine, I am going to stay right here on my knees until you say yes!"

Josephine turned to Aunt Effie and Grandmother. Their smiles seemed to say, "All right, you've teased him long enough." Josephine looked at me with love and affection in her eyes. "All right, Charles. You may get up from your knees. I will stay and marry you!"

The sun, as if on cue, burst forth from the clouds once more. It shone even more brightly than before. As she smiled at me, the halo returned to Josephine's hair.

I jumped up from where I knelt and ran to the door, "James! James!" I yelled into the hallway. I need not have raised my voice, for the startled butler was standing just outside the door with Belana. "Bring a bottle of the colonel's champagne. We're going to have a toast!"

I ran back to Josephine, who was now standing, and spun her around in a circle by both hands. Her skirts swept out behind her. She smiled and laughed. Aunt Effie and Grandmother stood and clapped their hands.

Unaware of what had just taken place, Mary Alice entered the room. She was joined by Ethne and Matthew. All three wore looks of confusion.

"What's going on? Have we missed something?" asked Ethne.

"We're getting married!" I shouted.

Josephine held out her hand. Mother's emerald sparkled in the sunlight. Ethne and Mary Alice voiced their approval. Their expressions turned to joy. Ethne hugged Josephine.

"Oh, how wonderful! I have always wished for a sister. Welcome to the family," she said.

Offering his congratulations, Matthew shook my hand and patted my back. Cousin Mary Alice smiled meekly and joined Aunt Effie standing by the settee.

As we laughed and congratulated each other, James arrived with the champagne. He was followed by Belana, who carried a tray of champagne cups. James expertly popped the cork from the bottle and poured the bubbling wine into the cups. We drank a toast to Josephine's and my marriage. The whole family began to laugh and talk at once.

Josephine and I walked out onto the piazza. I held her hands and gazed into her emerald eyes. She felt so soft and smelled of rosewater. I took her in my arms and held her close. As I kissed her, wisps of tangerine clouds melted into the horizon. The blueberry evening sky blossomed, first with magenta, then raspberry. In the west, the sun sank low to the horizon. In the east, the evening star rose and smiled her approval. Soon her sisters would join her and populate the nighttime sky.

Josephine put her arms around my waist and laid her head upon my chest. "I think this is the most beautiful time of day, the hours just before sunset," she said. "The work is done, the family is gathered around, and everyone enjoys the fruits of their labors."

I held Josephine close as her words rang in my head. I knew whatever came, we would be together from this day fourth. Still, I had to wonder, with the war surely coming, were these the hours before sunset for our civilization?

THE LATE UNPLEASANTNESS

The late winter and early spring of 1861 were overflowing with hopes and dreams. The world seemed to be rushing along at a frantic pace. My family and friends, like everyone in South Carolina, were swept away by the swelling tide of Southern patriotism. There were speeches and rallies in the streets. There were demonstrations that bordered on riots. We wondered and dreamt what the future might hold.

Contrary to popular belief, we in the South did not fight a civil war. We never, at any point, desired to overthrow the government in Washington. Our desire was to leave the Union in peace and govern ourselves, as we believed best for us.

What we did fight was a war for Southern independence. One may call the conflict "The Late Unpleasantness," "The War for Southern Independence," "The War Between The States," or "The Great Lost Cause," but those of us who are Southern born and bred and who fought for the glorious lost cause will forever find it hard to accept the term "Civil War."

We in South Carolina were a proud people, proud of our history and our accomplishments, proud of our culture and the way of life that we had built. However, pride, idealism, arrogance, and stubbornness—and we were all of those things—can blind people. It was certainly pride and arrogance that led us down the road to secession. It was secession, not slavery, that caused the

War Between the States. The war, in the minds of the Northern citizens, was directed at the issue of slavery.

President Lincoln promised not to free the slaves in states where slavery already existed. The president would write, "My paramount object in the struggle *is* to save the Union; it is *not* either to save or to destroy slavery." It was ironic that Lincoln eventually broke that promise by issuing the proclamation freeing the Negroes. The irony was not lost on the South that he freed the slaves only in those states that were in rebellion. The slaves in the North would have to wait until December 6, 1865, when the Thirteenth Amendment banned slavery, to claim their freedom.

With events being what they were, Josephine and I decided not to delay our wedding. We chose to be married in April. Unfortunately, we picked April 11, 1861, for our wedding day.

The appointed day dawned sunny and pleasant. The last of the azaleas blushed in the garden, and the listless breeze in the magnolia leaves whispered the promise of summer and long, lazy afternoons on the piazza.

Since neither Josephine nor I were spring lambs, we decided that a big, fancy wedding would be inappropriate. I did not wish to play the bashful, nervous bridegroom, and Josephine had no interest in being a blushing bride. We both agreed upon a small, intimate ceremony at Saint Michael's. It was Aunt Effie who insisted on a supper and ball at her townhouse afterward. Reluctantly, Josephine, who was staying with Aunt Effie, agreed. I went along with their decision.

"Both of your parents would be shocked!" said Aunt Effie. "It's bad enough that you chose to marry so quickly and to invite so few guests to the ceremony, but to deny Charleston the chance to share in your happiness would be viewed as very selfish."

On the day of our wedding, Aunt Effie's household was in the chaos one would expect preparing for the festivities. We were to be married at five o'clock in the afternoon at Saint Michael's. The ceremony would be followed by supper at Aunt Effie's house and a ball commencing at nine, also at Aunt Effie's.

Dressed in our wedding finery, we decided that it would be a grand idea to have our image preserved for posterity on this special day. As our carriage pulled from the curb, I was glad to leave the fussing and hubbub behind. We took the carriage to the bend at King Street, where the photographers plied their trade.

We chose George Cook's studio at 265 King Street, not too far from where The Abby had been. Mr. Cook was generally agreed to be the best photographer in Charleston. We climbed the stairs to the studio. The reception room was papered with red wallpaper and paneled with dark wood. To our right there was a seating area where there sat several handsome rosewood chairs and a rosewood settee. A gentleman with mutton-chop whiskers, wearing a long leather apron, welcomed us from behind a glass counter. The counter was lined with images of famous people, as well as the likenesses of half the residents of Charleston. They peered at us from velvet-lined cases or little gold frames.

The gentleman in the leather apron introduced himself as Mr. Samuels. He proceeded to instruct us as to what products were available for purchase. There were frames of gold or wood. We could have our image made on glass or metal. We could order prints of the photographs we had taken. We could order cases of leather with red or blue velvet linings or cases of Gutta-Percha with different designs embossed on them. Aunt Effie, who kept interrupting Mr. Samuels, was only too eager to advise us.

"Now you each should have a photograph taken alone and then have one taken together, and don't forget, you will need at least two-dozen *carte-de-visites* of you both together to send to friends and family who cannot make the wedding," advised Aunt Effie. "And, Charles, I want a nice photograph of both of you for my drawing room table."

I chuckled to myself as I paid for the photographs. Silently, I wondered if Aunt Effie was in league with the photographer.

It was decided that Josephine would be photographed first. She chose to stand in front of a plain background. She held her wedding bouquet in one hand the other resting on a short, fluted, ionic column.

Mr. Cook himself arranged the sitting and took the photograph. He fussed with her dress and arranged her hands and head. When he was pleased with the tableau, his assistant moved an iron contraption with a clamp on the top behind Josephine. He rested her head in it so that she would not move.

"Now, keep perfectly still. Do not move, Miss St. John, while I check the setting," instructed the photographer. He disappeared underneath the black silk cloth covering the camera. "Ah that's it...lovely, lovely. Now raise your head. That's it. Now look a little to your right...just a little more...and...perfect!" continued Mr. Cook. He came out from behind the camera, walked over to Josephine, and readjusted the stand holding her head. He returned to the camera and checked under the black silk cloth one last time. Emerging from beneath the cover, he took his watch from his vest pocket. Looking at Josephine, he opened his watch.

"Okay, we are all set. Hold very still." He removed the cover from the front of the camera and began to slowly count. "One, two, three..."

I looked at Josephine standing there so still in the afternoon sunlight. How beautiful she looked.

Aunt Effie had pinned white gardenias in her hair. She looked as though she wore a halo. I thought to myself, *My angel, how could I have waited so long to make you mine?* At that moment, her eyes met mine. She smiled a haunting, winsome smile. I smiled back. For a second the world stood still.

"And thirteen. Thank you very much. That is it, Miss St. John." Mr. Cook's baritone voice broke the trance.

The photographer took the plate from the camera and washed it through a series of liquids from the bottles on the table. "Now, watch this," he said. With a pair of large tongs, he laid the plate in the last tray of liquid, and the image of Josephine began to appear on the metal plate, first in negative, then turning to positive. Aunt Effie and Josephine crowded closer to get a better view.

"Ah, lovely," said Mr. Cook. "Would you like to see, Mr. McGuire?"

I leaned closer to inspect the photograph. There was the image of my angel smiling back at me, that moment fixed forever on a piece of metal plate.

The rest of that afternoon and that evening are a blur. There was pleasant chatter as we drove from King to Meeting Street to Saint Michael's. I remember stopping at the mausoleum in the churchyard where Mother and my brother were buried. We left a bouquet of flowers at the door as we said a brief prayer. Grandmother, Mary Alice, Ethne, her husband, and about fifty of our closest friends were waiting inside the church. I remember the sunlight streaming through the windows. I remember music, promises, whispered *I dos*, and the smell of incense mixed with gardenias. I do not remember the ride back to Aunt Effie's. I do not remember the wedding feast or the toasts.

I do remember Josephine floating through the room, rustling in her gray taffeta. She looked radiant as she accepted the congratulations of our friends and neighbors. I remember my friends slapping me on the back and wishing me well as we drank one too many toasts.

I recall Aunt Effie taking us both by the hands and leading us into the ballroom, telling us to stand at the head of the room. The band began to play, and there was music. The doors to the ballroom opened. Josephine and I greeted our guests as they entered two by two for the grand march. When the march had finished, we lined up for the Virginia reel. We danced and waltzed and did the polka till we were quite out of breath.

At four o'clock, the festivities were coming to an end. The band was playing the last waltz. Suddenly there came from the harbor a thunderous boom! The house rattled, and we ran to the piazza to see what had happened. At first, we thought Aunt Effie had arranged for a wedding fireworks display. Then another flash and an unearthly scream like a firecracker pierced the still morning air. A brilliant blast of light lit the area where Fort Sumter sat. Several people on the street below were running in the direction of the noise in the harbor.

One of the guests called to a man in the crowd.

"What's all the noise?"

"It's war!" cried the man in the street. "General Beauregard has fired on Fort Sumter, and our boys are going to rid us of the Yankees once and for all. We're going to blow 'em back north where they belong."

A murmur went through the startled crowd in the ballroom. A few of the ladies began to cry. Many of the men cheered. Josephine and I looked at each other and then at Aunt Effie, who had suddenly gone very pale and quiet. We all knew what this meant.

Three days after we fired on Fort Sumter, on the morning of April 15, President Abraham Lincoln called for volunteers to help suppress what he called the rebellion.

When the news of Lincoln's call for troops reached us in Charleston, the lid blew off the pot. The call to arms and the thirst for blood was on the lips of everyone. Our boys had been ready for this day for some time. They had been forming regiments, drilling, and making up fierce-sounding names for their fighting corps. There had been heated discussions as to the color and design of their uniforms and about who would lead them into battle. Everyone was eager to run off and pursue the great, grand adventure of our generation.

Afraid that the fighting would soon be over, most of the bucks in town could not wait to chase down and shoot a passel of Yankees.

Should a young man, however, have any reservations about signing up, the young ladies had their ways of convincing him. They would tease him and refuse to kiss him or marry him until he signed up.

The ladies threw themselves into the war effort with a zeal that surprised many of their men folk. Those who could sew organized sewing drives to make uniforms and bandages. Those who could not sew would knit socks and scarves by the dozens. The ladies organized parades, bazaars, and socials to send our brave boys off to fight. The whole city, it seemed, had war fever.

The attack on Fort Sumter prompted four more states to join the Confederacy. In April of 1861, with Virginia's secession, Richmond was named the Confederate capital. In the North, the cry from Union headquarters was, "On to Richmond!" For the next four years, a succession of Northern commanders struggled desperately to do just that—get to Richmond.

The morning we learned of Lincoln's call for troops, Josephine begged me to leave for London and take her with me before it was too late.

"This is not our fight, Charles," she said. "We can go to London or Paris and wait this whole mess out. Why wait here until the world goes to hell?"

I must admit that I thought about the idea. Then I thought about Grandmother. Her family had been among the founding fathers of Charleston. My mother and Aunt Effie's family, whose ties to the South ran deep, were also a part of me. Despite my years in England, this was my home and these were my people.

I could never leave Aunt Effie and Grandmother behind, and they, of course, would never abandon Charleston to the Yankees.

To turn my back on South Carolina and Charleston would be an unpardonable sin. I would never be able to return. If I had learned one thing at my Grandfather's knee, it was that your home and your family matter above all else. To lose them was to lose everything. No, I would have to stay in Charleston and see this through.

I thought for a brief moment Josephine would leave me and return to London until the end of the war. I am sure that she thought about it. I pleaded my case. Ethne's husband was busy with his family and a new practice. Grandfather was gone, and Mary Alice's father and brothers had all joined up the first month. I was the only male left to care for our family. Should anything happen to me, I explained, Josephine would be the only person strong enough to see to the welfare or the women of our clan.

Above all, Josephine was logical. She could see that I was right. She agreed to stay, and I agreed not to fight. I managed to keep that promise for two years.

Early in the conflict, the Confederacy won a sweeping victory at Manassas under the command of Generals Johnston and Beauregard. In May of 1862, General Jackson pushed Union forces back across the Potomac. In June of the same year, Robert E. Lee was placed in charge of the Army of Northern Virginia and successfully protected Richmond.

By March of 1863, the men who only a few years ago had been eager to fight grew tired of the game. They realized that this conflict might go on for quite some time. There was no one left at home to help with the planting and harvesting. Their families needed them back home. Desertion became rampant.

Since men were not signing up to fight, the first conscription act was passed, making all men between the ages of twenty and forty-five liable to be called for military service. Paying a fee or finding a substitute could avoid service.

The act was seen as unfair to the poor, and riots in working-class sections of New York City broke out in protest. A similar conscription act in the South provoked a similar reaction. The conflict became "A rich man's war and a poor man's fight."

One afternoon early in April, in 1863, I was in the office at Grand Oak going over some papers when I was interrupted by Cuff. He knocked excitedly on the door to the office.

"Masta Charles, your cousin, Masta Rutledge, is here an' he done bought some mighty important people with him."

"Thank you, Cuff," I said.

As Cuff left the room, Josephine entered. "Charles, your cousin, John Rutledge, is here with Senator Chestnut. What is going on?"

I assured her that I had no idea, and, with my curiosity aroused, I told Cuff to show our distinguished visitors into the parlor.

My cousin stood as I entered the room. "Charles, how good to see you," he said, crossing the carpet to shake my hand. John was actually my second cousin on my grandmother's side.

"This is a most unexpected surprise. This must be important for you to have made the trip from town," I said, returning the handshake.

John smiled at me. "Have you met Senator Chestnut?"

"Yes, I have." I bowed and offered my hand. "Senator, my wife and I had the pleasure of making the acquaintance of you and Mrs. Chestnut at the Alston's home last December."

The senator returned my handshake. "Yes, I remember. How is your lovely bride?"

"At the moment, she is fine. I would expect her continued good humor will depend on the reason for your visit," I said, smiling.

The other men in the room laughed. We all knew too well the iron magnolia and the velvet glove. Life was much simpler when our wives were happy.

"May I offer you some brandy or a little wine, perhaps?"

The gentlemen in the room nodded.

I poured four glasses of wine and distributed them to my guests. They took the wine, and as I offered one to my cousin, he said, "No, thank you, Charles. Actually, we have come to ask you a very important favor and to make you an offer we hope you will accept."

The Senator agreed. Setting his glass down, he began. "Mr. McGuire, I'll get right down to business here. As you know, our troops have been successful in repelling most of the enemy's advances. We have driven them steadily northward, but there is still much work to be done. You are, I am sure, aware of the current difficulties facing us here in Charleston. The blockade of our ports is making supplies difficult to get. Many of our men are getting tired of fighting, and desertion is becoming a concern, and then there is that damnable proclamation freeing the Negroes.

"I must swear you to secrecy on this matter, but I have it in good authority that General Lee and the glorious Army of the Confederacy will soon engage the Yankee army on their home turf. If we are victorious, we will surely gain the support of England and France. If we fail"—the senator looked at his feet—"if we fail, I fear we shall have to see this fight through on our own. Surely you can see the gravity of this situation, Mr. McGuire."

"Certainly, Senator. I can very well see your point, but I am not sure what you want from me."

"Charles"—Cousin John stepped forward—"we are going to need a strong cavalry if we are to beat the Union in the North. We are going to need more horses, more troops, and experienced men to lead them. And, well, everyone in South Carolina knows that Grand Oak has some of the finest horses in the state." The gentlemen in the room all nodded in agreement.

"I see," I said, beginning to anticipate where this was going.

Senator Chesnut gave John a look as though he had spoken too much.

"Mr. McGuire," the Senator continued, "if we are going to win this war, we are going to need great soldiers and greater men to lead them. Everyone is aware of your experience leading the workers at your family's business in England, and your work on civic committees in the state speaks for itself. We need leadership skills and minds such as yours to beat our enemy. We need superior animals such as you have bred here at Grand Oak; we need money to outfit our troops. Quite simply put, Mr. McGuire, we need you and what you have to offer."

"Hear! Hear!" shouted the men in the room as they stood and lifted their glasses in my direction.

"I don't know what to say," I said.

Cousin John spoke up. "Just say yes. I'm going to sign up. Your brother-in-law, Matthew, is signing up, and, hell, Charles, half the family has already gone off."

"Gentlemen, I am flattered, but I am needed here."

I thought about Matthew joining the war effort and possibly making my sister a widow. I could see Cousin John's mother's face when she heard her only son was going off to war. Perhaps if they were going to fight, it might be better if I went with them to look after them.

Then I remembered my promise to Josephine. "I promised my wife I wouldn't fight."

"Hell, Charles," said John. "The South needs you. Josephine will understand. Remember who you are. Your family founded this state. They fought for your freedom. You owe it to their memory to fight for South Carolina now."

John was right. Like it or not, I was a part of this place, and it was surely a part of me. Water from the Ashley ran in my veins. South Carolina and I were like wisteria and jasmine intertwined on the trees in the woods. They could not be untangled without destroying one or the other.

Senator Chestnut's voice interrupted my thoughts. "Mr. McGuire, if you will agree to join us in our effort to advance on the North and to supply us with horses, which we are willing to pay for, the Confederate government and President Jefferson Davis himself are prepared to offer you a commission as a major with the cavalry in the Army of Virginia."

What could I do? What could I say? My country needed me. Josephine would have to understand. I set my shoulders, lifted my chin, and squared my jaw. I made my mind up. At that moment, I was seduced from the bed of Venus to become a knight on the field of Mars.

Later that afternoon, when I informed Josephine of the conversation in the parlor, she did not seem surprised.

"Charles, I have long known that South Carolina would call you from me," she said. "She has always been a mistress with whom I could not compete. Why do you think I kept returning to England? Do what you have to do. I will see to things here, and I'll take care of the family."

"You're not angry at me for going back on my promise not to fight?"

"It was a promise I had no right to ask you to make."

I held her close and looked into her eyes. I said, "I don't know what I did to deserve such a wonderful, understanding partner. I love you, Josephine."

"I love you too, Charles. Just come back to me safe and sound."

The Eye of the Storm

There was much to be done before my departure. We had four short weeks to prepare. I would have to have a uniform made. I would need to get the horses ready. I would have to study the military manuals, for I fear I had very little idea of exactly what a major was supposed to do. I must set my business affairs in order and instruct Josephine as to what she should do. That month was the shortest month of my life, for seemingly overnight the time had come for us to depart.

Those under me and I were to comprise a new company—Company L of the First South Carolina Calvary under Wade Hampton. There would be, among others, Cousin John; a business associate, George Winthrop; Mrs. Humphies's grandson, Caleb; and my brother-in-law, Matthew. Jimmy and Johnny Murphy, who had already enlisted, would be transferred to my command. Several other young men from fine families would round out the unit.

It was agreed that I would supply nineteen thoroughbred horses at fair market value and a sum of money for supplies for my company. Since it was imperative that we travel quickly and efficiently, it was agreed that the officers would not take personal servants, as had been the custom earlier in the war. I would provide two of the Negroes from Grand Oak.

Big Jawn was too valuable. I would need him to protect the women if need be. I chose an older boy named Jordan and his brother, Peter; they would cook, clean, sew, and attend to what business we needed. In addition, I would supply and outfit my own horse. This would leave Grand Oak with one stallion, three bay mares, and six mules.

I chose to take my horse, Providence, with me. Providence, a gelding, was a magnificent saddle-bred bay with a white star on his forehead.

He had been born on Grand Oak, and I believe that he was one of the finest animals we had ever bred. He possessed a superior temperament and did not spook easily, a trait that would prove very valuable in battle.

He stood just a bit over sixteen hands high. Grandmother had unwittingly named him shortly after his birth. The delivery had been difficult, and for a moment, we feared we might lose both foal and mare, but as fortune would have it, they both survived. I related the story later that evening to Grandmother, who said, "By God's divine grace, he has been spared. It is providence."

"Providence indeed!" said Ethne. "What a grand name for a horse. Let Providence see you safely wherever you go." She raised her glass.

"To Providence!" we toasted. True to his name, Providence had borne me safely through fox hunts and races. He jumped beautifully and seemed to know what I expected of him before I asked. I was confident that now he would see me safe and sound through the coming conflict.

The ladies' auxiliary had organized a day of festivities to send us off. There was parade in the morning, a barbecue in the afternoon, and a ball that evening.

Everyone had agreed to meet at Grandmother's house on the day of the parade. We would ride to the corner of Broad and Meeting Streets together. The ladies would go in the carriage. My regiment and I would accompany the carriage to Meeting Street, drop the ladies off, and then we would ride to Market Street, where the parade would form up.

Before I knew it, I was standing at the top of the stairs of Grandmother's townhouse in my splendid new uniform. The entire household, black and white, as well as our guests, had assembled at the foot of the stairs to catch the first glimpse of me. I can still see everyone standing at the bottom of the stairs looking expectantly up.

Dressed in their Sunday best, the ladies were a rainbow of silk and taffeta. The servants also wore their best clothes. They added a festive note to the crowd assembled in the landing. The bright calicos of their head rags and skirts contrasted with the more somber grays of the uniforms of my fellow soldiers.

I have to admit I felt very proud. My uniform was made of the finest Richmond gray wool. The cuffs and collar of my jacket were yellow, the color of the cavalry. The fine gold stripe on my trousers and the triple Austrian knots on my sleeves identified me as an officer. The single star on my collar denoted my rank— a major. Around my waist was a sash of yellow wool with my sword belt over that. My white leather gauntlets with gold eagles embroidered on them were tucked into my sash, and a shiny new saber hung from my side.

My boots were polished to perfection, and I carried in my hand a fine, gray felt hat with a gold hat cord. I put my hat on, took the railing with one hand, my other resting against my sword, and paused on the third step. My family, standing in the landing below, broke into applause. Aunt Effie and Grandmother beamed with pride at my appearance.

Ethne put both of her hands to her mouth as her eyes teared up. Josephine smiled at me with approval. With my saber rattling and my spurs jangling, I descended the rest of the way down stairs. Smiling broadly, I felt like President Jefferson Davis himself.

Lizzie looked up at me and, in a dry voice, said, "Well, he sure ain't gonna sneak up on no one with all of that racket."

Ignoring her, I saluted the crowd at the bottom of the stairs. Everyone began to speak at once.

"Oh, Charles! How handsome you look. The captain would be so proud of you," said Grandmother.

"My, my, my, you remind me of your Uncle Henry. He loved his uniforms so," said Aunt Effie.

Ethne hugged me and said, "Oh, Charles, now all of the men I love are in uniform. Promise me you will all watch out for each other and bring yourselves home safely."

Even the servants added to the din. "Lordy, Masta Charles, you sure looks fine in that there uniform," said Mammy.

Cuff added, "I don't expect there's no finer looking officer in the whole Confederate Army."

I took my hat off and made a gallant sweeping bow.

Josephine walked up to me, put both of her hands of either side of my face, and kissed me squarely on the lips.

The men in the room whistled and the ladies blushed.

Josephine whispered in my ear, "I'll save the rest for later." Then out loud, she said, "We have some things for you in the parlor."

The family had gifts to send me off, things they thought I would need. Ethne gave me a beautiful canteen covered in gray wool. Grandmother gave me a pocket Bible to "see me through the tough times." My friends in my unit gave me a gold cigar case engraved with my initials. Josephine gave me a beautiful watch chain made from her hair. From the center of the chain hung a fob that, when opened, contained a picture of me on one side and on the other a picture of Josephine.

"I felt that this was as close as I could get to giving you a piece of my heart to take with you," she said.

I was touched beyond words.

Finally, there remained but one box left to open. It was from Aunt Effie. With obvious joy, she handed me a finely polished wooden box. I opened it, and inside was another box covered in leather. There was a shiny brass plaque on its top that bore my initials. I opened it to find a beautiful pair of brass shoulder-mop epaulets. They were very impressive, but I had not the heart to tell her that they had passed quite out of fashion.

"They were your Uncle Henry's. I am sure that he would want you to have them. I can sew them on in time for the parade," she promised.

The ladies, being not quite up on current military fashion, encouraged her to do so. "Oh, how fine you will look, Charles," said Josephine, as my friends smiled smugly from the corners of the room.

Figuring I could take them off once we left, I put Aunt Effie's feelings ahead of my own and said, "Sew them quickly. It's almost time to leave."

Later that morning, with the sun sparkling on my shiny, new, brass epaulettes, I led my company down Meeting Street. It was a most impressive parade; there were marching bands and fire wagons. The mayor and his wife rode with Senator and Mrs. Chestnut in a carriage decorated with ribbons and flowers. Several other dignitaries in fine rigs followed them. The home guard marched next with two of the young women's war relief groups following behind them.

Men, women, and children lined the streets and cheered us on. Little boys would fall in and march beside the infantry units until their mothers called them back to their sides. Older men cheered and waved from the sidelines, wishing that they too were young enough to join the adventure. The married ladies waved snowy white handkerchiefs from beneath colorful parasols.

I suspect that there was not a flower left unpicked in Charleston. The ladies, young and old alike, now held armloads of blossoms, scattering them before the trampling feet of the passing soldiers. The scene reminded me of Roman gladiators marching into the Coliseum. I shook the thought from my head and smiled gallantly; there was my family ahead cheering from the sidelines.

Josephine was first into the street. She held out a rose to me. I bent over, took the flower, and kissed her outstretched hand. Ethne was next. She tucked a flower into my stirrup and patted my boot. Aunt Effie tossed another rose to me. I caught it, waved, and tucked both flowers into my belt. From both sides of the street a shower of petals rained down on us like confetti.

Lost in the enthusiasm of the moment, I turned, smiling, to look behind me, just in time to see Aunt Effie. For a second, time stopped and the noise around me silenced. On her face, she wore the most peaceful, benevolent smile I have ever seen. Her eyes flashed blue in the sunlight. She held in her outstretched hand a blood-red rose. Caleb Humphries leaned down, took the rose, and, upon doing so and unnoticed by anyone but me, pricked his finger. A single drop of blood appeared.

Putting his finger to his mouth, he licked the blood from his finger and tucked the rose into the leather belt crossing his chest. I felt a pang of apprehension. Which of us would be the first to spill his blood for South Carolina?

We left to join the rest of our regiment the following day. We were to ride north toward Pennsylvania and Gettysburg, where we would rendezvous and join forces to push the Union army north.

The day of our unit's departure, the city was in a most gay mood. Everyone turned out and made a brave face as if life was the same as it had been before the war. The truth of the matter was that Charleston was beginning to suffer. I felt a little guilty at leaving Josephine and my family alone to cope with the changing tide of events in the city.

A few of the schools and churches had closed, and some sections of town were completely devoid of inhabitants. Slaves had begun to run off. With help now unavailable, many ladies found themselves having to do laundry, cook meals, and mop floors.

The city was so full of soldiers, it seemed like a camp. At the start of the war, the soldiers had been gentlemen and were most welcome. They had been feted and revered. The war, however, had made it possible for an entire class of men who would have never been accepted to find lodging in the city. A new "mobocracy," had seized control. Uncouth and vulgar, they were the scourge of society.

There had been a major fire in December of 1861. The fire had destroyed a large area of town. We had lost Secession Hall and the great circular church. Poor Mrs. Pickney had lost her family's handsome mansion, and Josephine had lost her mother's townhouse.

To the people in the North, Charleston was the ultimate symbol of rebellion. They felt that it was us personally who had been responsible for the conflict, and they cried for the total annihilation of our home. After the war ended, the Yankees clamored for images of our decimated city. Ironically, when Union photographers did come south, like vultures, to document the carnage and to pick the corpse of our humbled city, they photographed the fire-burned sections of town. They ignorantly documented them as evidence of the humiliation of Charleston by Union troops.

By spring of 1863, fewer and fewer blockaders were making it through the enemy lines, and inflation had become rampant. A spool of thread, which had cost five cents at the start of the war, might cost ninety cents now.

I remember Josephine buying a pair of wedding slippers as a gift for her goddaughter. She paid one hundred dollars Confederate for them. They would have cost only five dollars before the war.

Money and household items were becoming scarce, but this only brought out the resourcefulness in the townsfolk. Looking back, I suppose part of the fun was seeing just how far we could stretch supplies, clothing, paper, and the little things that made life civilized. We learned to make acorn coffee. It was a little bitter, but we got used to it. We used honey instead of sugar.

Occasionally, a blockade runner managed to sneak through the Union lines, and there would be a mad dash for the docks as the women folk competed for "just a pinch of sugar" or "just a few yards of cloth." It was amazing that the townspeople were able to communicate with each other so quickly.

This was the Charleston I left my family to cope with, but spirits were high, and we were confident we would survive. When I departed for war, I felt that the women would be safer in the town. General Beauregard was defending the city. The Yankees would never be able to enter! I wanted to leave Big Jawn with the women, but Josephine insisted that she could handle whatever the Yankees could throw at them. Big Jawn, she said, would be much more valuable at Grand Oak acting as foreman if there should be trouble. As usual, she made sense.

Our job in the cavalry was to be the eyes and ears of the army. It was our duty to check the accuracy of our maps, assess and report on the location and movement of enemy troops, and scout for food, supplies, and the most efficient routes for the infantry and artillery to follow.

We might ride behind and burn a bridge to keep the enemy from following, or we might ride ahead and harass the Yankee troops. One of our more unpleasant duties was to pick up stragglers and deserters.

We were just two days out when we came under fire for the first time. With Uncle Henry's epaulets still attached to my uniform coat, I was feeling somewhat full of myself. I fancied myself to be a classic Roman hero protecting his home and family. Surely, there were lovely maidens just ahead waiting to crown my brow with laurel leaves as a token of their gratitude.

I rode ahead of my men and charged up a hill. I reined Providence in and paused so that I could survey the field ahead. Down a slope to my right, the undergrowth thickened and ran along the edge of a fallow field. Fifty or so yards ahead of me was a stone wall, and beyond that was a field of young corn. To my left about twenty yards were several old growth trees. Overhead, a stout, gray squirrel refereed as a chorus of jays, joined by the sharp buzzing of the cicadas, argued loudly for possession of the oaks. I sat astride Providence with the sun shining on my face. I thought I must have made a fierce picture sitting on that hilltop.

I swelled my chest out with pride and inhaled the late spring air.

Suddenly there was a pop. Something whizzed by my ear and tore the epaulet from my coat. Providence reared, and I fell backward from my horse. He turned and ran in the direction of the rest of my company. I grabbed the epaulet and ran for the cover of the oak. I fired twice in the direction from where the shots aimed at me had come. Suddenly, from behind, I heard the pounding of hooves, and my men took the hill. I heard someone yell "Damn," and two men in blue coats sprang from the undergrowth and ran toward the stone wall. Several shots rang out, and the men fell headlong into the tall grass. I saw two men die, and the war became real.

Our second engagement with the Yankees came on June 9 at Brandy Station, Virginia. I put any romantic images of the honor and glory of war behind me. There are no words that can convey the horror and madness that is war.

I remember that first battle as having four distinct chapters.

It began as we sat astride our horses in the woods just behind a stone wall. Although the engagement was primarily a cavalry battle, there were also infantry troops in attendance. The cavalry was dispersed on either side of the infantry. Soldiers stood twenty deep the length of the barrier. Ahead of us stretched a field of the greenest grass we had ever seen. Here and there, clumps of white daisies nodded sleepily in the breeze.

A hawk circled lazily in the pale blue afternoon sky. Just beyond the field in front of us, running east to west, was a dusty, brown ribbon of road. On the other side of the road the grass continued. It blended into an apple orchard whose trees reached for the horizon.

The horses pawed the ground idly or nibbled on low-hanging branches. Everyone was deathly quiet.

The men in my command stared, their dusty faces focused on the road ahead of them. We knew the Yankees were marching in our direction. We had been told to wait until the enemy was close enough to see them plainly.

It was in those seconds just before grave danger, when looking death in the face, that we felt most alive. The grass was greener, the sky was bluer, and I could see every leaf on the trees and smell the dust in the road.

A small rabbit hopped along in the grass not too far from where we sat. Out of the blue, the hawk we had noticed earlier swooped from the sky and violently snatched the rabbit from the field. I wondered whom among us would death snatch like the rabbit from the field.

The second chapter was the call to arms. Abruptly, those same men who, moments earlier, had been so still, muscles tensed and waiting, now sprung to urgent action. There was smoke from the guns and cannons. The smell of dust and sulfur was choking. The yelling of men and the whinnying of horses deafened our ears. Confusion reigned supreme. In that moment, as the world went to black and white, it was as if the earth opened beneath our feet and hell belched forth a demon-filled cloud of ash and sulfur upon the godless landscape.

Whether the tempest lasted for minutes or hours, I cannot say. There were only images—snarling, sweaty, faces blackened by gunpowder; smudged flashes of blue, gray, and black passing by; the flash of a sword; the fire from a pistol—all of this punctuated by flashes of red, each image passing so quickly that the mind cannot process it.

The third chapter was when the call to retreat was sounded. The company regrouped to count the survivors and lick their wounds.

The gunshot and cannon fire stopped, and for a moment, the quiet was deafening. Then we heard it: the unearthly moan of the wounded sweeping across the fields. They raised their voices for help and water. They prayed that someone was left alive to hear their cries. The ambulance corps rode out to sort the living from the dead.

In the quiet of the late afternoon came chapter four. I rode across the battlefield. The grass was trampled flat, and the daisies lay stained with blood. Branches and leaves had been torn from trees by rifle fire. Men and body parts were scattered like toy soldiers on the ground. With battle weary faces turned toward heaven, the soldiers stared, unblinking, through vacant, open eyes into the fading sunlight. They seemed to be only sleeping; surely, if someone sounded the bugle, they would jump to life and fall into line. Then there were the horses—oh, Lord, the horses—lying on their sides. The soldiers had chosen to go into battle, but the animals had no choice. They went where they were led. I thought with regret about the horses I had sold to the army.

A lonely crow called from the edge of the woods. The hawk, a victim of a random bullet, lay beside the rabbit in the field. There was no more hunter or prey, no more blue or gray. There were no cries of victory or sobs of anguish, only silence, as united in death, brother lay beside brother on the green, broken, blood-soaked grass.

That night as we bivouacked in the shadow of an old abandoned house, we assessed the condition of our company. We had been very lucky. We had lost one man, Joseph Barrett. He would be buried on the field, and word would be sent to his family. Two other men had been wounded, and Matthew had been shot in the shoulder but not severely enough to impede his ability to fight. Most of the rest of us had multiple scratches and bruises. Thankfully, we had not lost any horses. On the positive side, it appeared we had gained a bugler. Cousin John rode into camp early that evening with the boy in the saddle behind him.

"What have we got here?" asked Caleb, lifting the boy from John's saddle.

"I found him wandering the battlefield," said John as he dismounted his horse.

Caleb led the boy over to where I sat by my tent. He was a fine-looking lad. His sandy-blond hair poked out from beneath a gray forage cap. He stood about five feet two and was solidly built with a pleasant square face. He was obviously not the son of a planter, but neither was he poor white. There was a coltishness about him, but one could tell he was from good stock.

He was wearing a dusty, patched, Confederate shell jacket and mud-soaked gray trousers that were two sizes too big. A shiny brass bugle hung from a strap over his shoulder. He looked too young to be a soldier.

I suspected that he had been outfitting himself from the clothing left behind on the battlefield. My uniform jacket hung over a chair behind where I sat, and my sword and belt hung over top of it with my sash and hat. The boy eyed them with admiration.

"You a real general?" he asked, his eyes widening.

I smiled at the promotion. "No, I'm a major. What's you name, son?" I asked.

"Hardy," the boy answered.

"Hardy, is it? Is that a first name or a last name?

The boy looked at his feet. "S'just Hardy, that's all," he said.

I deduced by his accent he must have been from inland North Carolina. "What were you doing wandering the battlefield all alone, son?" I asked. "Don't you know that could be dangerous?"

The boy looked at me square on. Without blinking his hazel eyes, he said, "I wanna be a soldier, sir."

"I see. How old are you, Hardy?"

"I'm twelve, but I can shoot straight, I know all about horses, and I ain't a scared of nothin'."

Caleb and John were standing by my side. Matthew, his arm freshly bandaged, joined them, followed by George and Jimmy.

"I know I'd be a real good soldier," Hardy continued.

"Looks like we got us a live one here," said George, ruffling the boy's hair.

Hardy pulled his head away and scowled at George.

"What about your family? Where are your parents?" I asked.

"My four brothers and my pa joined up the first year. They said I was too young to fight and I had better stay at home and look after my ma. Lost my oldest brother at Bull Run; then my pa and the youngest were killed, and we ain't heard 'bout Bill or Frankie. Ma took sick. I s'pose her heart done broke. She took to her bed and died. There weren't no one else to look after, so I left to be a soldier and maybe find my brothers."

There was a determination about the boy. He seemed much older than his twelve years. No child should have to face so much hardship alone. My heart went out to him. I was certain that if he had to, he would take on the entire Union army by himself.

"You realize that you have to be eighteen to be a soldier?" I said.

"I seen lots of boys my age fighting," he said. "Pa said I learn real quick, and Ma said I was the smartest outta the whole bunch."

"I see. Well, there's a lot to know about soldiering. It takes a long time to learn. Tell you what. Can you play that bugle you have there, son?"

Without saying a word, the boy lifted the bugle to his lips and played an impressive call to attention.

"Where did you learn to play like that?" I asked.

"Don't rightly know. I just kinda listened to the older boys and figured it out for myself," he answered.

"I see. That's really very good, Hardy. If you really want to be a soldier, you have to learn how to take care of the horses, clean the guns, and take commands. If you are really serious, we might be willing to teach you; but you need to start out slowly. How would you like to be our bugler and call the troops to arms till you learn about soldiering?"

The boy's eyes brightened, and he stood up straight. "You mean it sir?" he asked.

"Sure do, but you would have to promise me that you would stay in camp during the fighting until you are trained."

The men around me smiled at the boy's enthusiasm.

Hardy extended his hand. "Shake on it, sir? Pa always said that once you shake on it, you gotta deal, and there ain't no goin' back."

I shook the boy's outstretched hand. "Deal!" I smiled.

Despite the loss of life and the carnage of the battle earlier in the day, that evening was the most pleasant of the war. Hardy proved to be a ray of sunshine after the storm of battle. As we rode to Gettysburg, we had only a few short weeks to get to know him. We had outfitted him with Joseph's horse, but he still proudly wore his baggy, mismatched uniform. Hardy proved to be a natural horseman. The boy had a fine sense of humor and took the good-natured ribbing from the men in stride. True to his word, he learned quickly. He only had to be shown something once, and he could master the task. From that first day, there seemed to be a bond between us.

I had never really had a desire to become a father. Frankly, children made me uncomfortable. But there was something different about this boy. He was one of those rare individuals who, despite a common beginning, with the proper education and guidance, had the potential for greatness.

I wrote to Josephine about him. If we both survived the war and we could not find his family, I wanted to make him our ward.

By the end of June, we arrived to join the rest of our unit near a small farming town in Pennsylvania. The reunion and good-natured jocularity of old friends was overshadowed by the knowledge of the task before us.

The first two days of battle held their tribulations, but the third day of battle of Gettysburg was by far the bloodiest.

The day had dawned like the previous two—brutishly hot. By midmorning, the temperature was already in the nineties. At three o'clock in the afternoon on July 3, General Pickett gave the order to "Charge the enemy and remember old Virginia!"

With that, we rode into the eye of the storm and never looked back.

Our troops must have made a magnificent spectacle as the cavalry rode and the infantry marched, with battle flags unfurled, toward that clump of trees on the ridge.

The federal artillery opened fire on us, and there followed a storm of shells and bullets such as I have never seen. We closed our ranks to cover the gaps, and still the fire came. During the height of battle, the twenty-sixth North Carolina reached the stone wall.

At the top of the hill, the Union troops broke and began to scramble. For one brief, shining moment, we could see the face of victory as she smiled down on us. Alas, it was not to be. Replacements arrived to close the gap in the Union lines. The smoke of their rifle fire obscured victory's sweet face as she passed out of view.

Our dreams of triumph died with General Armistead and many of his brave men by a stone wall in a field in a tiny, unknown town in Adams County, Pennsylvania. Gettysburg was to have been our shining moment. Ironically, it turned out to be our high-water mark. Never again would the Confederate army set foot on Northern soil. We lost all hope of recognition of our government by the European nations. Straggling and limping southward, the Confederate army would last but two more years before uttering its dying breath in a farmhouse in rural Virginia.

Out of all of the men we lost in that battle, I am not sure why or even how God spared me that day. In the thick of battle, things began spinning faster and faster. The noise on the battlefield became louder and louder. Sound, sight, and smell seemed to swirl into one dizzying funnel cloud, then *bang*—a flash of light. I was galloping alone by myself across a field of green, green grass. The indigo sky was hung with clouds of purest white, and ahead lay a stream of clear, cool water.

I galloped toward the stream. Someone tapped me on the shoulder. I kept on riding. My unseen companion tapped me again, harder this time, on my chest. I turned to see who it was. I found myself staring straight into the face of Satan himself. The grass turned to ash, the sky to red, and the water turned to blood.

On a midnight-black stallion, the devil rode beside me in a Yankee-blue uniform, grinning mockingly. His stallion's hooves never touched the ground as he matched Providence pace for pace. A dust cloud of demons trailed in his wake.

I spurred Providence. "Faster, faster," I cried.

I could feel Satan's hot breath on our heels. We rode like the wind. The devil reached for me; I clung to Providence's neck. Satan threw a serpent into Providence's path. The horse faltered and stumbled, throwing me to the ground. I rolled onto my back too late; the devil was sitting on my chest. I couldn't breath.

With one last attempt, I grabbed him by the neck. He fell to the side, and we wrestled. I squeezed and I squeezed. Just as I could take no more, the sky opened and a sparkling pulse of light electrified the air. A figure in white descended as the devil withered and sank into the ground.

The light came into focus. A beautiful woman in a gown of dazzling white sat by my side on the grass. She looked so familiar. Why did I remember that face? I laid my head upon her lap. I stared at the blue, blue sky as she stroked my sweat-stained hair and whispered promises I could not hear. As I lost consciousness, I thought I heard my mother call my name. I was falling, falling, falling backward into large, fluffy, white cloud. I was at peace.

Evening came and the air turned cooler. The sounds in the distance faded away. My eyes opened. I could see the light draining from the evening sky like the life ebbing from the soldiers left behind to die on the field. Regaining my senses, I realized that I was lying at the edge of a wood. There was Providence, still wearing his saddle.

With horror, I saw a streak of bright red staining his coat. I tried to sit up, but something was lying across my chest. I pushed. The pain in my left shoulder was almost unbearable. Once more, I tried to sit up. I pushed harder. This time I succeeded.

The body of a Union soldier, his neck black and blue, rolled to the ground beside me. I stood and, with great effort, made my way to Providence. He turned his head and nuzzled my hand. I inspected his side.

Thankfully, the blood had not come from him. It was then that I looked down and saw my blood-soaked uniform. I had been hit twice. There was a hole in my jacket at my left shoulder. Blood oozed from the wound. Just a little lower also on the left side in line with my heart was another tear. There was no blood from this hole.

I put my hand to my chest and took from my pocket my cigar case. Imbedded in the gold was a single bullet. The case had saved my life. My shoulder would need attention. I had to get help. With a great deal of effort, I climbed onto Providence's back and headed in the direction of camp. I arrived just after dark. I lay, almost passed out from fatigue and loss of blood, slumped forward in the saddle, clutching my horse's neck.

I heard Jordan's voice yelling, "It's Masta Charles. He done made it back."

Soon there were two other men at my side. They grabbed me as I rolled down from Providence's back.

"Get him over here," someone ordered.

"Looks like he done been shot," said Jordan.

"Let's get him over here by the fire into the light and get his coat off. We need to see how badly he's wounded." That sounded like Matthew.

As I lay on the ground, the last thing I remember was someone tearing off my jacket and a voice saying, "Quick, I need water now."

The lady in white was back. I tried to ask her name. She just put her finger to her mouth and said, "Shhh." She stroked my forehead and told me to sleep. I smiled; now I remembered. Now

I recognized her face. I called her by name, and she nodded yes. She said, "Now sleep, my son, sleep. I'll be right here."

When I awoke the next morning, she was gone. It was Hardy's face, sleeping in a chair by my bedside, that greeted me. For a brief moment, as I looked at his innocent face, it was as if the war had not happened. He was me—a child again. A servant would be there in a moment to wake me.

I would go downstairs to find my family at the breakfast table. Grandfather would be sitting at the head of the big table in the dining room at Grand Oak, his pocket watch in his hand, waiting. I smiled. How naive we had all been.

"What does a soldier have to do to get a drink of water here?" I asked, my voice cracking.

Hardy blinked twice, rubbed his eyes, and toppled the chair as he leapt to my side. He fell to his knees and put his arms around me, crying, "You're alive! You're alive!"

Pain from the weight of his body against my shoulder shot through me.

"Hardy, my shoulder!" I cried.

He sprang up. "I'm sorry, Major. I'm sorry!" With tears in his eyes, he said. "It's just that I thought you'd left me like Ma and Pa and everyone else."

"I'm not that easy to get rid of," I said. "Besides, I promised to make you a soldier, and we aren't finished yet. We shook on it, remember?"

Hardy snapped to attention and saluted me. "Sure do, sir." He smiled.

Gettysburg had been costly. It cost us the dream of an independent South. It cost us the lives of many of our brightest and finest young men. It was, however, the personal loss that was the greatest to abide. The outcome of the battle was difficult to fathom. Jordan's brother ran off to join the Yankees. We lost eight men and nine horses. All of us were wounded, some more seriously than others. I had been shot twice. I would recover. Matthew's horse was shot out from beneath him. A second bullet had caught Matthew in the leg. He was hobbling about camp with a nasty-looking wound. I prayed it would not turn gangrenous.

It was, however, the task of writing letters to the families of the young men whose lives had been entrusted to me that was the most difficult to bear. Both Jimmy and Billy Murphy were gone. They had fallen side-by-side moments apart. Their families would later journey north to claim their bodies from shallow graves.

They would be reentered with honor in Charleston. The prophecy of Caleb Humphries's blood-red rose was fulfilled, and George Winthrop joined him on the field of honor. We never knew where they fell or where their bodies were laid to rest.

Three other young men in my company, heroes all, became permanent residents of Gettysburg that awful day.

With the battle lost and all hope of a victory on Northern soil gone, we turned our attention to the defense of our homeland. Troops would be needed to defend Richmond and others to defend South Carolina and home. The remnants of our battle-weary cavalry turned southward.

July 7 found us bivouacked near a little town called Monocacy Junction, about three miles southeast of Frederick, Maryland. Hardy and I had ridden away from camp to try to find food. We were in a fair-sized field. To our west, a long stone wall with woods behind it rambled down a short hill. Just a little piece ahead of us was a dead tree whose limbs hung over the wall. On one of those limbs perched the grandest, fattest turkey I had ever seen. I took my pistol from my belt, aimed, and dropped the bird with one shot.

"You got 'em, Major!" cried Hardy.

I jumped down from Providence's back to retrieve our dinner. "Looks like we'll eat good tonight." I smiled. I held the bird high so Hardy could admire our prize.

Suddenly there came from behind the wall a rapid series of sounds like the cocking of several gun triggers. A line of blue-clad soldiers jumped up.

"You best drop that bird, rebel," shouted one of the soldiers.

As three of them jumped over the wall, several others remained in position with their weapons pointed at me. Hardy sat stunned, watching from his horse.

"And you can toss that pistol over yonder while you're at it," sneered one of the men.

"Well, looky here. Looks like we caught us an officer," said another.

Then I made one of the great mistakes of my life. I turned to Hardy and shouted, "Run, boy, run!"

Hardy took off at a gallop.

I heard a soldier holler, "Shoot that rebel traitor! He's gettin' away! Shoot him!

Someone fired a gun. I saw Hardy's horse tumble. I reached for my pistol just as a rifle butt hit my head, and then the world went black.

I awoke hours later with a headache of biblical proportions and a goose egg on the side of my head. I sat up quickly and yelled "Hardy? Hardy, where are you?" Nausea overtook me, and I fell backward on to the cot.

I heard the soldier guarding me call, "Captain Hallowell, he's awake!"

A young-looking officer with a drooping moustache and eyes the color of his uniform entered the tent. To the sentry he said, "It's okay, Private. I've got it. Guard the door." He turned to me and said, "Don't worry, Major. The boy is fine. He had a few scrapes and bruises. The nurse is bandaging him up. You can see him in a minute. How are you feeling?"

"I feel like I've just been kicked in the head by a mule," I answered.

"I want to apologize for that," said the captain. "We are not barbarians. I assure you that the man who hit you has been punished."

With as much sarcasm as I could muster, I said, "Much obliged. Now, if you don't mind, I'll just collect my son and our horses, and we'll be on our way. You can keep the turkey for your trouble."

Trying to be pleasant, the captain smiled through his blond moustache. My sarcasm was lost on him. He said, "I'm sorry, Major. I can't do that. I have orders to have you both escorted to Fort Delaware."

"Fort Delaware?" I repeated.

"Yes, sir. We have a group of prisoners being shipped there tomorrow, and I am afraid you will have to accompany them."

A million thoughts raced through my head. I had heard about the horrors of the Yankee prisons that were little more then death camps. I would rather take my chances on the battlefield.

THE LAST MEASURE
OF INNOCENCE

One week after our capture, Hardy and I found ourselves standing at the number-one lock on the Chesapeake and Delaware Canal in Delaware City. We were waiting for the transport vessel that would take us to a place called Pea Patch Island and Fort Delaware.

If one had to be in a federal prison, Fort Delaware was the least of evils. The death rate in the average camp ran from around 20 to a high of 24 percent. Fort Delaware, with its rate of just over 7 percent, fell well below the average. Still, the sanitary conditions and the lack of health care, aided by the overcrowding on the island, encouraged the spread of disease. In addition, many of the men now coming in were already ill or wounded.

Barely above sea level, Pea Patch Island was home to a most impressive, well-armored, stone fortress. On the northern side of the small island was located the prisoner's barracks. A series of open, mosquito-infested trenches that were no more than open sewers crisscrossed the exposed, marshy fields. One balanced one's self cautiously across a makeshift boardwalk of creaky old lumber to a rabbit warren of hastily constructed barracks that were home to the prisoners. These un-insulated wooden boxes were oppressively hot in the summer and brutishly cold in the winter. The men slept without mattresses, ticks, pillows, or even a little straw, stacked shoulder to shoulder, three bunks high.

On the northwest side of the island was the mess hall where the scraping from the hog's troughs that passed as food was served twice a day.

The privies were located on a wharf over the river. One reached them by a narrow wooden bridge. Inside the long buildings were holes cut in the floor for the waste to drop into the river below. On the southeast side of the island were located the homes for the married officers and their families. Nearby to the east, construction was underway for a chapel, which would be finished in the fall.

Until my incarceration in Delaware, I had spent little time in the North. I had conducted business in New York City and Philadelphia but never stayed more than two or three weeks. I had been a guest in many fine homes and found the companionship and hospitality most agreeable. I had visited Newport with Aunt Effie and found the people pleasant and welcoming. However, Delaware seemed to be another matter. I suppose that that observation is somewhat unfair as the soldiers from the fort were not native sons. Most of the soldiers in the garrison had never seen combat. I found them to be arrogant, cocky, pusillanimous, self-anointed demigods who liked to bully men who were either unarmed or too weak to fight.

The civilians were not much better. Tourists would hire fishing boats to take them the short distance across the river. The fishermen, realizing that there was more money to be made by hiring out their boats, were only too happy to oblige. They would pass slowly so that visitors from the mainland could "step right up and observe, in person, the poor, wretched rebel soldiers!" They came by the boatload to gawk and point at us, as though we were no more than animals in a cage. We were surrounded by people who saw us as less than human. According to their perspective, we were either a burden that took them from their own self-perceived importance or a diversion to entertain or pity.

Inside the fort, for the prisoners, boredom was rampant. To pass the time and fight the monotony, I taught Hardy to read and write. We read from the Bible Grandmother had given me. Writing presented a different challenge. Paper was scarce, but I managed to procure a small amount for my personal use. As I wrote to Josephine weekly, Hardy practiced his penmanship. I had no way of knowing that not one of my letters reached Charleston.

Because of my close, professional ties to England and my rank, the paranoid Yankees thought that I might be sending messages in code or, worse yet, personally financing the war effort. They classified me as a prisoner of state, thus rendering me ineligible for parole. They regularly questioned me about bank accounts that I had in England and the exact nature of the businesses that I owned. Not believing me, they held on to every letter I wrote.

I wondered why Josephine never answered my letters. I told myself that the mail out of the South was unreliable or that the postmaster at the fort was lying about my getting any mail. I told myself anything except what I feared may be the truth.

In the fall of 1863, disaster struck. As the first frost of October signaled the end of the growing season, the smell of wood fires and decaying leaves drifted across the river and in through the iron bars, stretched across the windows of the fort. Suddenly, without warning, smallpox, like fire through a cotton shed, ran rampant in the prison population. By the beginning of December, over 860 Confederate prisoners had succumbed to the infection. Most of the Union soldiers had been vaccinated against the dreaded disease and were not as likely to contact the sickness. I felt a strange mixture of guilt and relief that, due to the fact that I was an officer, I was not quartered in with the general population in the main barracks. The higher-ranking officers were garrisoned in the main fort so that we could not encourage the rank and file in rebellion. The living conditions were definitely better inside the walls of the fort. Hardy, due in part to his age, had been allowed to stay with me in my quarters.

In order that we might be spared exposure to the sickness and disease that ran rampant through the camp, Hardy and I kept to ourselves as much as possible. Still, we were required to take our meals in the prisoners' mess. Twice each day we made our way through the swampy fields to division seven to eat our meager fare. Each day I wondered would today be the day we would become ill.

Realizing that the epidemic would wipe out the prisoner population of the island, the Union doctors began to inoculate the prisoners. By December, the outbreak seemed to be under control.

Delaware was a place that knew not only the heat of summer, but also the deep-freezing cold of winter. By December, most mornings we awoke, shivering, to find ice thick on the inside of our window. The river had frozen completely over. Were it not for the great blocks of ice that the tide threw upon the mud surrounding the island, it looked as though one could walk the one and one-eighth mile over the smooth frozen water to freedom on the mainland.

We passed the winter concentrating on Hardy's education. We were able to borrow a few books from the officers' library, and we continued writing lessons on whatever scraps of paper we could find. I was even successful at teaching the boy a little French. Just as Hardy had been an apt pupil when it came to soldiering, so, too, did he take well to academics.

Thus engaged, Hardy and I passed the winter. In May, the boy turned thirteen. I regretted that I had nothing to give him.

There was a gentleman named Isaac Handy detained at the fort. The Reverend Handy was a Presbyterian minister from

Portsmouth, Virginia. He was a political prisoner. He was considered a threat because of his pro-Southern sympathies. He reminded me a little of Moses with his flowing hair and beard. We had become close friends. From somewhere, the good Reverend produced a small book entitled *How to Be Gentleman*. He wrapped it in newspaper and gave it to the boy. Hardy was so excited. He studied that book and could eventually recite it word for word. There was no doubt in my mind that one day this boy would be a great man.

Throughout the early spring and summer, we watched and waited as prisoner after prisoner was exchanged. Repeatedly, because of my status a prisoner of state, Hardy and I were excluded from the lists.

The early part of 1864 saw the population of Pea Patch swell to about sixteen thousand souls. Without their superior officers, and without the drilling and fighting, the prisoners abandoned the military routine and returned to their civilian way of life. Men who had been barbers cut hair. Men who had been cobblers repaired shoes.

There was a chess club, a debating society, and a theatrical club in the barracks. Just as in civilian life, there was the gambling, fighting, and drunkenness. These problems were generally handled by the prisoners themselves.

With the approach of summer, the heat and humidity began to make themselves felt at Fort Delaware. The crowded conditions, poor rations, and the unsanitary conditions assured that the two hospitals erected on the north end of the island were always full. More than a few prisoners noticed how many of their comrades never returned from a trip to the hospital, and so they refused medical attention, opting instead for home remedies. This action was the cause of much more spreading of disease. Despite the fear of illness and the harassment from the Union soldiers, life on Pea Patch went on as usual.

In late June, a rumor washed over the island. Fifty prisoners were to be paroled and shipped to Charleston, South Carolina.

The morning of June 24 dawned exceptionally warm and humid. Hardy and I dressed hurriedly and ran to read the list. My name, along with Hardy's, appeared on the register for parole. Oh, what joy, what rapture! We were going home!

Our euphoria was short lived. That evening after our meal, we returned to our quarters and retired. Around two o'clock in the morning, Hardy awakened me.

"Major, I don't feel so good. I think I'm gonna be sick," he said.

There was a pale blue light coming through the cell window. I lit the lamp by my bed and walked over to where Hardy lay. The poor boy was soaked in sweat. He started to heave, and I quickly grabbed the chamber pot by the bed. Hardy lost his supper into the pot and fell backward onto his bed.

"Major, am I gonna be all right?" I could see the fear in his eyes.

"Of course you are, son," I answered. I walked over to the washbasin and soaked a towel in water. I wrung the towel out and returned to his side. I laid the cool cloth on his hot forehead.

"I don't think we're ever gonna find my brothers. I expect they've been done in by the Yankees. I'm all alone," he said.

"Nonsense. I'm sure we'll find them. But, Hardy, if we don't, you are not alone. You can come and live at Grand Oak with Josephine and me. You'll be our son."

Hardy coughed violently. "Honest?" he said.

"Honest," I answered.

"Will you tell me about Grand Oak?" he asked.

As I told him stories about home and life on the river, Hardy closed his eyes and drifted into an uneasy sleep. I extinguished the lamp and sat by the boy until the first light.

By sunrise, Hardy had the chills. I had seen enough of other men dying of any number of illnesses to be concerned. I sent one of the guards for the doctor. The doctor looked at Hardy and called for two attendants.

"Get this boy out of here and to the hospital immediately," he ordered. He turned to me. "Major, you had better come with me."

Stunned, I followed the doctor to the hospital. When we arrived, he ordered me to wait while he examined Hardy. After what seemed like an eternity, the doctor entered the room where I sat waiting. He walked over to where I sat and removed the spectacles from his gray eyes. He looked sadly at me. "I'm afraid the boy has malaria," he said.

I felt as though the floor dropped out from under me.

"I'm not going to lie to you. It doesn't look good, but it is hard to tell. The first few days are critical. He is young. He may pull through. I am afraid I will have to keep you both here for observation."

I barely heard these last words. I jumped from my chair. "I have to see him," I said.

The doctor stood and pressed his hands on my shoulders, forcing me back down into the chair. "You can't right now. I gave him something to make him sleep. We will take good care of him."

We would not be able to move Hardy while he was ill. I would not leave him behind. Two days later another officer and private took our places aboard the ship as it sailed for Charleston. We did not know it at the time, but that would be the last of the prisoner exchanges until the end of the war.

For the next two weeks, Hardy drifted in and out of consciousness. He never failed to smile when he opened his eyes and saw me sitting by his bedside. I told him stories about Josephine, Aunt Effie, and Lizzie. I told him about the cotton we grew, the horses we raised, and the mills in England. I promised him an education and a grand tour when he finished.

One night, Hardy awoke from a troubled sleep.

"Major! Major!" he cried.

"I'm right here, Hardy," I answered.

"I'm awfully cold." He coughed. "But I don't feel the pain no more."

"Do you want me to get you anything?"

"No. Just tell me a story."

I began to tell him about the time Josephine stowed away on her father's ship dressed as a boy, when suddenly he said, "It's Stuart."

"What's that, son?" I asked.

"My last name. It's Stuart," he repeated. "Major, you won't forget me, will you?"

"Of course not. Don't talk silly. You're going to get well and go to Grand Oak with me."

"Mama said as long as the people you love remember you, you will live on in their hearts."

"You're going to be all right." I tried to smile.

Hardy coughed. It didn't sound good.

"I know," he said.

I stood up. "I'm going to go get the doctor."

"No, don't leave me. Finish telling me about Josephine and how you thought she was a little boy," he pleaded.

I sat back down and began again with my narrative. Hardy closed his eyes. As I spoke, I brushed the hair from his forehead. He felt so cold. He coughed again softly, opened his eyes, smiled brilliantly at me, and then he was gone.

Hot tears welled into my eyes; I shook him like a rag doll. "Hardy, don't go!" I cried.

I let his limp body fall to the cot and ran for the doctor. He came quickly.

"What is it?"

"It's Hardy. You have to help him," I pleaded.

The doctor felt the boy's pulse. He shook his head slowly and laid Hardy's hand across his chest.

"I'm sorry, Major," he said.

I was mad with rage. I jumped up and started overturning tables and throwing things about the room. The doctor called for help. Two soldiers wrestled me into a chair.

"Major, take it easy. He's gone. There is no more we can do," said the doctor.

I had watched men die as I shot them. I had seen my friends killed and maimed before my eyes. I had found soldiers and horses lying dead and bloated along the roadside. I had watched my beloved horses massacred on the battlefield. Through all of this, I had never, never shed a tear. I had seen the gates of hell, and somehow I had survived. But this, this was more than my heart could stand. At that moment, the war, with all of its violence, putrefaction, and death, became undeniably real.

I could not turn my face from the carnage any longer. With Hardy went the last measure of innocence and humanity that I possessed. I buried my head in my hands and wept as I had never wept before.

The following day was the worst of my life. Hardy had to be laid to rest quickly because of the malaria. They bought a wooden box for him. I washed his face and hands and brushed his hair. I put his blanket in the box and dressed him in his tattered uniform, of which he was so proud. I asked that my saber that had been taken from me when we were sent to the island be returned to me so that I might bury it with Hardy. I viewed the act as signifying the end of my fighting and the graduation of Hardy to manhood. My request was granted. I placed the hilt of the saber in his hands, with the blade pointing down to his feet. I kept his bugle so that I would always have a piece of him. I folded the blanket around him.

They nailed the top on the box and took him to the pier. I was determined to go across the river and make sure that they respected him and offered a prayer, but Captain Ahl was against the plan.

"We can't present you with an opportunity to escape," he said.

It was Reverend Handy who came to my rescue. The good reverend argued my case before Captain Ahl.

"Surely, sir, the man has suffered a great loss. He is not thinking of escape right now. I will personally guarantee his return if you will permit him to go to the burial with us," pleaded Reverend Handy.

Captain Ahl finally agreed but with the promise that if anything happened, he would have both our heads. We committed Hardy to the cold, sandy soil of Finn's Point, New Jersey, so far from his family and friends. I felt at least some comfort in knowing that he was in the company of so many brave men, soldiers of the South. Surely, now he was one with them.

After Hardy's funeral, I was returned to my cell in the fort. It had been three weeks since that dreaded night that Hardy took ill.

For three days, I sat alone and wept. I ate no food and drank very little water. On the fourth day, Reverend Handy came to see me. He found me sitting on a chair by the window with my head in my hands.

"They tell me you're not eating, Major. If you don't start taking better care of yourself, you're going to be joining that young boy over there in New Jersey," he said.

I raised my head and looked at the reverend through watery, bloodshot eyes. Slowly, I shook my head from side to side. I returned my head to my hands.

"Major, you must have family and friends back home to live for. They have to miss you very much. They wouldn't want to see you suffer like this," continued Reverend Handy.

An image of Josephine on the day of our wedding flashed through my mind.

"God has called the boy home to be with his family—" began the Reverend.

I jumped up so violently that I overturned the chair in which I sat. "God! God!" I shouted. "What kind of a God murders a young boy's family and turns him out into the world alone? What kind of a God sits back and watches men pick up guns and swords and clubs and hack each other to death? What kind of a God strikes down a thirteen-year-old boy? There is no more God. He doesn't care about us. He's dead, dead and lying by the side of the road somewhere, rotting with soldiers and horses."

Not wanting Reverend Handy to see the tears running down my cheeks, I turned and looked out the window. I wiped my face with the back of my hand.

The reverend sat calmly on the end of my cot, his hands folded on his cane. He shook his head sadly. After a moment, he spoke.

"I assure you, my son, that God is indeed alive and well. It's hard to understand his plans for us. We don't know why he does what he does. Jesus said only the Father knows the hour. He knows the hour for each of us. Major, you need to realize it was Hardy's time. His work here was done."

I paused for a moment, letting his words sink in. "Don't you find it ironic that after being around all of those battles and all of that fighting that the boy should die here in this hellhole from a disease that he never should have come in contact with?"

"Yes, I do," said Reverend Handy. "But Hardy is safe now, safe from war and disease. Nothing can harm him ever again. He has gone ahead to prepare a place for you at Jesus's table."

I thought of my mother and my grandfather. I remembered hearing those same words as we laid them to rest. I had believed those words once upon a time. I believed I would see them all again one day. I remembered the man I was so long ago.

With tears in my eyes, I looked at the minister.

He smiled and said, "Right now you're hurting, my son, but you're not angry with God. You're hurting because you were left behind."

He was right. I felt my anger subsiding.

"Do you remember telling me about your family's business?" the reverend asked.

"The plantation?"

"No, the other one, the one in England."

"Yes."

"And what is it that you do?"

"We manufacture fabrics."

"Right. I want you to think about the tartans and the paisleys and all the rich tapestries that you weave," the wise man continued. "When you weave the designs, you don't just use bright-colored threads; you use blacks and browns and grays as well. Correct?"

Puzzled where the reverend was going with this, I said, "Of course we do. The designs wouldn't be very interesting with just the bright colors."

"Well, did it ever occur to you that perhaps life works the same way? That it is the good and the bad times that make us who we are? Maybe God weaves our lives just like a fine tapestry, with dark and light threads all running together. It's not until the weaving is finished and you step back and look at the finished design that you see the beauty of all of the colors side by side. Maybe we have to wait till he's finished to see the whole picture."

I began to cry once more. This time it was not from bitterness. This time I knew I would be all right. I would survive.

I realized that Hardy had been a part of my life for only a little more than one year, yet he had affected me so profoundly. I thought I was teaching him, but all the while, it was he who was teaching me. He taught me that I could love a child. I would make a good father. I would like to leave a legacy for the future. I prayed that it wasn't too late, and I would find a way to honor Hardy's memory.

An Uneasy Truce

As I sweated through the summer of 1863 at Fort Delaware, Josephine sat down and began to pour her heart out in letters to me. She didn't mail them; there was no way to get them out of South Carolina. She kept them instead, tied in a bundle with one of her hair ribbons, until I came home and she could read them to me in person. I would not learn until later that on August 22, at 1:30 a.m., Union troops found a new way to harass the citizens of Charleston. They aimed their 16,300-pound, eight-inch Parrot gun at Saint Michael's steeple and fired into the city. Before dawn, the "Swamp Angel," as it would come to be called, would send sixteen shells into the city. Aunt Effie's house on Legare Street was fortunately out of range of the shells, but the screams and resulting explosions from the shells were no less demoralizing.

It is difficult to express the psychological stress the almost daily shelling would eventually take on the citizens of Charleston. As the days passed, the shelling continued for what seemed an eternity. Many of the civilians had already left before the campaign had begun, but those who remained moved from the city's lower regions to areas out of range of the federal guns. To those who stayed behind, the sharp scream and the whiz of the shells passing overhead was a fearful sound. The townsfolk would lie in their beds at night, windows ajar, and wonder if they would live to see the morning light.

By September, the entire town was on edge. Even the head-strong, normally calm Aunt Effie was affected by the shelling. A few weeks into the bombing, Aunt Effie and Lizzie began to see Yankees behind every tree and bush. Convinced the unsavory element that now roamed the city posed a threat, Aunt Effie seldom left a room without someone by her side.

Mrs. Harriet Hudson Humphries had lived next door to Aunt Effie since I could remember. Mrs. Humphries was a short, plump woman with a strawberry complexion and a shock of unruly white hair. She had been widowed some years before the war when, during a thunderstorm, her husband, attempting to secure a loose shutter, lost his balance and fell from the third-floor window to his death.

In their youth, Aunt Effie and Mrs. Humphries had been best friends. As the friends entered matronhood, they vied for the crown of dominance in their social circle. We all smiled and kept our distance while the pair quarreled like siblings fighting for the last piece of cake at the dinner table. After Mr. Humphries death, Ms. Harriet lost all interest in running the affairs of Charleston. The crown went, by default, to Aunt Effie, and peace settled over the two households.

Mrs. Humphries had a mule named Tobias on which she lavished all of the affection she had once shown her dear, departed husband. Tobias, a moody, temperamental animal, was small for a mule, only about ten hands high. Mrs. Humphries had a diminutive cart to which she would hook the mule on market days. Off through the streets of town she would ride with Sally, who was her housekeeper and cook, by her side.

Perhaps Tobias's bad attitude had something to do with the fact that Ms. Harriet had taken to dressing the mule on holidays and market days—humiliating for the mule, hysterical for the townsfolk.

Depending on the occasion, poor Tobias might be wearing a flowered silk scarf fluttering in the wind. He might wear hats ranging from a particularly ugly sunbonnet to a large leghorn hat covered in red paper roses or, on a more patriotic whim, a Confederate forage cap and collar, complete with sergeant's stripes.

We would sit on Aunt Effie's piazza sipping tea and smile at the trio as they made their way home along the street. More often than not, as they returned from the market, Sally would be walking in front of Tobias, pulling him. He would be pulling the cart, and Ms. Harriet would be sitting on the seat of the cart with a broad smile on her florid face. I can still see her holding the reins in her tiny, gloved hands and wearing a hat, which matched the poor mule's.

One evening in late September, Aunt Effie remembered that she had left her mother's hand-crocheted afghan on the line in the backyard. Convinced that the thieving soldiers or Yankees would steal the treasured heirloom, she sent Lizzie to retrieve it. Lizzie returned after a few moments without the afghan, complaining that she was afraid to go out into the yard at night alone.

"There's nothing to be afraid of, Lizzie," said Aunt Effie. "Go light a lantern and get me a shawl, and I will go with you."

Lizzie disappeared down the hall and returned with the shawl and a lantern. There was a full moon that night, but the clouds obscured its light.

Occasionally the moon would peek through the clouds, illuminating the mist and bathing the landscape with shafts of pale blue light. There was a low fog as well, which only added to the eerie gloom of the evening. Aunt Effie marched assertively through the twilight across the lawn, holding aloft the lantern. Lizzie followed a pace and a half behind. Suddenly, she let out a piercing scream, scaring Aunt Effie, who dropped the lantern, extinguishing the flame.

"Now look what you've done, you silly girl! What are you squealing at?" cried Aunt Effie.

"Over there! Yankees, they've come to get us!" screamed Lizzie hysterically.

"Oh, bother, I don't see any Yankees, Lizzie," said Aunt Effie.

"Over there, there by the gate! I can see his hat," Lizzie cried.

Aunt Effie squinted in the direction Lizzie had pointed. Just then, the clouds parted momentarily allowing the moonlight to reveal, sure enough, a lone figure in a big straw hat standing just outside the gate. The stranger appeared to be stumbling as if he were drunk.

Effie and Lizzie turned and ran screaming toward the house only to be stopped at the door by Josephine, Grandmother, Ethne, and Mary Alice, all of whom had been roused into action by the first scream.

The ladies, except for Josephine, who had her gun in hand, were carrying an odd assortment of weapons with which to fend off the Yankees. Grandmother had her knitting needles, Ethne had a fireplace poker, and Mary Alice had a bust of Shakespeare taken from the fireplace mantle.

Josephine could out shoot many of the men in town. When she hauled out her Smith & Wesson, everyone scattered because they knew she meant business. Bolstered by reinforcements, Aunt Effie and Lizzie fell in line behind the ladies. Josephine pushed between them, hoops in one hand, gun in the other. She strode bravely across the lawn toward the stranger at the gate.

The moon reemerged, and the tip of a straw hat appeared floating above the top of the still-fastened gate. Wondering how many more of them there might be, she spoke in a brave firm voice.

"Whoever is there, this is private property. Please identify yourself or leave at once. I have a gun, and I'm not afraid to use it."

All of a sudden, several things happened in rapid succession.

The moon once again disappeared behind a cloud just as one of the Swamp Angel's shells found its mark and exploded in the next block.

The gate flew open, and the figure behind it stumbled into the dark yard.

Aunt Effie, finding courage in numbers and convinced that the Yankees wanted to steal her mother's blanket, lunged for the clothesline, shouting "Not my mother's afghan, you don't."

Lizzie, at the sound of the shell exploding, believed she had been shot by the Yankees, screamed loudly, and fainted.

Josephine, thinking she was being fired upon, took aim and dropped the figure at the gate in his tracks with a single shot.

The body hit the ground with a sickening, dull thud. Everyone froze where they stood. The clouds once again parted.

The pale full moon illuminated the backyard. The women edged hesitantly over to the body. Laying there in the moonlight with a single bullet right between his eyes was Tobias, Miss Harriet's poor mule. A worn straw hat lay beside him on the ground.

Knowing Miss Harriet would be inconsolable at the loss of her animal, there was a brief moment when the ladies contemplated burying the mule in the garden and letting Miss Harriet think the hapless animal had wandered off on its own. But, believing honesty to be the best policy, and shovels being scarce (the slaves had taken them to the edge of town to dig trenches for the soldiers to hide in), the ladies elected to tell Miss Harriet in the morning.

As expected, Miss Harriet did not take the news well. When Aunt Effie broke the sad tale of Tobias's demise, Miss Harriet called Josephine a "murderer" and declared it was bad enough putting up with the siege, but all the town needed was another loose cannon at large.

After "the murder," the ladies decided that it would be better to take their chances with the Union Army in the country than to put up with the ire of Mrs. Humphries. Aunt Effie closed the house in town and the ladies retired to the country.

The party arrived safely at Grand Oak on September 21, 1863. Unlike so many other fine homes that dotted the countryside and lined the riverbanks throughout the South, Grand Oak would survive the war. The reason for this fortunate turn of events was that Josephine had shot poor Tobias that fateful September night. It was that incident that made Aunt Effie and everyone else decide to retreat to the relative calm of the country and leave the pandemonium of the city behind. This move would change the course of history for our beloved home.

Once they were settled inside the big house, the women decided that they could better defend themselves if they stayed in groups or pairs. "Safety in numbers," Aunt Effie would say. It was Josephine's idea to move the beds from the upstairs rooms to the double front parlors that overlooked the river. Sleeping together in the same room would make it easy to watch out for each other. Every evening at dusk, they would close and fasten the shutters and draw the heavy velvet curtains, believing they could keep out the Yankees as easily they could vanquish the winter chill.

Once they had secured the house, they would light the gas lamps and build a cozy fire. They would spend the winter evenings taking turns reading while the others knitted socks and mittens or sewed for the men on the front lines. Sometimes they would entertain each other with an evening of music. When music or sewing did not occupy the ladies' time, they might play a game of whist or some other popular card game of the day. For a few brief hours, there was no war or sorrow.

With this routine firmly established, they passed away the long winter months of 1863 warm, secure, and safe within the walls of Grand Oak.

One warm spring morning in early May of 1864, the peace and quiet of Grand Oak was shattered in a most spectacular fashion. For two days, everyone had been listening to the deep rumble of what they believed to be thunder in the distance. The skies had been dull gray and filled with ominous clouds, but rain had not come. A blustery wind from the west bullied the angry clouds and set them in turbulent motion. They passed overhead, like chariots bearing the gods of the Acropolis on some urgent errand. As evening fell on the second night, the clouds thickened and the wind shifted to the north.

"It won't be long now," said Aunt Effie. "Look how the trees are turning their leaves upside down asking for rain. And the swallows are circling low to the ground too. That's a sure sign of rain."

"Perhaps we should send Big Jawn to see that all of the animals are in," said Mary Alice.

"I'm sure everything is taken care of, Mary Alice," said Grandmother, sitting in her rocking chair and knitting by the fireplace. "Besides, dear, the animals won't shrink if they get wet in the rain."

Mary Alice looked crossly at Grandmother; she started to tell her that she knew the animals wouldn't shrink, but before she could finish her sentence, she was interrupted by a loud crack of thunder, which caused everyone in the parlor to jump. Seeming to shake the very foundation of the great house, the thunder echoed through the parlor and down the hallways. The deafening roar was followed by a mighty gust of wind and a brilliant flash of lightning.

The latter ripped through the clouds in a blinding flash. Almost as if they had been slashed open by the lightning, the clouds parted, spilling their heavy burden of wind-driven water on the landscape below. The ladies quickly fastened the shutters and drew the drapes against the tempest.

The rain remained heavy for hours. Several times during the night, Josephine thought she heard men shouting or horses whinnying. She looked around at the peaceful scene before her. The soft glow of the fireplace cast a golden glow over the room. Everyone had been lulled sound asleep by the rhythm of the rain. Josephine decided the sounds were just her imagination and soon she drifted off to sleep.

By the next morning the rain had stopped. Brilliant sunshine and clear blue skies replaced the clouds from the previous two days. The birds chattered in the trees outside, and there seemed to be a lot of noise on the front lawn not too far from the house.

Mary Alice pulled open the drapes and the early morning sun shone through the slats in the heavy oak shutters. Just as she had done every morning for the last six months, Mary Alice unhooked the iron fasteners and opened the shutters to let in the fresh morning air. Suddenly she gave a strange, strangled cry and backed into the room, both hands clutching her throat. Everyone in the parlor rushed to the window to see what had upset the poor girl so. There on the lawn, as far as the eye could see, were tents, hundreds and hundreds of tents. They had sprung up overnight, like mushrooms after the spring rain. There were soldiers too, Yankee soldiers, scurrying about in a great deal of urgency.

Josephine, taking charge, addressed the group. For once, everyone was silent.

"Everybody just sit quietly here in the house. I'll take Big Jawn and find out what is going on," she said.

Josephine called for Big Jawn. It was not long before his immense frame could be heard thundering from the back of the house to where she stood waiting for him in the front parlor.

"Child, just where do you think you are going"? asked Aunt Effie.

"I'm going to find out who is in charge and what is going on," said Josephine.

"And who is going to look after us if something should happen to you?" Aunt Effie asked.

"Don't worry, Aunt Effie," Josephine said in a calm, soothing voice. "If they meant us any harm, they would have stormed the house by now."

It was Lizzie who spoke next. "But, Miss Josephine, suppose they thought the house was empty? When they find out it's not, they will come for us."

"There are so many of them, we can never hold them off," Ethne said.

"Everyone just be quiet until I return, and everything will be all right," said Josephine. With that, she marched out the front door and sailed down the steps with Big Jawn in tow.

As Josephine and Big Jawn made their way across the front lawn, it became apparent what had been happening in the countryside for the last two days. Unbeknownst to those at the plantation, what had sounded like thunder in the distance had actually been cannon fire. A battle had been raging several miles upriver from the house. Wishing to get the wounded out of harms way, the Union forces had removed them to a location away from the fighting. Scouts had found the relative peace and quiet of the homestead a safe location in which to locate their field hospital.

The westerly wind had blown the sounds and smells of battle away from the house. The direction of the wind had changed overnight, and the smell of gun power hung heavy in the air replacing the scent of flowers. There was a muffled moan from the wounded, who cried out for water or aid. The wounded seemed to be everywhere on the great lawn, and soldiers scurried about, sorting out those in need of the most urgent care and dispatching them to the operating tents on stretchers.

After questioning several soldiers, Josephine got the location of the commanding officer's tent. She went to pay him a visit. There was a sentry standing at the open flap of the tent. He inquired as to reason for Josephine's visit. She informed him that she was the mistress of the house and that she would like to speak to whoever was in charge.

"One moment and I will announce you," said the guard.

Standing outside, Josephine and Big Jawn could hear pieces of muffled conversation. The sentry came back and motioned for Josephine to enter the tent.

As she entered the commanding officer's tent, Josephine bade Big Jawn to wait for her outside. The officer was busy at his desk going over some papers.

Without looking up the officer in charge, a captain, said, "Yes, what is it?"

"I'm sorry. Perhaps this is a bad time," said Josephine. The fact that she was annoyed by the captain's curt reply did not show in her voice.

The officer looked up from his papers startled to hear a woman's voice. He stood quickly, knocking his pen from his desk.

"Begging your pardon, ma'am. I was expecting a gentleman. My guard failed to tell me that it was a lady waiting to speak to me," he said.

The captain was a pleasant-looking man with nice, even features. Josephine noticed that his eyes were the same shade of Yankee blue as his uniform. A few strands of blond hair had fallen across his forehead, giving him an almost boyish appearance. In an effort to make himself look older, the captain had grown a large, drooping mustache, but it only seemed out of place on a face so young.

"I'm Captain Thomas J. Hallowell. How can I help you?" he asked.

"I'm Mrs. Charles McGuire," said Josephine, extending her hand.

The captain took her hand and shook it.

She was relieved that Captain Hallowell at least seemed to be a gentleman.

"I and the ladies of the house were wondering what is going on here."

"I am sorry to disturb you and your family, but we have been fighting nearby. We needed a place safe from the battle to treat our wounded," said the captain.

"I see," said Josephine. Weighing her options and realizing she had no other choice, she decided right then and there to offer the hospitality of the plantation to the Union army as if it had been her idea to invite them there all along.

"Then please allow me to welcome you and your staff and soldiers to our home. How long may we expect you to stay?"

"That's difficult to say right now, ma'am. We'll have to wait for supplies and till these men are strong enough to travel," said the captain.

"Very well. Unfortunately, we do not have much to offer, but please let us know if we may assist you," offered Josephine.

With that simple offer, she unknowingly insured the future and the survival of our home.

Back at the house, Josephine related the details of her conversation with Captain Hallowell to those anxiously assembled in the parlor. She braced herself for the flood of criticism she knew would follow. Before she could finish, everyone spoke in loud, excited voices.

"Josephine, you can't mean we are going to welcome these men into our home," said Ethne. "You must realize that you are embracing the same soldiers who have attacked our homeland and fired upon our cities and made our lives unbearable."

"Let us not forget what they have been doing to Charleston!" said Grandmother.

"And what is to happen to us when they have eaten all of our food and run off our animals?" added Mary Alice.

"My dear, surely you could have found some way of letting them know they are not welcome here," said Aunt Effie.

Defending her decision, Josephine said, "Just what would you have me do? I can't order them off the property. And even if I could, how would we make them leave?"

"Well, then perhaps we should leave," said Ethne.

"Yes, we could take the servants and children and the things we need to survive and disappear into the night when they are all sleeping," said Mary Alice.

"First of all, we are not prisoners. We are free to come and go as we please. We don't have to sneak out in the night. Secondly, even if we had to leave, just how far do you think Aunt Effie and Grandmother could walk? If we take a horse and carriage out, the army will only confiscate it," said Josephine.

"Thirdly, even if they could travel by foot, where would we go? We can't go back to Charleston; it's not safe. We are better off staying here. I weighed all of these options in my head. The only way to survive is to play along with the Yankees. Like it or not, they are here to stay for a while, and we will just have to wait this thing out. I have made my decision!" With that, Josephine turned and left the room. Everyone sat in disbelief.

"Well, I don't like this one little bit," said Mary Alice.

"Now, now, she means well. She thinks she is making the best choice for all of us. She does make sense," said Aunt Effie.

"I still don't have to agree with her," snapped Mary Alice. She rose and went to the veranda to sulk.

The ladies sat in the parlor and discussed what had just happened. Josephine was correct; there was really nothing they could do to send the army on its way. Grandmother reminded everyone there wasn't any sense in poking a hornet's nest. Yes, the best thing to do was for everyone to try to get along until the soldiers left. The women could just busy themselves with their household chores, keep the doors locked, and pretend the army wasn't outside.

Deciding that peace began at home, Grandmother went to find Josephine to tell her she would support her. Aunt Effie and Ethne went to find Mary Alice and soothe her feelings. They found her standing at the corner of the porch, leaning against one of the columns and observing the scene before her on the lawn.

There seemed to be less confusion than there had been earlier this morning, but there was still plenty of activity. The soldiers were crossing the lawn with a little less urgency than before. They walked back and forth carrying men on stretchers, while others limped about on wooden crutches or sticks cut from trees. Other men just lay beneath the trees and called out for water. The air, too, was different.

So far, the ladies had been spared seeing the war up close and personal. Things were difficult in Charleston, and the shelling had been unnerving, but now the war was at their doorstep. Strange new smells had replaced the familiar scents of the grounds. There was the acrid stench of gunpowder. There was also the smell of blood, sweat, and wet canvas in the air, and there was something else, something unfamiliar, something cruel. It was the smell of death! The war had come to Grand Oak. Mary Alice wished with all of her heart she could be anywhere but here right now.

Joined by Aunt Effie and Ethne, who stood in silence, Mary Alice watched the soldiers go about their work from the safety of the wide gallery.

After several minutes, Ethne said, "It terrifies me to think these could be our men. Yankees don't look so different when you see them up close like this."

"You are right, Ethne. They don't look any different. Maybe we are being selfish. After all, everyone of them is somebody's son," said Aunt Effie sadly.

With that, Mary Alice burst into tears and ran crying into the house.

For two and a half days, through the high, wide windows veiled by lace curtains, the women watched the soldiers busy themselves on the lawn. Sometimes they would go out and walk from one end of the porch to the other to take a little air and observe the drama taking place before them. Swept along in the tide of events, their feelings began to soften. They began to feel sorry for the men on the lawn. After watching the soldiers go about their daily chores, it became clear that they meant the women in the big house no harm. A feeling of consciousness took over and the conversation turned to how they might help these poor men and boys.

It was Aunt Effie who finally decided she had seen as much as she could bear.

"We have sat here long enough! Yankees or not, we can't just sit here and watch these men die. We have to do something," she declared.

The ladies all agreed that there must be some good in everyone, and perhaps by helping these soldiers, they would ensure the good Lord would see to it that the Northern women would take care of their men and see them safely on the road home.

As the days progressed, it was touching to see how everyone found their own way of helping the army camped around their house. Led by Aunt Effie, the ladies rounded up all of the old bed linens and excess cloth they could find. They cut them into strips and rolled them for bandages for the wounded. Mary

Alice seemed to have a real gift for nursing, and she threw herself into the task of caring for the wounded with a passion that surprised everyone.

After a few days, even the servants and former slaves joined in the efforts to help. Mammy, Lizzie, and the female servants boiled water for baths and washed clothes for the soldiers. The males who were left on the plantation helped with the horses and hunting up food. The ladies began taking turns visiting the sick and wounded and writing letters for those who could not write for themselves.

Most of the soldiers professed their love for mothers and sweethearts, telling them not to worry and that they would be home soon. Others left instructions for how to handle things if they should die.

There was one young soldier who was too injured to write. It was obvious that he would not recover from his wounds. As he lay dying, he dictated his last words to Aunt Effie, who sat with tears in her eyes and pen in her hand.

She felt angry at the waste of so young a life, but she didn't let it show on her face. The soldier told how he was sorry never to see his parents again. He told them not to worry; he was in the company of friends, and he regretted that he would never see his unborn child or hold his young bride again. He had barely finished speaking when he breathed his last. Aunt Effie gently held his hand for a moment then closed his brown eyes. She wept bitterly over his lifeless body. Before they carried him out, Aunt Effie cut a lock of his hair and took two of the buttons from his torn uniform to send home with the letter.

There were other soldiers too who did not live through the ordeal. As many of them as could be were shipped home to their families for burial. The others were buried near a grove of persimmon trees by the stream that ran a fair piece from the main house.

There was also much to be done to care for the recovering soldiers and for the two doctors and the nurses attending to them.

The slaves set long wooden tables, under the limbs of the old oak; here they served meals for the officers. Young Captain Hallowell had taken to eating here with the ladies of the house. One evening, during dinner, Aunt Effie realized that the captain, who was usually so confident and well spoken, seemed to stutter and look at his feet whenever the ladies were around. She realized Mary Alice in particular seemed to have captured the young officer's fancy. Aunt Effie decided to keep her eye on the pair.

Food was not as plentiful as it would have been before the war. In fact, it was downright scarce. Now with so many more mouths to feed, it was even more precious, but everyone made the most of what they had. Ethne said it reminded her of the story of Jesus feeding the crowds with only a few fish and a couple of loaves of bread.

One morning two weeks after the army had arrived, Ethne, Mary Alice, Lizzie, and Aunt Effie were finishing their morning chores when they noticed several men walking at a brisk pace toward the house, one of whom they had not seen before. Concerned, they called for Josephine.

She came with Grandmother to the door. Josephine walked across the porch and stood on the top step of the veranda. She watched, arms akimbo, as the soldiers approached the house. She had the feeling that the man who was leading was somehow very familiar. As they got closer, she realized that the man walking in front was a very famous general in the Union army. She recognized his weather-lined, bearded face from an illustration she had seen in the paper before she had left Charleston.

"Good morning, ladies. May I sit with you for a moment?" asked the general.

"Yes, by all means," said Josephine. She motioned the soldiers onto the porch. The general, followed by Captain Hallowell and two other officers, mounted the steps to the gallery. They removed their hats and bowed to Josephine.

"Please have a seat. May I offer you all some tea?" she asked politely.

"We wouldn't want to put you out, ma'am," said Captain Hallowell.

"It's no trouble at all," said Josephine with a pleasant smile. "Lizzie, would you run into the house and have Isabelle bring us tea and some cups please? And have Big Jawn bring us a few extra chairs."

Not wanting to miss what was being discussed on the porch, Lizzie contemplated telling Miss Josephine to get her own tea, but knowing she could not get away with impertinence with Josephine as she could with her mistress, she thought better of it and grudgingly complied with Josephine's request. As she disappeared into the hallway, she mumbled something under her breath about Mr. Lincoln freeing the slaves. The girl emerged a few moments later, still mumbling but with two extra chairs. She was followed a few moments later by Isabelle, bearing a large, wooden tray on which sat the tea and cups for the general and his men. She was followed by Big Jawn, carrying two more chairs.

"I'm afraid we can only offer you chamomile tea," explained Josephine. "I am sure you know any other type of tea is impossible to come by, but we grow our own chamomile here."

Captain Hallowell made introductions as Josephine poured tea for the officers. Once everyone had been served, she surveyed the men on her porch. Everyone seemed calm and relaxed except for the poor captain. He was fidgeting, and small beads of perspiration were starting to show on his forehead. He would stare at his shoes, then at Mary Alice, then back at his shoes.

It was at that moment that Josephine realized that Mary Alice was looking back and smiling.

Josephine was not the only one to notice the captain's infatuation with Mary Alice. The general, it seemed, also realized what was going on. He sat with an amused smile on his bearded face. The obvious discomfort of the young captain reminded him of his own first romance.

Aunt Effie cleared her throat, bringing Josephine and the general's thoughts back to the present.

"Honey?" asked Josephine.

"Beg your pardon, ma'am?" stammered the general.

"Honey. Would you like some honey with your tea? I would offer you sugar, but we haven't had sugar for ages," said Josephine.

"Yes, honey would be fine," said the general, regaining his composure.

Curious as to the reason for this visit, Aunt Effie turned her attention to the general.

"One would assume this is more then just tea and biscuits with the lady of the house. What brings you to our home this morning?"

Taking a sip of his tea, the general seemed slightly caught off guard by Aunt Effie's directness. He swallowed his tea, cleared his throat, and began to speak.

"Captain Hallowell and his men here have been telling me how helpful you ladies have been to our troops while they have been recuperating. As a matter of fact, the captain tells me that you ladies have done more for morale then can be imagined."

"Nonsense," interrupted Aunt Effie. "We just did what any God-fearing Christian women would have done."

Josephine shot Aunt Effie a look that said, "Let the man finish," but it was lost on Aunt Effie, who had found her voice. And once she started talking, it was difficult to get a word in till she had made her point.

Aunt Effie continued, "Make no mistake, we don't approve of what you are doing. But we saw these poor boys camped out on the lawn all shot up, some of them bleeding and dying, and so far away from their mothers and sweethearts with no women to care for them, and well, we just got to worrying about our men. Caring for your soldiers took our minds off our men folk for a spell. We have been writing letters for them; it would break your heart to hear some of them talk. We have been playing music and cards, and we have been feeding them too! Yes, we have! And heaven knows these boys can eat! Why, I don't expect there's a deer or rabbit within miles of here now. I believe they have hunted these woods clean out."

As the general listened to Aunt Effie, an amused smile played on his lips. It was easy to imagine he was hearing the voice of a favorite aunt of his own scolding him for some past misdeed.

"And, well, it just didn't seem right to lock ourselves in the house and leave these poor boys all alone without any female company to brighten their days," continued Aunt Effie.

"Aunt Effie," interrupted Josephine, "I am sure that the general is a busy man. Perhaps we should let him tell us why he is here."

"Oh, that's quite all right, ma'am," said the general. "I feel as though I'm right back at home with my family. I must confess, you have made me a little homesick. It's been several months since I have seen my wife and children."

"And that's you own fault!" scolded Aunt Effie. "You men need to make peace with each other instead of charging about the countryside, shooting each other up, and scaring women and old folks half to death! It is a crime what you are asking these young men to do."

"Aunt Effie, please!" begged Josephine.

"Well, I can't help it, that's how I feel. A lot of these boys are away from home for the first time with no one to care for them, and I'll bet that a lot of people up north feel the same way."

The general chuckled. "I wish it was that simple, but I am afraid there will be a lot more fighting before we have peace." His face grew serious as he continued.

"I believe we could bring an end to this conflict so much quicker if only everyone showed the compassion for each other that you ladies have shown for my men. Words cannot express my gratitude, and I have come here today to thank you personally and to ask if there is anything that I can do to repay you kindness."

Sitting on the edge of her chair, her head erect and her tiny hands folded on her lap, Josephine thought for a moment. Perhaps these Yankees, for whom she had so much contempt, had some good in them after all.

"There is one small favor I would ask of you," she said.

"If it is within my power, I will gladly grant your request," said the general.

She leaned forward in her chair. "We would appreciate it if you could use your influence to make sure the house and barns are not burned or looted and that we are left with our livestock."

The general's eyes filled with admiration as he regarded this plucky Englishwoman before him. "I think I can arrange that," he smiled. "I will write the necessary letters this very morning. Is there anything else?"

Aunt Effie started to speak, but Josephine, fearing what she might ask the of the officer's generosity, cut her off.

"I think that will be sufficient," she said.

Not sure to whom Josephine was speaking, Aunt Effie sat quietly with a puzzled look on her face.

"Very well then. My men and I will be leaving by the end of the week. If there is nothing else, I think our business here is complete."

The general rose to his feet, as did the officers around him. He bowed to each of the ladies on the porch in turn, and as he faced Josephine, she leaned forward and extended her hand. The general took her hand in his and looked into her eyes.

"Madam, I thank you and your family again for all you have done for our troops. I will do all that I can to insure the safety of your family and your home. I would hope that we can all meet again another day, under more pleasant circumstances."

"I am sure we shall," said Josephine with a pleasant smile.

"Gentlemen," said the general, putting on his hat. The men, except for Captain Hallowell, started down the steps.

The general turned to address Captain Hallowell. "Captain, are you coming?"

Captain Hallowell shuffled his feet nervously and said, "With your permission, sir, I will be along shortly."

The general smiled to himself. "Very well then. Carry on. We will see you back at camp." He tipped his hat to the women assembled on the porch. "Ladies." With that, he and his men were off.

By now everyone on the porch except for poor Lizzie, who had returned and now sat by Aunt Effie's side, had caught on to what was happening. Josephine, wanting to give the young people a few moments to talk through their feelings, made an excuse to get everyone into the house.

"Ladies, I think we should go inside," said Josephine.

"But, Miss Josephine, I'm tired. I've been working all morning with Miss Effie and Miss Ethne, and it's so nice on the porch. Can't we just sit here awhile?" whined Lizzie.

"Inside right now!" insisted Josephine.

Knowing by her tone that Josephine meant business, everyone except for Mary Alice and the captain made for the door. They were clearly annoyed at being herded like sheep. With a great sweeping of cotton and petticoats, they filed into the hallway of the house.

Alone together at last on the porch, Captain Hallowell turned to Mary Alice. He took both of her hands in his. He found the courage to look deep into her gray eyes; she was smiling and returned his gaze before casting her eyes modestly downward. They stood like this for a moment while the captain gathered his courage and collected his thoughts.

Standing in the hallway, sensing their curiosity, Josephine said to the ladies, "I trust I can leave you all alone for a few moments and that you will respect the privacy of these young people!"

The entire group, eyes looking downward, suddenly found something very interesting to contemplate on the carpet and mumbled, "Yes, ma'am."

With the matter having been settled to her satisfaction, Josephine helped Grandmother upstairs to take a nap. Left alone in the quiet of the cool hallway Aunt Effie, Ethne, and Lizzie exchanged mischievous glances then scurried into the parlor and tiptoed quickly over to the open window.

The morning had been warm with gentle breezes blowing, so all of the windows and shutters had been opened wide to allow fresh air into the house. The windows on the river side of the parlor were double wide and slid into the wall so that in the summer when they were open, if there was nothing in front of them, you could walk right through onto the veranda.

The birds chattered in the trees outside. Just as the ladies had hoped, one could hear scraps of the conversation from the porch. The soft spring breeze carried the sound intermittently into the room through the lace curtains.

In front of one of the windows in the parlor sat an old Chippendale settee that belonged to Grandmother. It had been a wedding present from her Uncle William of Charleston and had been in his family for generations. The settee had been in Grand Oak since the house had been built. When the slaves had carried it up the front stairs, one of them lost their grip and dropped it.

The settee slid to the bottom of the porch steps, breaking the two back legs. Not wanting her uncle to think she had been careless, Grandmother had never told him what had happened. She had simply had the legs repaired.

Nobody was allowed to sit on the settee except for Uncle William on his visits to see Grandmother. As the old man sat sipping his tea, Lottie would sit nervously watching and praying that the repairs held.

It was in front of this same settee at the window that the ladies gathered to eavesdrop on what the captain was saying to Mary Alice. Their presence was concealed by the lace curtains.

Aunt Effie, Ethne, and Lizzie struggled to hear the conversation on the porch, but the fact that the couple was speaking in hushed tones made it difficult to understand what was being said.

The bird's song and the rustle of the leaves masked every other word, making it even more difficult.

"I can't hear," said Aunt Effie.

"I can't see," said Lizzie.

"You don't need to see. You already know what they look like, simple child," scolded Aunt Effie.

"*Shhhhh!* Be quiet. They'll hear you," said Ethne.

Leaning closer to the settee, Aunt Effie decided that it would be just as easy to kneel on the seat and lean over the back so she could keep her ear to the open window. She was soon joined by Ethne and Lizzie, who crowded closely together in this highly undignified position. Not wanting to miss what was being said, the ladies leaned closer to the open window. Just as they had hoped, the gentle breezes carried voices clearly from the porch into the room.

"My dear Mary Alice," began the captain. He paused for a moment and then continued. "Ever since I first set eyes on you, I thought that you were the most beautiful lady I had ever seen. You were bringing water to the soldiers on the lawn, and you moved so gracefully amongst them. The sun was shining on your hair, and you smiled and found some nice thing to say to each person you helped. I thought at first that nobody on earth could be so kind and beautiful. When I realized that you lived here, I knew that your family would never approve of my feelings for you, so until now I have kept them to myself. I have thought of little else but you since that day I first saw you, and my admiration for you has grown day by day as I have watched you nurse my men back to health. Now that I am leaving, I find I cannot bear the thought of never seeing you again. I would never expect that you could feel for me the way I feel for you, but would you consider writing to this humble soldier?"

"Why, Captain Hallowell," said Mary Alice. "I would be honored to write to you." She glanced demurely downward. "I must confess that I have thought about you as well. I will always remember the first time you smiled at me with those blue eyes of yours."

The captain smiled and lifted Mary Alice's chin with his hand until their eyes met. "Is there someone I should ask for permission to write to you?"

For a brief moment, a chill ran through Mary Alice as she realized she was not sure where her father or brothers were. They may even be dead at the hands of the very army that the man before her represented.

She opened her eyes and looked at Captain Hallowell. When she saw the love shining in his eyes, all thoughts of doubt melted like ice on a warm spring day.

Mary Alice looked away. "My father and brothers are away at war. Josephine is in charge of the household. I suppose that you should ask her," she said.

"Very well," said the captain. "I will ask her this afternoon."

With that, the captain touched his hand to Mary Alice's face. Turning her face to his, he leaned toward her. Mary Alice closed her eyes.

"What's going on? What's happening? I can't hear anything!" said Lizzie.

"I think that scoundrel is going to kiss her," said Ethne. She still didn't trust these Yankees.

"*Shhhh!*" scolded Aunt Effie.

It was at this moment that Josephine came back into the room. A look of curiosity came over her face as she paused in the doorway, unable to understand the reason for the unladylike position everyone had assumed on the settee. Suddenly it hit her. They were listening to Mary Alice and Captain Hallowell.

So engrossed were they in the events unfolding on the gallery that they did not hear Josephine at the door to the parlor.

"Aunt Effie, you should be ashamed of yourself," admonished Josephine. "All of you come from that window at once!"

Josephine's voice cracked like a whip. The three women on the settee nearly jumped out of their skins. Ethne and Lizzie turned their heads to see where Josephine was standing. Aunt Effie lost her balance and fell forward. With a resounding crack, unable to support the weight on its back legs any longer, the settee broke.

"*Oh! Oh!*" cried Aunt Effie.

As the settee slanted dangerously toward the open window, the ladies, with a great flailing of arms, made a mad grab for something to stop their fall. Ethne, who had been kneeling on one side, grabbed at the lace curtains, which came loose, pulling the rod with them.

Lizzie, kneeling on the other side, made a wild grab at the fern stand, but came away with only a handful of leaves. The plant and the stand on which it sat teetered precariously then tipped over as well. With a loud crash, the curtains, the plant stand and fern, the settee, and everyone on it tumbled out onto the veranda like a basket of laundry, landing at the feet of the stunned couple.

The young people on the porch stood frozen where they were and turned crimson.

After the fiasco on the veranda, Mary Alice was embarrassed and humiliated. She was sure she would never see the captain again and that she would become an old maid. However, true to his word, Captain Hallowell returned later that afternoon with the letter from the general and to ask for permission to write to Mary Alice.

Trying his best to be professional in light of the morning's events, the captain clicked his heels, saluted Josephine, and then extended the other gloved hand, in which he held the letter from the general.

"With the general's compliments, ma'am," he said in his most businesslike tone.

"Thank you." Josephine took the envelope from the captain's hand. Trying not to show her amusement, she said, "Won't you please have a seat for a moment? I would like to have a word with you."

"I would prefer to stand," said the captain.

Josephine found the young officer's attempts to conceal his embarrassment regarding the morning's events very amusing. She decided to try to put Captain Hallowell at ease.

"I feel I must apologize for the actions of my kin this morning. They meant no harm. They were just looking out for Mary Alice."

The captain looked down at his feet and reddened the incident still fresh in his memory.

"No offence taken, ma'am," he said. "I know they meant no harm."

"Well, all the same, I hope you won't think too harshly of them," said Josephine.

She gave him a moment to collect his thoughts, but he stood in silence.

"Well, if there is nothing else, I would wish you and your men a safe trip to wherever you are heading," said Josephine.

The captain snapped to attention. "There *is* one other matter I would like to discuss with you, Mrs. McGuire."

Josephine smiled, "Yes. What is it, Captain Hallowell," she said softly.

"I would suppose by now you are aware of my feelings of affection for Miss Mary Alice," said the captain.

"I had my suspicions," said Josephine, trying not to look too amused.

The captain stuck out his chest. Finding courage in love, he continued with an authority that, considering how mild he had been concerning Mary Alice up till now, impressed Josephine.

"I have had these feelings of affection and admiration for quite sometime now, and after talking with Mary Alice this morning, I feel that it is safe to say that she feels the same way. We both feel that we have a great deal in common. I understand that her father and brothers are away at war, and since I cannot ask either of them for their consent, I would like to ask your permission to write to her, and if I survive this war, I would wish to call on her."

"I see," said Josephine. She thought for a moment before continuing.

"Captain Hallowell, if you had asked me this three weeks ago, I would have to have said no. But as all of us here have gotten to know you and your men, we have come to realize that the values which we hold in common are greater than the differences which separate us. We all are fighting the fight of our lives right now. We both are fighting for principles in which we believe. It really is not an issue of who is right or wrong anymore. This cost of this fight is too dear. The issue now is how can we bridge our differences and bring peace between our families and friends?

"To deny you and Mary Alice a chance for happiness because the two of you find yourselves on opposing sides of this battle would be wrong. One cannot choose where the heart leads one. I feel that there is no better place to start building that bridge to peace than with you and Mary Alice. I give you my blessing."

"Thank you, Mrs. McGuire. Thank you. I promise you will never regret your generosity," said the captain, shaking Josephine's hand enthusiastically. "I can't wait to tell her the good news. When may I see her?"

"Why don't you wait here, and I will find her for you," said Josephine.

"Thank you, ma'am," said the captain.

Josephine turned to fetch Mary Alice. She looked up to see her standing in the open doorway. "Mary Alice, I didn't see you standing there," she said.

Mary Alice entered the room. She crossed to where the captain stood and took both of his hands in hers. She gazed into his eyes and smiled. He returned her gaze. Josephine couldn't help but feel that there was something very different about the girl. The girlishness in her seemed to be gone, and in its place was a new self-confidence.

"I have heard the entire conversation," said Mary Alice, "and there will be no need for the good captain to write to me."

A look of surprise and shock crossed the faces of both Josephine and the captain.

"But I thought you wanted to correspond with the captain," said Josephine.

Still holding his hands and looking into his eyes, Mary Alice continued, "There is no need to write to each other because I plan on leaving with Captain Hallowell the day after tomorrow."

The captain's jaw dropped. This was much more than he expected. With one swift movement, he grabbed May Alice, swept her off her feet, and twirled her around the room.

"Mary Alice, we need to discuss this," said Josephine. "Captain Hallowell, set Mary Alice down and give us a moment alone please."

The captain set Mary Alice down.

"Thomas, stay where you are," said Mary Alice. She turned to Josephine and said, "There is nothing to discuss. My mind is made up. I want to be a nurse and follow the troops."

"Need I remind you that there are plenty of Confederate troops that need nursing?"

"I know," said Mary Alice very sincerely. She was now looking into the captain's eyes. "But they don't have Captain Hallowell."

"You can't just run off. Why, you're not even married. You haven't even thought this through. I'm responsible for you, and I forbid it."

Mary Alice turned to face Josephine. For the first time in her life, she neither whined nor threatened. She met Josephine's eyes as an equal and said, "I am twenty years old. I appreciate that you have been looking out for me, but I assure you that I am capable of making my own decisions. You cannot tell me what to do any longer…or was that all just an untruth, what you said about not choosing where the heart leads one and building peace through love?"

Josephine felt herself caught by her own words.

"As for not being married…" She turned to Captain Hallowell. "Darling, there is a chaplain with your company, is there not?"

The captain, not believing his good fortune, nodded yes.

Without waiting for a proposal she said, "Then it's settled. If Captain Hallowell will have me, we can be married here tomorrow."

The captain shouted, "Yes! Yes!" as he hugged Mary Alice.

It took some convincing to get Grandmother to allow Mary Alice and the captain to be married in the house, and still more convincing to get everyone to attend the wedding. Ethne's children, of course, were delighted to play dress up. The children had no concept of the politics involved with this union.

Even though they had developed a sympathy for the soldiers, Grandmother, Aunt Effie, and Ethne had been against letting the Yankees into the ballroom. To camp out on the lawn was one thing, but to welcome them into the house was another. As my wife, Josephine was now head of the household. Her major concern was the preservation of the estate, and so she approved of having the ceremony inside, Yankees and all.

"I would invite General Grant himself into the ballroom if it would save the house and the animals," said Josephine.

"All the same, I'll bet the captain is turning in his grave right now," said Grandmother.

An uneasy truce was called as the next morning Mary Alice and Captain Hallowell were married in the ballroom at Grand Oak. As the ceremony concluded, a small group of soldiers played music. Captain Hallowell's comrades congratulated him and his new bride.

Captain Hallowell walked over to thank Josephine for all she had done. She was standing in front of a full-length oil painting of herself in a lavender gown. The captain noticed the painting of Josephine and then turned his attention to the other paintings in the room. When he came to the portrait hanging opposite of Josephine's, his face showed an expression of surprise.

"Mrs. McGuire, who is the man in the painting hanging over the fireplace?"

"Why, that's my husband, Charles," said Josephine.

"I…I know that man."

"I don't see how you could, Captain Hallowell. Were you ever in Charleston before the war?"

"No. It's from someplace else." The captain suddenly went white. "Oh, Mrs. McGuire, I'm so sorry."

"What is it?" asked Josephine.

"Your husband and a young boy were captured at Monocasy Junction. I was ordered to send them to Fort Delaware with the prisoners from Gettysburg. He was in our camp. I...I...didn't know," he stammered.

"Was he wounded? How was his health?" begged Josephine.

"He was fine. My unit caught him and the boy foraging for food."

Then something unexpected happened. Josephine reached out to Captain Hallowell and hugged him. "Oh, thank you, thank you," she cried.

Confused, the captain looked at her. "Mrs. McGuire, I'm not sure that you understand. He's in a federal prison in Delaware."

"No, Captain Hallowell. It is you who does not understand. I have not heard from my husband in over ten months. I was afraid he was dead. If he is being held prisoner, he is surely still alive. He is safe from being killed in battle."

The captain did not want to ruin Josephine's euphoria at the news of my capture, but he knew the condition of some of those prison camps. He had seen the suffering and sickness. He was aware of the hunger and boredom. As a soldier, he knew that any warrior would rather face death in glory on the battlefield then waste away in a dark, filthy prison. The captain felt guilty for his part in my predicament. He managed a smile and vowed to himself he would make this right.

With Mary Alice and Captain Hallowell waving good-bye from the front column, the Union army left Grand Oak the next morning.

Trial by Fire

As the Union army departed from Grand Oak, Josephine turned her thoughts to how she would manage the plantation. Mary Alice would be missed. She was young and healthy, and every pair of hands was needed. Grandmother was too old to do any of the hard work that now needed to be done. In addition, fourteen slaves had marched off with the army. Josephine was unable to convince them to stay.

Months earlier, twenty of the field hands had run off when news of Lincoln's proclamation reached the plantation. The loss of the slaves was not the only problem Josephine faced. The stable master had gone home to England shortly after I left for war. The overseer and his wife and children left that same week. The house servants, Mammy, Isabelle, Cuff, Big Jawn, and our cook and her daughter were still there.

The cooper and his family stayed, as did the blacksmith and his wife. That left only three field hands and the old slave woman, Sarah, to see to all that needed to be done. Of the seventy-eight or so people who once lived at Grand Oak, just fourteen adults remained.

The only livestock left at the plantation consisted of four horses, a pair of sheep, one cow, a calf, a dozen or so chickens, and three young pigs. The house servants were useless, as were the ladies and children, when it came to caring for the animals.

Both the cooper and the blacksmith felt that it was below them to labor like a field hand or care for animals, but they put forth a valiant effort and did what needed to be done.

Thankfully, the vegetable garden was in. It would need tending during the summer. Most of the household would help in that task. Josephine had seen to it that the cotton crop had been planted. There would be far fewer acres than usual, but at least there would be some income in the fall.

Josephine believed that due to the aid the family had given the Union army, they would be safe. The letter she now held declaring the house off-limits from retribution was an additional insurance policy. She was soon to learn that unlike the troops that had bivouacked around Grand Oak, not all soldiers and officers were gentlemen.

By autumn, all of South Carolina and the entire South was suffering. The Union blockade was working, and nothing now got through the lines. The residents of Grand Oak worked as they had never worked before, putting up vegetables and smoking meat for the winter ahead.

One day in late September, several Union soldiers on horseback rode up the long driveway to the house. Cuff ran excitedly to find Josephine.

"Miss Josephine! Miss Josephine! They is Yankees comin' up the road."

Josephine ran to the front door. Sure enough, charging up the dusty roadway were a dozen men in blue coats. As she called for Big Jawn, Josephine smoothed her hair and straightened her dress. She took the letter written by the general from the hall table and slipped it into the pocket of her dress; then she slipped her gun in the belt around her waist. She walked through the door onto the front portico followed by Big Jawn, who held a shotgun. Upon seeing Josephine and the big black man standing at the door, the soldiers reigned their horses and came to a stop.

The man in the lead removed his hat. He said, "Afternoon, ma'am."

Josephine looked down at the man before her. He was unshaven and his uniform was caked with dry dust. On his sleeves was a pair of what Josephine guessed to be sergeant's stripes.

"Good afternoon. May I help you?"

"Well yes, ma'am. We're scouting food for the army," said the sergeant.

"I'm afraid we haven't any to spare. We have a houseful of people, and we need everything we have."

The sergeant turned to the soldiers behind him and laughed. "Isn't that funny?" He turned back to face Josephine. Putting his hands on the pummel of his saddle, he leaned forward and smiled at her. "Well, now, that don't sound very neighborly. What about all that Southern hospitality I heard about?"

One of the other men laughed. "You s'pose they ain't heard 'bout it out here in the country, Serge?"

"Maybe you're right, Wallace," the sergeant said. He spat on the ground and looked at Josephine. "Well now, little lady, we don't see as you have any choice in the matter. You see, we're authorized to take what ever we want from you rebels. We got a hungry army to feed. It's gonna take more than a couple of darkies and a little white woman to stop us. Boys, why don't you go around back and see what you can find while I keep the little lady company here?"

Four of the soldiers started to dismount as two others spurred their horses.

"Stop right there!" cried Josephine with a force that surprised even her.

The soldiers stopped where they were.

"In the first place, we are not Southerners. We are English. In the second place, we have a pardon from one of your commanding officers. It says that you are not to touch the house or livestock."

"Is that so?" said the sergeant.

Big Jawn stepped forward. "If Miss Josephine say it is so, it is so. She be telling you the gospel."

The men laughed. "I don't know. Does he sound English to you boys?" asked the officer.

"He don't, but she sure don't talk like no one I ever knew," said Wallace.

"Okay, lady, let's see this pardon you got."

Josephine took the paper from her pocket. She handed it to Big Jawn and took the rifle from him.

"Here, hand this to the sergeant," she said. She cocked the rifle and pointed it in the direction of the soldiers.

Big Jawn descended the steps and walked over to the man on the horse. Eyeing him suspiciously, he handed him the letter. The sergeant tipped his cap back and began to read.

"Well, I'll be a son of a…" he said.

He finished reading the document and handed the paper back to Big Jawn.

"I'm sorry, ma'am. Looks like you was telling the truth. We didn't mean no harm. Unfortunately, we still gotta feed our men. Tell you what, we'll just have a look around and take only what you can spare."

"I told you we can't spare anything," said Josephine.

"I appreciate that, ma'am, but like I said, we got an army that's starving. I gotta feed them. Men, let's ride around back and see what we can find. Don't go in the house and don't hurt anybody."

Twenty minutes later, Josephine watched helplessly as the soldiers traveled down the road from the house in the direction from which they had arrived. They carried with them eight of the chickens, the calf, all but one of the pigs, two of the horses, and one of the sheep. They had also helped themselves to the vegetable garden. Josephine was grateful that the Yankees didn't know about yams or okra. These they left.

Choking back tears of rage, she watched the men disappear. "Good riddance!" she shouted with impotent rage.

Once the soldiers were out of sight, Josephine went back into the house. The moment she entered the hallway the family flooded from the parlor to her side. She was in no mood to deal with them. Her head was spinning with thoughts of her own.

Everyone spoke at once. "Are they gone? Did they take all of our food? What are we going to eat all winter? Are they coming back? What are we going to do?

Josephine turned to face them. "I don't know," she said angrily. "I can't do everything around here. I'm tired of being the only one with answers. Stop your whining and leave me alone!"

With that, she stomped off down the hall slamming the office door behind her.

The ladies stood in the hall with their mouths open.

"That girl's got gumption! I like that," Grandmother said. She turned to the rest of the family. "No use standing here in the hall. She just needs a good cry, that's all. She'll be all right."

The next morning Josephine called the family together. As they sat in the parlor, servants and family alike stared expectantly at Josephine.

"The house looks too inviting," she began. "We need to make it look like she is on her last legs. Big Jawn, I want you to take the field hands and go to the entrance of the property. Since we can't lock the gates, I want you to dig out the foundation under one side of the brick piers that held them. Pull the brick wall down over the road leading up to the house.

"I want you to build a fire around the base of both walls so they look like they have been burned. Cut whatever small trees may be by the gate so that they fall over the road. Then I want you to go into the woods and drag whatever branches you can into the lawn and road. Try to make it look like no one has been up the drive in months."

To the cooper she said, "Israel, you and Cuff close the shutters on the second floor. Get some old boards from the barn and nail them over the outside shutters. Whatever windows are not shuttered, paint over with black so that they look like they are missing when you see them from the river.

"The rest of you, I want to go into the woods and drag as much kindling as you can to the river side of the house. Pile it all up in a row along the porch."

Everyone just sat and looked at Josephine as if she had gone mad.

"Lawdy, Miss Josephine, you ain't goin' to burn the house down, is you?" said Mammy.

"No, I'm not going to burn the house down. But when you see it from the river, I want to make it look as though it has been burned. We will light the kindling on fire and then cover it with wet palmetto leaves. When the fire gets good and smoky, we will fan the smoke in the direction of the house. The smoke will turn the pillars black, and the house will look like it has been on fire."

Beginning to see her plan, the family smiled at Josephine's ingenuity.

"Any questions?" she asked. They all shook their heads no. They knew better than to question. Josephine was back to herself and in charge once again.

By that evening, the transformation was complete. Grand Oak, having once been one of the showplaces on the Ashley, looked as though it was in ruins.

As the autumn of 1864 progressed, the news reaching Grand Oak became increasingly worse. As we lost battle after battle, storm clouds gathered over Atlanta. The wind began to whisper a new name: *Sherman!* The wind gained strength until it became an unstoppable hurricane destroying everything in its path. On the morning of November 14, Sherman departed the smoldering ruins of Atlanta. He vowed not to stop until he reached the sea. Charleston was put on alert.

Charleston was viewed as the cradle of secession and the heart of all that the South stood for. Only Richmond, the capital of the South, was more hated. The ladies were terrified. General Lee had promised to defend the city to the last house, the last man, woman, and child, if need be. However, where, oh where were General Lee and his army now that Charleston needed them? They need not have worried, for it was not Charleston that was Sherman's destination.

William Tecumseh Sherman vanished into the Georgia countryside, like a water moccasin when it disappears under the surface of the water. No one knew, except those unfortunate enough to be in his path, where he was or when or where he would resurface. His path of destruction was no accident. He had taken with him the tax and census records from Atlanta. He knew the exact location of the most profitable plantations and villages in his route. He and his troops pillaged, burned, and looted the best of what Georgia possessed. What his men could not carry off, they destroyed, leaving the people left behind to starve on the barren land. His desecration of Georgia was complete and final.

On December 22, Sherman and his army of demons surfaced in Savannah. Fortunately, Savannah did not suffer a fate similar to that of Atlanta. Sherman planned to depart the city on January 15. Once again, Charleston went on alert. However, fate smiled on Charleston a second time, for on February 18, the menace headed north for our state capital, Columbia. All that probably saved us from Sherman's wrath was the fact that January had produced incessant rains, flooding swamps and raising streams.

The flooding delayed the army's crossing the Savannah River until early February. In addition, the rain-swollen creeks forced the army to cross higher than originally planned.

Sherman's advance on Columbia was so rapid that troops for the defense of the capital could not be gathered in time. Beauregard was in command in Columbia. However, he promised much but did little. As the rear defenses under Wade Hampton evacuated Columbia, they set fire to the cotton crop that had been stored up. A high wind carried burning embers to the rooftops, setting them on fire. In a few brief hours, our beautiful capital lay in ruins. All that remained to complete the devastation was for Sherman to set fire to the arsenal outside of Columbia. With this accomplished, he headed for Fayetteville, North Carolina, leaving in his wake a smoking trail of desolation nearly forty miles wide.

As vile as Sherman had been, there was an even greater threat to the civilians in the army's path—bummers! Bummers were scavengers, often the lowest, most despicable, loathsome class of vermin masquerading as human beings. They writhed like snakes from the head of the Gorgon Medusa, spitting their venom on anyone they came in contact with. Just like Medusa's hair, cutting one of them down only seemed to cause two more to spring up to take its place. They traveled in front, beside, and behind Sherman's wake. They knew no mercy.

As the news of Sherman's march through Columbia reached Grand Oak, believing the threat to be behind them, the family breathed a little easier. Perhaps Josephine's idea had worked. There had been no more visits from the army. The appearance of the house had certainly produced a response from the neighbors. They had been relieved to find that despite its exterior, the house had not been burned and ransacked.

With the coming spring came the thought of life renewing itself. The war couldn't last much longer. The meager cotton crop was stored in the sheds. There were more chickens since a few eggs had been left to hatch. The last sheep, alas, had been Christmas dinner, and the poor cow was now in the smokehouse, but at least there were two horses left in the barn. The family was getting to the end of the vegetables that had been put up, but soon the growing season would bring new life to the earth.

One late February morning, the family was about their chores when there came from the house a piercing scream. Josephine dropped the basket of eggs she had been collecting and ran in the direction of the house. As she came from behind a large azalea bush, she could see two dirty, ragged men standing on the gallery. The meat from the smokehouse lay where the first man had dropped it on the floor by his feet. The second man held Ethne by the arm.

Aunt Effie stood with the children frozen by the door.

"Come on, now. You can be a little more friendly than that, missy. I ain't seen a pretty li'l thing like yew in a long time. I just wants a kiss, that's all."

Ethne was struggling madly and beating the man with the fist of her free hand.

"Go on. Show her who's boss, Jack," taunted the other man.

Jack grabbed Ethne's free arm and yanked her close to his face. She could feel his hot breath against her. His thin lips parted in a sneer, revealing yellow-pitted teeth.

"Come on now. It's time yew played nice, before I have to hurt you. It would be a shame to mess up that there pretty little face."

Ethne spat violently at the man. He slapped her with such force her head snapped to the left. Ethne felt her knees give out, and she passed into unconsciousness.

Josephine yelled from the lawn, "What do you think you are doing? Leave her alone!"

"Well now, what have we got here?" growled the man who was watching. "Looks like we got us a woman for both of us."

"I said leave her alone and get off my porch! Effie, hurry and take the children inside."

As Josephine ran to the steps, Aunt Effie and the children quickly disappeared into the house.

"Now that's mighty brave of you, but what are you gonna do?"

Josephine stopped a few feet from the bottom step. She pulled her gun from her waistband and pointed it at the man holding Ethne.

"I told you let her be."

The man threw Ethne against the railing. She fell like a rag doll to the floor.

"Now, honey, you don't wanna do that. We got two to one here."

Suddenly from around the corner of the house came Big Jawn and Cuff, both with rifles. Israel and Isaac, the blacksmith, came running across the lawn. They stopped when they saw the men on the porch.

"Ain't that a somethin'? She done got her darkies fightin' her battles for her," said Jack's accomplice.

Big Jawn pointed his cocked rifle at the men on the veranda. "I done killed white trash like you before, an' I ain't scared of doin it again!"

"That so?" said Jack. With the speed of lightning, he grabbed the gun from his belt, aimed it at Big Jawn, and fired.

Josephine aimed her pistol and shot Jack, hitting him in the shoulder and causing him to miss. Big Jawn fired. He hit the man standing next to Jack, striking him in the arm. The man yelped in pain as he grabbed his arm and ran down the steps across the lawn toward the barn.

With his good arm, Jack pointed his gun at Josephine and fired. She dropped her gun and fell backward onto the lawn. With three steps, Big Jawn was up the stairs. Jack tried to fire. His gun jammed.

Holding his rifle by the barrel, Big Jawn swung it with all of his strength. The force of the blow to the man's skull was so great that it crushed his head like an egg, almost severing it from his body.

By now, Isaac and Israel had reached Josephine where she lay on the lawn. They knelt beside her on the grass.

"Miss Josephine's done been shot. We has to get her up to the house quick," yelled Isaac.

He picked her up in his arms and started toward the house. Suddenly, a third man came galloping from the direction of the barn, riding one of the last two horses left on the plantation. He led the second horse by a rope hastily tied around its neck. The man who had been shot in the arm ran to him yelling, "Them darkies done killed Jack. We gotta get outta here!"

The man on the horse stopped briefly enough to allow his companion to jump on the second horse's back.

As he galloped off, he shouted, "You ain't gonna get away with this! You all gonna regret the day you was borned."

With that, the two men galloped off. Cuff fired at the men. This time he did not miss. He shot the man who had been on the porch in the back. The man tumbled from the horse. The horse reared, changed direction, and headed for the river. Big Jawn fired at the third man. The bummer joined his accomplice face down on the lawn.

Once the last shot was fired, the ladies, who had been watching from the inside of the house, came running to the door.

Ethne was lying on the porch floor. Beside her, a man lay face down in a pool of blood. Isaac came running across the lawn with Josephine's limp and bleeding body. At first, they all thought both women had been killed.

Big Jawn yelled to Isabelle, "You, woman, get the women folks in the house right now!" Isaac continued up the stairs with Josephine as Isabelle and Aunt Effie dragged Ethne into the house.

Big Jawn walked over to where the man who had been on the porch lay face down in the grass. He saw the man's hand move toward the gun lying beside him. Big Jawn fired his rifle at the man's head, and his hand moved no more.

Aunt Effie would later tell Josephine the story of how she had been shot and what had transpired during her lapse from consciousness.

Realizing that Ethne had only fainted, Aunt Effie said, "Lizzie, run quickly and get my medicine bag."

For once Lizzie did not talk back to her mistress.

"Isaac, bring Josephine into the parlor, lay her across the bed by the window, and then wait for us in the hall. Mammy, Isabelle, come quickly. We need to get Josephine's clothes off to see how badly she is hurt," ordered Aunt Effie.

As Lizzie returned with Aunt Effie's bag, Ethne's three small children sat terrified at the foot of the stairs. When Aunt Effie appeared in the doorway to take the bag, they ran for her skirts.

"Aunt Effie, Aunt Effie, are Mommy and Aunt Jo going to die?" they cried.

"Hush, children. No, no, don't worry. Everything's going to be all right. I need you go with Lizzie so I can take care of everything." She turned to Lizzie. "Take the children to the other side of the house and keep them busy."

Aunt Effie rummaged through the black leather satchel. She pulled a small, brown bottle from the depths of the sack. She opened it and passed it beneath Ethne's nose. Ethne's eyes fluttered and she coughed.

"Welcome back, my dear," said Aunt Effie.

Ethne tried to speak, but she couldn't get the words out.

"There, there now, my child. Everything is all right. You've just had a little fright, that's all. Everyone is okay. Not to worry, the Yankees are gone. We are safe. You just lie here while I attend to Josephine. Isaac, go and fetch Miss Ethne some water then sit here with her till I come back. Do you understand?" asked Aunt Effie.

"Yes'm," he replied.

Aunt Effie hurried to the parlor. Grandmother was sitting in a chair by Josephine's side. She held a blood-soaked cloth on Josephine's shoulder. Mammy and Isabelle had opened Josephine's blouse but upon seeing the bullet hole in her shoulder had been afraid to move her.

"Lordy, Miss Effie, the poor girl done been hit right in the shoulder. What we gonna do?" cried Mammy.

"The first thing we have to do is find the bullet," said Aunt Effie.

She walked over to where Grandmother sat by Josephine and said. "Move the cloth. I need to see the wound."

Grandmother complied. Aunt Effie inspected the injury from different angles. "I can't tell if the bullet is still in her."

Aunt Effie took a pair of scissors from her bag. Expertly, she cut through Josephine's blouse and chemise.

"I still can't see enough to tell," she said. "I need to roll her on her side so I can cut more of this dress off. Isabelle, come over here and put your hands one behind her neck and one at her waist and then gently roll her so her left side is up."

Josephine moaned softly as Isabelle rolled her onto her side.

"Easy now, don't hurt her," said Aunt Effie, her hopes soaring as she noticed a small, bloodstained hole in the material of the back of the dress. Aunt Effie continued cutting away fabric. Once Josephine's flesh came into view, Aunt Effie exclaimed, "Yes. Praise the Lord."

"What is it, Miss Effie?" questioned Mammy.

"It's an exit wound," said Aunt Effie. "That means the bullet passed clean through her and we won't have to look for it."

Aunt Effie dug into the medicine bag. She produced a clear glass bottle filled with a red-orange powder. The label read *cayenne*. Euphemia took a small porcelain bowl from the bag. The servants watched spellbound as she poured a little of the cayenne into the bowl and added a dried yarrow leaf. Expertly, she ground them into a fine powder.

"Now I need a glass of water," said Aunt Effie.

Isabelle handed the water to Euphemia, who mixed a small amount with the powder. The servants watched as next Aunt Effie took a couple of the cloth strips that had been cut for bandages from her bag.

She dabbed the cloth in the mixture and applied it first to Josephine's shoulder in front and then to her back.

After that, she pressed wads of cloth soaked in the remaining liquid to each of the wounds before she bandaged them.

"The cayenne will stop the bleeding, and the yarrow will prevent infection," she said. "Now, Mammy, get a pillow behind her head. We have to elevate her for a minute. Isabelle, lay her on her back. We need to wake her up."

The servants did as they were told. Euphemia mixed a little more cayenne in a glass with water; then she waved the smelling salts under Josephine's nose.

Josephine shook her head, and her eyes blinked open. "*Umph, umph,*" she cried.

Aunt Effie brushed her forehead. "There, there, my dear. Everything's going to be okay."

Josephine looked around the room. "Where am I? What happened?"

"You're in the parlor, my dear. You've had a little mishap, that's all. Nothing to worry about. Right now I need you to drink this," said Euphemia, holding out the glass of water laced with cayenne.

Josephine drank the liquid. She made a face.

"Oh, what is that?" she asked.

"It's a little cayenne and water. It will help stop the bleeding from the inside," said Aunt Effie.

"Now I remember! I was shot. Was anyone else hurt?" asked Josephine.

"Big Jawn killed a couple of them white trash Yankees," offered Mammy. "But the rest of the family, they is okay."

"I am afraid they may have gotten away with at least one of the horses," said Aunt Effie. "There was a third man; he came riding like Sherman through Georgia when he heard the shooting. He was leading the second horse by a rope. The man who had been on the porch jumped on the horse, but Cuff shot him. The man fell to the ground, and the horse took of in the opposite direction. I don't think they got any of the food though."

"Is the thief dead?" asked Josephine.

"Yes. Big Jawn made sure of that."

"Good!" said Josephine. "I wish they were all dead."

The conversation was interrupted by an urgent cry of "Fire, fire!" coming from the lawn.

"Josephine, do not move! You will start bleeding again. I will handle this. Miss Lottie, do not let her out of that bed! Do you hear me?"

Grandmother shook her head yes. Aunt Effie ran to the hallway followed by Isabelle and Mammy. Ethne and Isaac were already running out the door.

Thinking he smelled smoke, Israel had gone to check on the barn. When he could see no smoke coming from the building, he went outside. It was then that he saw the cotton storage sheds blazing fiercely down by the river. As he ran to the house to alert the family, he saw that the hen house was also on fire. He ran as quickly as he could to summon help.

"Miss Uphemie, the Yankees done fired up the cotton and the hen house!" cried the smith excitedly.

Aunt Effie could see the smoke coming from the direction of the storage sheds. "Lizzie, Lizzie, come quick!" she yelled. As Lizzie appeared in the hall, Aunt Effie said, "Quickly, put the children in the parlor with Josephine and Miss Lottie, then take Ethne and get the chickens out of the hen house. Everyone else, follow me to the barn. We can't put the fire out in the cotton sheds, but we can keep the barn from catching fire."

Ethne and Lizzie ran for the hen house. Aunt Effie and the former slaves, followed by the house servants, ran in the direction of the barn.

Ethne and Lizzie arrived at the hen house to find most of the right side engulfed in flames. The chickens were squawking excitedly.

"Lizzie, we have to get the chickens out," said Ethne.

"I know you don't expect me to run into a burning building to fetch a couple of chickens," said Lizzie.

"Of course not, let's go to the door on the other side and shoo them toward the side not burning. They will come flying out," said Ethne.

With a great deal of effort, the women were able to herd the chickens out of the building to safety on the lawn. Once the hens were safe they ran to the barn to assist the others.

The family had formed a line from the troughs to the side of the barn closest to the cotton sheds. They passed buckets of water from person to person from the troughs until they reached the person closest to the barn. The water was then thrown against the side or hoisted to the top of the building, where one of the men threw it across the roof. The buckets were then handed back down the line to be refilled. There was a storm gathering, and the wind was picking up from the river.

The firefighters could see the sparks and ash flying, from the cotton fire, as if they were alive.

Just as it appeared that soaking the barn enough to keep it from going up in flames might be working, the plantation bell began to ring urgently.

"Big Jawn, come with me. The rest of you, keep working," cried Aunt Effie. With her dress pulled up to her knees and her hair streaming straight out behind her, Euphemia, followed by Big Jawn, ran in the direction of the house.

As the house came into view, Aunt Effie was horrified to see that clumps of burning cotton had settled into the top of the great oak on the lawn. In addition, several other trees had tufts of burning cotton in their branches. That was not the worst of it. Some of the clumps of burning cotton had landed on the roof of the house. The roof was on fire!

The sight was truly horrific to behold. Deep, black thunderheads rolled in the angry sky. A wicked dry wind blew dust and flame in all directions. The tops of the trees blazed with burning cotton as tongues of flame snaked across the roof. Aunt Effie screamed for the people at the barn to come at once and bring their buckets. Not bothering to wait for them, she and Big Jawn ran into the house and up the stairs.

On the top floor, they reached the narrow stairway that led to the attic and the widow's walk. Soon they could hear the others running up the stairs. They opened the glass windows on the widow's walk and stepped carefully onto the roof.

There were large holding tanks that collected rainwater, which funneled through a system delivering water to the inside of the house. Once again, the family began a bucket brigade, using the water from the storage tanks. Just as they seemed to be making progress against the flames, the wind began to pick up carrying more burning cotton to the roof. The water was making the steep pitch of the roof very slippery, and the wind made it hard to keep their balance. Without warning, there came a loud crack of thunder. It frightened Lizzie, causing her to lose her balance and fall. She began to slide from the roof.

"Help me! Help me!" she screamed. She slid into Aunt Effie, knocking her down as well. The two women slid toward the edge of the roof at an alarming pace. Big Jawn, who was farthest out on the roof, grabbed on the shingles as best he could and braced himself. The women slid into him. His grip held, and their flight from the roof was halted.

Another clap of thunder signaled the start of a deluge of rain. Afraid to move, the three people trapped on the roof held fast as the wind and rain did their best to dislodge the trio from the roof.

It was Isaac and Israel who came to their rescue. They had been closer to the water tanks at the top of the roof when the rain had started. Israel grabbed two long lengths of rope that had been coiled on the attic floor. One he tied around Isaac's waist and the other end to a beam just inside the window.

The second rope was also secured to a beam. A stinging rain lashed Isaac as he slowly crept to where Lizzie and Aunt Effie lay trapped with Big Jawn. He tied the rope first around Lizzie just under her arms.

"Okay, haul 'er up," he yelled to Israel.

With great strength, the man pulled Lizzie across the roof to safety. Isaac, held in place by the rope, kept Big Jawn and Aunt Effie from slipping any further. Israel tossed the rope back down to the three people still on the roof. Next Israel pulled Aunt Effie to safety; then Isaac and Big Jawn made their way to the open window of the widow's walk.

Once inside, they joined the others who lay panting and frightened on the floor. Everyone was soaked through to the skin, but thankfully, the rain had put out the last of the flames. The house was safe.

Four hours later, the ladies stood on the riverside gallery. Aunt Effie, Lizzie, and Ethne had changed into dry clothes, but they were still shaken. Josephine had rallied from her encounter with the Yankees. She stood on the porch with her arm bandaged and held in a sling. Grandmother had brought the children outside so that they might see what was on the horizon. Even the house servants stood in silent awe staring at the heavens.

There in the sky was one of the most brilliant rainbows ever to grace the South Carolina sky. It appeared to start near a grove of trees at the edge of the garden and make a complete arc to an unseen field on the other side of the river. In the clean calm after the storm, it was hard to imagine the violence of a few hours previous.

"Well," said Josephine, "we've seen plagues and famine. We have shared our home with our enemies and then had to defend ourselves from them. We've been spared the wrath of Sherman, but we had to commit murder to save ourselves. Now we have been tried by fire. There isn't much else to test us. Maybe this is God's way of saying its over."

Big Jawn, Isaac, and Israel did not share the ladies reverie on the veranda. There was still work to be done. While the sun sat that evening, an Anhinga bird with wings spread wide officiated as three more bodies found their way into the swamp. Much to the disappointment of a mother alligator and her hungry brood, who lamented the loss of a good meal, the men made sure that no one would know that the bummers had ever been on the property.

The next morning, Josephine, accompanied by Big Jawn, surveyed the plantation. The cotton crop and the storage sheds were a complete loss, as was the chicken coop. The chickens, thankfully, had survived. They could be relocated to one of the empty slave cabins. The bummers had indeed tried to set the barn on fire. Thankfully, the flames had not caught on. There was also evidence that they had tried to fire up some of the slave cabins. Thankfully, the damage was minimal.

Josephine thanked Big Jawn for all that he had done. Wearily, she turned to go up the steps. Suddenly she heard a horse's hoof beats coming across the lawn. Quickly she spun around, expecting to see the entire Union army. To her relief, running toward the house was the horse that the last bummer had tried to steal.

"Thank God," she said. "At least we will have transportation."

The "trial by fire," as Josephine called it, was the last time that Yankees would set foot on Grand Oak. But alas, our family had not seen the last acts of Northern aggression against us. In mid-March, Euphemia received a devastating letter from the wife of the overseer at Sycamore Hill.

Euphemia sat on the veranda with Josephine, Ethne, Grandmother, and the children. Once, their days had been taken up with writing letters or planning parties and visits. There was no topic more important than the latest issue of Godeys or Petersons. The whole world was neat and well ordered. Each new day promised more of the same.

Now life was a struggle just to survive. Leisure time was at a premium. Grandmother insisted that everyone, black and white, rest for an hour exactly at four o'clock each afternoon. Isabelle would round up whatever treats she could find and serve them with tea of chamomile or lemon balm. She would leave the cups and saucers on a table on the veranda before she went to the kitchen to join the other servants.

As Grandmother would pour tea, the ladies would try to pretend that the war had never happened. One afternoon, during this ritual, Cuff came from inside and handed Aunt Effie a letter.

"Miss Uphemie, I was told to give you this right away," he said.

Aunt Effie opened the envelope and read silently to herself.

"Well? Tell us, what it is!" the ladies said all together.

Aunt Effie's eyes began to fill with tears. She handed the letter to Josephine. "I cannot finish it, my dear. Would you please read it to me?"

Josephine took the letter from her hand and began to read:

Dear Mrs. Scott,

It is most difficult to find words, but I must write to tell you of the news at Sycamore Hill. As you may have heard, General Sherman's army passed through Goose Creek in February. The Union Army came charging up the alley to the plantation in a venomous cloud of dust. There were hundreds of them. They swarmed over the house and lawn like a plague of locusts sent to Pharaoh. Mr. Hammond, the children, and I ran to the front door when we heard them. The officer in charge told us that his troops were hungry and wanted to be fed. We told them that there was no food.

The officer ordered us from the house and made us all sit under a tree in the yard. Some of the soldiers actually rode their horses up the steps and into the house. We could hear furniture crashing and glass breaking as they looked for valuables or hidden food. The officer in charge ordered the table and chairs taken from the dining room and brought outside to the yard.

A group of freed Negroes acting as servants to the soldiers took the silver candle sticks, the glass decanters, and china and set the table. They found the chickens and what meager food we had left. It was cooked and served to the officers as they sat at the table on the lawn. We thought for a moment the house may be spared. Then one of the officers laughed and said, "I don't know, men. I think it needs to be cooked a little more, don't you?" The other men laughed and shouted, "Hear, hear!" The officer in charge ordered, "Fire her up, boys!" The men sat fire to the house. There was nothing we could do.

The devils sat and drank your wine and ate the last of our food as they watched the house burn. When they finished eating, they flung the plates and glasses into the inferno as they laughed and joked. They picked the chairs up and threw them into the fire as well. They then tied a rope to your mother's beautiful mahogany table and pulled it across the lawn by horseback until it fell apart. When they had finished with this awful deed, the officer in charge ordered all of the buildings on the property fired up as well.

They made us sit and watch helplessly as the house and buildings around us burned. When the flames reached their zenith, the officer turned to us and said, "That's what we do to traitors! You best be off before we do the same to you."

Mr. Hammond rode out a few days later to see if there was anything that could be salvaged. We had hidden your mother's silver tea service and a few other valuables in a stone recess between the original house and the west wing addition.

We found the hole when we were doing some maintenance on the plaster. We had also taken some of the paintings from their frames and rolled them up and put them with the other valuables. Whether or not they survived, I do not know. Some of the walls are still standing, but it will take a lot of effort to get to the hole between the walls.

I apologize that we were not able to better defend the house and property that you left in our charge. All of the Negroes had run off; there was only my husband the children and me, and we were frightened for our lives. What could we do? We took the children and ran. We made it safely to town and my sister's house, but, oh, Mrs. Scott, there is nothing left for us to eat. We are all most desperate.

It is my sincere hope that you and your family are safe and in better shape than we. May God deliver us from our enemies, feed us in our desperation, deliver us all into the light.

Your obedient servant,

Mrs. Robert H. Hammond

Josephine finished reading. Everyone sat in silence on the veranda. They all shared one thought: how lucky they had been that Grand Oak had not been burned. At least they a roof over their heads.

After a moment, Aunt Effie dabbed her eyes and said, "I guess I am homeless now."

Josephine took her hand and said, "Oh, Aunt Effie, you will never be homeless. You have a place here at Grand Oak with all of us. And besides, I am sure that the house in town is fine. The Yankees will never get into Charleston."

An Unexpected Visitor

As my family dealt with the Yankees in the South, I was dealing with them on their home ground at Fort Delaware. If things had been bad before, they were even worse now. With the collapse of the Dix-Hill Cartel came the end of all prisoner exchanges. The population of the island remained consistent. In addition, due to malnutrition and fatigue, most of the new prisoners were ill when they arrived. As if this were not enough to deal with, there was a new regiment of guards installed at the fort, the 157th, Ohio.

Having been in service for only one month prior to their assignment, they were as green as green could be. Their conduct toward the prisoners was ghoulish and mean spirited. They were no more than bullies. There was no honor among them. They delighted in confiscating personal property and firing upon us with no provocation whatsoever. They were given to drunkenness and quarrels among themselves.

As their cruelties became more pronounced, the whisper of escape became increasingly common. After all, it was only a one-and-one-eighth-mile swim that separated us from the mainland and freedom.

Many of the men were too ill to swim; others did not know how. That did not stop an ingenious few from trying. Those who made it to the water would use logs or boards to paddle across the river. There was one resourceful fellow who tied several empty canteens together and floated to freedom. It was this ingenuity and the unrest among the prison population that inspired the creation of Special Order 157. The order gave the guards permission to detain, search, or discipline the prisoners for any reason, real or imagined. General Schoepf ordered that "the sentinel must enforce his orders by bayonet or ball."

Life had been difficult before Special Order 157, but now it became unbearable. The guards were free to take pot shots at us, without fear of reprisal, whenever they pleased.

I found myself becoming a prisoners' rights advocate. I fought for equal treatment of all of the residents on the island. Many issues needed to be addressed. The new chapel was finished, but even though they had built it, the prisoners were not allowed to worship there. Letters often arrived with pages missing, and items sent to us through the post, with no explanation, disappeared before they were delivered. When disputes occurred between the rank and file, we arranged for the Confederate officers to hear the cases and recommend punishment.

I worked with several men who were literate to teach those who could not to read. Like a common criminal, I was watched at every moment. I had always been suspected of being a troublemaker.

The authorities dangled the possibility of parole before me, like a carrot before a mule. It would be mine if I would take the oath of allegiance to the Union or tell them where the money was hidden for the Confederacy.

Repeatedly I denied any monetary assistance to the Confederate government, and I refused to take the oath.

General Schoephf and Captain Ahl were now, more than ever, certain that I was up to no good. Just as a cat watches a mouse hole, they watched my every move, waiting for me to betray myself.

Except for those terrible days leading to Hardy's passing, life at Fort Delaware, to this point, had rolled along at a snail's pace. April of 1865 would prove to be anything but dull.

Our fight would soon be over. The news of the end of our struggle for an independent South would reach my loved ones at Grand Oak and me at Fort Delaware in very different ways. At Grand Oak, the news of Lee's surrender was passed quietly, tearfully, from hand to hand, so that each member of the family could read for themselves that terrible headline: "Lee surrenders to Grant at Appomattox."

The ladies, with tears in their eyes, sadly shook their heads and embraced as they consoled each other.

The news of the fall of Richmond and the inevitable end of the war was delivered to the prisoners at Fort Delaware with a violent explosion of guns and cannons. The only thing that made our shock and disbelief bearable was the knowledge that soon we would be going home.

April 3 started quietly like every other day at the fort. Brilliant, blue skies and mild temperatures heralded the coming spring and summer. By late afternoon, there came a great scurrying of troops. It became apparent that something was up. We began to wonder if there was an attack coming. Was the Confederacy on its way at last to rescue us?

A little after 7:00 p.m., we found out.

There came a roar such as I had never heard. In a sheet of flame and a cloud of sulfur, all 156 guns in the casements fired at once. As the resulting explosion shook the entire island, a burning acrid wall of smoke obscured the setting sun. General Schoepf wanted to give us a wake-up call that we would never forget. Soon after the discharge of the guns, a dispatch was read to all of the prisoners. Richmond had fallen and our beloved Confederacy would soon follow. Throughout the night, news was shouted and celebrated in a loud, drunken frenzy. If the guards had been undisciplined bullies before, they were even worse now. Any sense of duty or decorum they may have felt disappeared with the news of the beginning of the end.

Unlike the Union army at Appomattox, who, when the end did come, would show respect to their opponents for a battle well fought, the soldiers at Fort Delaware became more arrogant, abusive, and cocky with each passing day.

Four days after the fall of Richmond, I was in my cell over the sally port when a guard came to tell me that I had an unexpected visitor. At first, I did not believe him. I had been allowed no contact with the outside world since the start of my incarceration. My captors wanted to take no chances on my passing information to the South.

"Who is it?" I asked.

"Actually, there are two of them—a man and a woman. Some folks from the sanitary commission," the guard replied.

The sanitary commission had been founded by citizens and clergy to provide necessities and to see to the fair treatment of prisoners of war. In addition, the commission staffed field hospitals, raised money, provided supplies, and worked to educate the military and government on matters of health and sanitation.

"You best look good, too. The woman's a looker, and she's with a preacher man."

"What do they want with me?"

"Don't know, don't care. I was just told to fetch you; that's all."

I could not imagine what their interest in me could be. I was afraid that this might be a trap to try to get me to divulge any information. I washed my face, brushed my hair, and put on a clean shirt and my uniform jacket. I had no idea what to expect.

I was taken downstairs to a private cell that served as a hospital room for the officers. The room was sparse but very clean. There was a bed on the back wall. Two wooden chairs and a small table with an oil lamp comprised the remaining furnishings.

Originally, the room must have been used as a holding cell for disciplinary reasons, for a heavy oak door with a window and bars guarded the entrance to the room. A woman dressed in black sat in the chair closest to me. A man wearing the dress of the clergy stood beside her. The minister thanked the guard and asked, "May we have a few moments of silent prayer alone with the prisoner?"

The guard turned and left the room. I heard his key turn in the lock. We could see the back of his head through the bars as he stood outside the door. As the minister turned to face me, I was struck by the intense blue of his eyes. I had the distinct impression that we had met before.

The woman stood and lifted the veil from her face. She put her finger to her lips, shook her head no, and whispered, "Shhh!" I thought I was losing my mind. The woman looked amazingly like Mary Alice.

Aloud, she said, "Good sir, we have come to offer you the wonderful news of Jesus's saving grace. Are you ready to accept him as your Lord and Savior?"

Not knowing what else to do I said, "Yes."

In a loud, authoritative voice, the reverend began an invocation from his Bible. The private, satisfied that my visitors were not enemy spies, left the door and went to his post at the end of the hallway.

Once the guard was out of earshot, Mary Alice grabbed me and hugged me.

"Oh, Charles, we have missed you so much. I am so glad you are safe."

I must admit I was surprised at the change in the girl. She seemed so different from the spoiled, selfish little girl I remembered. She was also not generally given to displays of emotion such as this.

"Oh, but where are my manners? Cousin Charles, I want you to meet my husband, Reverend Thomas Hallowell."

The reverend extended his hand. "Actually, we have met, sir, once before in a little town called Monacasy Junction.

I pulled my hand back. Now I realized who this man was. He had shaved his moustache and changed his uniform, but there was no mistaking those blue eyes. He was the person who was responsible for sending Hardy and me to this place. It was his fault that Hardy was dead.

"Mary Alice, how could you? You've betrayed your family and everything we fought for. Get this man out of here. Guard!" I yelled.

Mary Alice grabbed my arm. "Please, please, Cousin Charles, listen to me."

I heard the clicking of the guard's boots as he ran to the cell. He stuck his head through the bars of the door. Turning his head away, the reverend began to cough. Mary Alice said urgently, "Please, we need a glass of water quickly!"

As the private ran for the water, Mary Alice begged, "Please, Cousin Charles, hear us out. Let us explain."

"There is nothing you can say to me. You have betrayed us all," I said.

"You don't understand. We have come all this way and put ourselves at risk just so we could help you escape," pleaded Mary Alice.

"Please, sir. I love Mary Alice. She is my life. Give me a chance to make up for what I have done," implored the reverend.

My mind raced. I stood with my fists clenched. I was furious, but I kept silent as the guard returned with the water.

Reverend Hallowell continued his coughing spell. Mary Alice took the water from the guard and gave the reverend a drink. When he finished, he smiled at the guard and said, "Bless you, my son. I am fine now."

The guard returned to his post at the end of the hall.

"Major McGuire, it is true I was at Monacasy Junction, and I did sign the papers that sent you and the boy here, but I was only following orders. Believe me, I would much rather have released you. I am not a fighter. I never wanted to join the army. My father was a soldier. Imagine his disappointment when, before I came along, my mother presented him with six daughters. I am his only son; he was adamant that I follow in his footsteps. I had no choice but to pursue a military career. I always had difficulty reconciling myself to the hardships that the war caused to people on both sides. When I saw how Mary Alice put aside her feelings to care for my men, I realized that I too had a choice. I resigned my commission in the army and joined the ministry. I am not ordained yet, but I will be soon. I want to try to undo some of the heartache that I have caused."

He seemed sincere. I remembered how the young man before me had apologized for my treatment at the hands of his men. He had not been as barbaric as some of the soldiers I had met. Perhaps he did deserve a chance.

"Mary Alice, what were you doing in the North? I thought you were at Grand Oak with the rest of the family."

"I was, Cousin Charles. Thomas's unit was ordered south shortly after Monocasy. They were engaged in two days of fighting not far from the house. When the army retreated, they camped around Grand Oak."

"Fighting at Grand Oak? Is everyone all right?" I asked.

"Yes, yes. Everyone is fine," said Mary Alice. "Josephine and I nursed the soldiers. Aunt Effie and Ethne wrote letters for the men who were recuperating. Josephine saw to it that the servants kept the men supplied with water and helped to fix what food we could find. Everyone got along fine. When Thomas's commanding officer came to camp, he told him how we had helped to save the unit. The general asked what he could do to thank us. Josephine said they could leave us and the animals alone in peace."

I laughed to myself. I could see Josephine standing up to the Union army.

"When the army left, the general gave Josephine a letter saying that the house and everything around it was not to be touched," explained Mary Alice.

"Before we left," continued Thomas. "We were married by our unit's chaplain in the ballroom at your home. I was looking at the painting of your wife when I noticed the one hanging across from it. It was then that I realized who you were and what I had been a party to. That was when I determined to set this straight. I managed to get your name on one of the exchange lists, but you were not on the boat when it reached Charleston. I couldn't find out what happened. Finally, I discovered that the boy had died and that you were still here."

"That is why I missed the boat. Hardy was too ill to travel, and I couldn't leave him behind," I said.

"Major, I am so sorry. If I could bring the boy back I would, but the best I can do is to get you out of here."

"And how do you plan to sneak me out past the guards?" I asked.

"Simple, you are to switch clothes with me. I will lie on the bed like I am crying. Mary Alice will tell the guard that you are overcome by your conversion and that you need a few moments to recover. Then, wearing my clothes, you will accompany Mary Alice to the mainland, where we have someone waiting to help you make your way south."

"But how are you going to get free?" I asked.

"When the switch is discovered, I will simply say that I was misled as to the true identity of my traveling companion and that the two of you overpowered me."

"I suppose it could work. Are you sure that you will be all right?" I asked.

"They won't doubt me when they find out I was a captain in the Union army," said Thomas.

Reverend Hallowell and I changed clothes. He lay down on the bed. Using the rope that had been tied around the minister's waist and a scarf from Mary Alice, we bound and gagged him. I pulled the reverend's black hat low on my head to help disguise myself. Mary Alice gave me a black scarf and said, "Hold this to your face and cough a little so they can't see your beard."

Once the switch was accomplished, Mary Alice called for the guard.

"Pardon me, sir. We are ready to leave."

As the private unlocked and opened the door, I held the scarf close to my face. I looked down at the floor and coughed.

"What's the matter with him?" the guard questioned.

"Oh, it's nothing. Just the dust and dampness. He will be all right once we get out into the fresh air," said Mary Alice.

"No, I mean the major," said the guard, pointing at what he believed to be me.

Mary Alice leaned close to the guard. In a very soft voice, she whispered, "He has just found God and is repenting for his sins. He just needs a little time alone to ask for forgiveness, that's all."

I was impressed with the ease with which she thought up the lie.

"Oh," said the guard. He locked the door behind him and escorted Mary Alice and me to the boat dock and freedom.

Later that evening, the Reverend Thomas Hallowell would sit in General Schoepf's office and tell the sad tale of how he was fooled by a young woman posing as a Sister of Mercy so that she could help free me from prison. He would testify how I knocked him over the head, stole his clothes, and left him bound and gagged on the bed. He vowed that he would find us one day. That part of the performance was true.

I set foot on the mainland for the first time in over a year. I could scarcely contain my jubilation at being free. A waiting carriage took us to a large two-story brick house just outside of town. There were many people sympathetic to our cause in Delaware City. The owner of the house was one of those people.

My host explained to me that I would not be able to stay inside the house in case someone should see me. I was welcome to sleep in the barn, where I would find a horse and saddle. I was not to worry about returning them. I thanked my host and made my way to the barn. To my amazement, the horse that had been provided for me was none other than my beloved Providence. The family had managed to talk one of the sergeants into letting them buy him before he was sent off to the army.

I was told that it would not be safe for me to be seen in either a Union or a Confederate uniform. The best disguise would be to travel in the minister's frock that I was now wearing. I was given a small leather sack containing ten silver dollars and the name of a family that would help me when I found my way to Maryland.

Mary Alice brought supper to me in the barn later that night.

"Mary Alice, I am sorry I was so angry earlier. I can never you repay the two of you for what you have done. How are you and your husband going to find each other?"

"Tomorrow I am to go to the Quaker meeting house in Wilmington to wait for him there."

"Do you want me to take you?" I asked.

"No, Cousin Charles, you mustn't. It isn't safe. They will be looking for you. Mr. Howe will see that I get there safely."

I looked at Mary Alice with pride. Her family would be so pleased at the way she had turned out.

"Cousin Charles, I am sorry I was such a selfish girl growing up. I hope you will forgive me," she said.

I smiled at her. "There is nothing to forgive."

"And Thomas, I love him so. Do you approve of my marrying him even if he is from the North?"

"How could I disapprove of the man who helped get me out of that awful place?" I said.

Mary Alice hugged me. "Thank you so much, Cousin Charles. When this is all over, we will all be together again. I promise."

"I hope so. You know that both you and your husband will always have a home at Grand Oak," I said.

Mary Alice looked at me shyly. "What if there are more than just the two of us?" She smiled.

It took a moment for the meaning of the statement to sink in. "You mean…"

"Yes," she said. "You're going to be a third cousin!"

I hugged her close and offered my congratulations.

"Shouldn't you be getting in from the night air then?" I asked.

"Yes, I suppose. It's just hard to say good-bye."

"I understand. Don't worry; we will all meet again at home as soon as this mess is over."

"Please tell everyone I miss them," said Mary Alice.

"I will," I promised.

Mary Alice stood and kissed my cheek. I hugged her good-bye. As she reached the door, she turned and took a package from the basket that had held my supper.

"Oh, I almost forgot to give these to you," she said. "One of the officer's wives said she was sorry about your boy and that your treatment on the island was disgraceful. She took these from the trash and saved them. She was hoping to give them to you before you left."

Mary Alice handed me a bundle of letters. I recognized the handwriting immediately. It was mine! Not one of my letters had been mailed. Poor Josephine, she must be worried sick.

The Long Road Home

I was on my way the next morning before sunrise. I had no wish to jeopardize the safety of those who had helped me by staying any longer in my host's barn than necessary. I was certain that a search party would be organized to look for me. I need not have worried, for my fears were unfounded.

Sitting on General Albin Schoepf's desk were papers absolving my family and me from any complicity in aiding the Confederate government. On April 12, in a small town in Virginia, the war would end, rendering my pardon unnecessary. I would have been free to go home. Two days after Lee surrendered the army of Northern Virginia to Grant, an assassin's bullet would end President Lincoln's life. The country would have more pressing matters about which to worry than an escaped Confederate officer. There would be no one coming to look for me.

I was eager to put Fort Delaware behind me. At first light, I saddled Providence and headed south. In the eastern sky, the breaking dawn unfurled ribbons of light in shades of pink and aqua. In the west, the last stars faded from the navy blue sky while a fingernail moon balanced on pencil-point treetops before melting into the horizon. The air was crisp and fragrant. Our breath made little clouds of white that dissipated in the morning breeze. Overhead, the birds sang symphonies to Flora, the goddess of spring. In gratitude, she clothed the crabapple trees with fragile pink and white blossoms and strewed our pathway with a mosaic of wildflowers.

All around us, the blushing, naked earth was eager to clothe herself in a fresh mantle of green. I felt as if I was being born again with the new season. Ah, blessed freedom! How I had dreamed of this day.

As I rode through the greening countryside, I contemplated the miracle of rebirth surrounding me. In the midst of this season of resurrection, it was difficult to believe that another world, my world, was uttering its dying breath.

I had not expected to be making this journey alone. I had imagined that the trip home would be a victory ride with my regiment and Hardy. I did not know what had become of my men or how many of them were still alive. Hardy was gone. I had no idea if my family was safe. There was no way of knowing if my home was still standing.

I forced myself to look ahead. I had to take the seeds left from the previous year's harvest and plant my future. That which had been harvested had been consumed or laid away; it could not be bought back.

My second night of freedom, I spent at a simple clapboard farmhouse that was home to a widow and her three small daughters. Her husband and son had been killed in the war. The family had been Southern sympathizers. The woman and her daughters had vowed to honor their loved ones by helping Southern soldiers make their way home to their families. I was touched beyond words that they were so eager to share their modest fare with me.

I spent the night in a storm cellar behind the house, and by sunrise, once again, I was gone. I left three of the silver dollars I had been given by Mary Alice wrapped in my handkerchief for the family. It was not very much, but I hoped it would ease their way. The next two nights I spent under the stars. It was chilly, but I had survived colder nights than this. I could not bear to be a burden on another family who had so little to share.

The city of Richmond had fallen. The Yankees now were everywhere. They were in Petersburg, Farmville, Hopewell, and Appomattox. It seemed there was no way to avoid them. I kept to the east, along the coastline, hoping I would not come across them.

By late afternoon of the fourth day, the steady drizzle of morning gave way to a soaking rain. The rain turned the heavily rutted roads into a sea of mud, making them almost impassable. In the early evening, I came across a small, two-story, brick dwelling. A plume of charcoal-colored smoke rose from the house's ramshackle chimney. Shafts of light sliced through its tightly fastened shutters.

To the left of the house was a large hickory tree. Approximately twelve feet from the ground, nailed to the tree trunk, with the ends pointing south, was a horseshoe. This was a safe house. They were part of the network. I had been told before I left Delaware that I would be able to recognize homes or inns that would shelter Confederates by a horseshoe nailed to a tree in just such a fashion.

A so-called underground railway running south to north taking slaves to freedom was whispered of by civilians and abolitionists. Unknown to most people who were not Southerners, there was also a Southern equivalent running from the North to the South. The network had two different paths. The first helped Confederate spies and prisoners make their way home. The second was more diabolical; it returned to the South and captured freedmen and slaves who had escaped. Many of these people were then resold into slavery.

There was an entire network of Southern patriots who had sworn to help anyone who had fought for the Great Lost Cause get home safely. Their credo was "Least We Forget." It was an anagram. When the letters were rearranged, they spelled, "Great Slow Feet." When a traveler knocked on the door to a safe house and said, "I have walked here with great slow feet," the person answering the door replied, "Least we forget," and they knew that they were safe.

I tied Providence's reins to the railing, walked onto the porch, and knocked on the door. The door was answered by a woman in her early thirties. Her eyes were red and swollen. She dabbed a handkerchief to her nose. She appeared to have been crying.

"I'm sorry, Reverend," she said. "We have been waiting for you."

I was not certain what she meant. "I apologize for bothering you, ma'am," I replied. "I have walked here with *great slow feet.*"

The woman opened the door wide. "*Least we forget,*" she said as invited me in.

"Please forgive me, friend. You are welcome. What we have we are honored to share."

I shook the rain from my hat and coat and stepped into the hallway of the house. As the woman closed the door behind me, four small children came running from the parlor to my left. They stared up at me expectantly with hollow eyes. I smiled at them. The youngest smiled back as she ducked behind her mother's skirt.

"Forgive me, Reverend," said the lady as she curtsied. "I am Mrs. Harper. These are my children, Anna, Robert, Samuel, and Joy. Though I suspect that it is little Agnes that you have come to see."

"Say hello to the good reverend," instructed the children's mother.

"Hello, Reverend," the children said in unison.

"Where is Mr. Harper? Isn't he with you?" she asked.

"I'm sorry, I don't understand. Why should your husband be with me?"

"Are you not the new minister from town?"

"No. I am making my way home to South Carolina from Delaware," I explained.

"Oh, forgive me!" said Mrs. Harper. "My husband went into town to find our new minister. We need him for our dear little Agnes."

We were interrupted by the sound of boots on the front porch. The door opened to reveal a stocky, dark-haired man with a beard standing just outside the threshold. Looking down at the floor, he stomped the mud from his boots on an old rug by the front of the door.

Without glancing up, he said, "Ain't no use. He ain't arrived yet. Don't know when he'll be here. We'll just have to manage by ourselves." As he entered the house, his eyes looked up and saw me. Surprise registered on his face. "Oh, you're here!"

"Reverend, I'm sorry. I didn't get your name," said Mrs. Harper.

"It's McGuire," I said.

"Reverend McGuire, this is my husband, Samuel Harper."

Mr. Harper extended his hand. "Reverend, we sure are thankful that you're here," he said as he shook my hand.

"Samuel, Reverend McGuire is just passing through. He is a Confederate, least we forget," said Mrs. Harper.

"My apologies," said Samuel. He nodded slowly in understanding. "The Lord does provide. Welcome, Reverend. Has Mrs. Harper told you of our loss?"

"No," I said.

"It's our youngest, Agnes Dei," he said.

I recognized the meaning of the name. "Lamb of God," I said.

"That's right. She was our little lamb, a miracle baby. She came four weeks early. We were so thankful when she made it through the first eighteen months. She took ill two weeks ago.

They ain't no doctors in town. They all left to help the army. We nursed her the best we could, but we lost her two days ago. We were waiting for the new preacher to get here so we could have her baptized, but he never came. Thank God he has brought you here. You can baptize her for us."

My heart almost stopped; the air seemed to leave the room all at once. I had never anticipated having to perform any sacraments. Up until this moment, I had not realized what a coward I had been, hiding behind a minister's frock. Would God ever forgive me?

My mind raced, *What would be the greater sin—to impersonate a priest or to disappoint this family who looked up me with such relief on their faces?* Then, as I remembered the soldiers lost in battle, the answer came to me. There had been no minister to speak for my men. I had entrusted their souls to the Almighty by reading from my Bible. I would perform the sacrament and, at a later date, when the real minister came to the congregation, I would advise him of what I had done. He could rebaptize the infant and offer a prayer of remembrance in secret if need be.

"Let us go and see Agnes," I said.

We sat with the child through the night. Together with her parents, I offered prayers for little Agnes. I remembered my mother and my grandfather. I remembered Hardy. I looked at the peaceful faces of the family gathered around. They had put their faith in God, and he had sent them me. Maybe I was supposed to be here all along. Perhaps God was using me to ease this family's pain and suffering.

The next morning, under a brilliant April sky washed clear by the previous day's rain, we stood in the buttercup-strewn field behind the family home. I had attended enough baptisms that I had no difficulty remembering the words.

From memory, I asked, "Hath this child been already baptized, yes or no?"

The family replied that she had not.

I began to recite those old familiar words from the *Book of Common Prayer*.

> Give thy Holy Spirit to this infant, that she may be born again, and be made an heir of everlasting salvation; through our Lord Jesus Christ, who liveth and reigneth with thee and the Holy Spirit, now and for ever. Amen.
>
> Dearly beloved, forasmuch as all men are conceived and born in sin, and our Saviour Christ saith none can enter into the kingdom of God except he be regenerate and born anew of water and of the Holy Ghost.
>
> I beseech you to call upon God the Father, through our Lord Jesus Christ, that of his bounteous mercy he will grant to this Child that which by nature she cannot have that she may be baptized with water and the Holy Ghost, and received into Christ's holy church, and be made a living member of the same.

Opening the Bible Grandmother had given to me, I continued.

> They brought young children to Christ, that he should touch them; and his disciples rebuked those that brought them. But when Jesus saw it, he was much displeased, and said unto them, Suffer the little children to come unto me, and forbid them not; for of such is the kingdom of God. Verily I say unto you, whosoever shall not receive the kingdom of God as a little child, he shall not enter therein. And he took them up in his arms, put his hands upon them, and blessed them.

I dipped the water from a silver bowl Mrs. Harper had bought from the house. She had dressed little Agnes in a white christening dress. She stood beside me holding the tiny baby in her arms. I anointed the baby's head with the water.

"Agnes Dei Harper, I baptize thee in the Name of the Father, and of the Son, and of the Holy Ghost. Amen."

Next, I read the words that I had read for too many friends in the recent past. "I am the resurrection and the life, saith the Lord: he that believeth in me, though he were dead, yet shall he live; and whosoever liveth and believeth in me, shall never die." When I had finished, I sprinkled some of the remaining water on the child's small coffin.

I ended by reading the Twenty-third Psalm. When the reading ended, we joined hands and sang "Amazing Grace" as the breeze whispered "Amen" through the grass.

Later that morning, as I prepared to leave, Mrs. Harper came running down the steps of the house. She carried a few pieces of bread and some dried apple slices wrapped in a cloth. "Here, these are for your journey. We can never repay you for your kindness," she said.

"Mrs. Harper, I can't take this. You need it to feed your family," I said.

"Nonsense. God will provide, just like he sent you to us." She smiled sweetly at me. I thought of Josephine, and I was eager to be on my way.

I looked up to see Mr. Harper standing on the porch with the children. They waved. I waved back.

I looked at Mrs. Harper and smiled, "God bless you, and peace to you and your family."

"And to you. We will be praying for your safe return home, Reverend McGuire."

"Thank you, Mrs. Harper," I said, tipping my hat.

I put my foot in the stirrup and threw my other leg over the saddle. I waved good-bye and was on my way. I thought about that day in my cell when Reverend Handy had come to see me and I had declared God was dead. I regretted uttering those words. I wondered what the reverend would think if he could see me now.

As I made my way south, it became increasingly apparent what the cost of this conflict had been.

We had fought bravely and lost. The altercation was now in the past. One fourth of our male population had been sacrificed on the altar of honor and glory. Our most beautiful towns and cities, our finest homes and public buildings, all had become funeral pyres to the Great Lost Cause.

No longer would the sight of men and hometown boys marching with the sun gleaming off brass buttons of their handsome uniforms as they passed cheering crowds stir the hearts of young and old. Gone were the days when we would flirt across gaily decorated ballrooms or linger in magnolia-scented twilight. No longer would sweethearts pine for the return of their lovers, for they would not be coming home.

Our best and brightest minds were dead or imprisoned. We had squandered the promise of a generation of our young men. We were now a people of shattered dreams, ruined homes, and maimed, broken, tin soldiers. We had become a nation of widows and orphans.

The farther south I traveled, the more complete the devastation became. Entire towns and villages lay in ruins, their residents scattered to the four winds. The blackened towers of brick chimneys stood eerily silent amidst skeletal remains of farmhouses that had once been plump and ripe with life and productivity. Bridges had been burned, rails had been torn up, and the deep ruts that the heavy artillery had cut into the roadways rendered them almost impassable. The stench of death lay across the land as vultures circled in the sky.

Yet, even in all of this death, there was resurrection. Grass had begun to grow in the ruts along the road. Poppies and violets clothed the fresh graves of the dead, and honeysuckle and jasmine began to claim the blackened ruins of once proud dwellings.

As I rode home through my desolate homeland, there was plenty of time to contemplate what we had done. At the beginning of the conflict, each side, convinced of our righteousness, had prayed to the same God. We both asked for the same thing: victory. The North saw themselves as liberators of the slaves, defenders of the sacred Union of States, and guardians of the high moral ground. To the South, slavery was a part of God's plan for humanity.

The white population gained grace by caring for and educating the Negroes. The Negroes gained civilization and Christianity. Liberating the Negroes from Africa gave us a mission, a purpose; it gave us justification. There were those who questioned the humanity of slavery, but many of those people viewed it as abuse by the few who mistreated their slaves rather than abuse as a result of the institution.

Then, somewhere in the conflict, as we lost battle after battle, popular opinion began to shift. We began to question; was slavery a sin? If so, it was not the only one we had committed. We quarreled amongst ourselves, we were impatient, and we took advantage of our neighbors. We made a mockery of the commandments. We broke the Sabbath; we killed our brother; and the most holy of all commandments, we did not treat our neighbors as ourselves. Surely, this could not be the reason for our defeat, for the North was guilty of the same trespasses.

No. We in the South were God's chosen people. God had granted us success and prosperity. Our civilization was the envy of the world, and instead of giving thanks, we had been proud, boastful, slothful, and corrupt. We had showered wrath upon our brothers. God had set them upon us like the plagues of Egypt, and we were humbled.

If earthly triumph was granted to the people of the North, then moral triumph would become the legacy of the Southern people. If God handed his chosen people defeat, then misery would become martyrdom. The Bible said that, "The first shall be made last, and the last shall be made first." Maybe by humbling the South, God was insuring that his chosen people would be first in his heart and first in the kingdom of heaven.

As I continued my journey home, unable to find civilian clothes, I continued wearing the liturgical garments I had been given. I was greeted at every turn by people and families who were only too eager to share what little they had. Thankfully, I managed to avoid being called upon to administer any more sacraments. What I found were a people eager to believe that God had not abandoned them. I was touched beyond belief. Families had been broken apart, their houses of worship destroyed, and their towns and villages decimated by loss, yet somehow all of this had only seemed to galvanize their faith. They waited and listened for a sign that God had not abandoned the South to her enemies.

I was thankful that for a few brief hours I was able to sit with them and assure them that God was still there watching over them. I would read to them from Matthew: Who of you by worrying can add a single hour to his life...Consider the lilies of the field they neither labor or spin...Oh ye of little faith, do not worry about tomorrow for tomorrow will worry about itself.

Sometimes when I was alone, after I had been offering comfort to these poor forgotten people, I would cry. I cried with regret for my loss. I cried for the men I had killed. I cried for Hardy. I cried for the South. I did not feel guilty for the deception I was party to. I tried my honest best to offer comfort and hope to the people I met. I had not chosen this charade; it had been visited upon me. Perhaps this was God's way of cleansing my sprit before he sent me home, for in helping my countrymen,

I was able to calm the waves of anger and resentment that kept my heart from finding peace.

Soon I had put Virginia and North Carolina behind me. What joy and rapture I felt as I crossed the border to my beloved South Carolina. It would only be a matter of days until I was back at Grand Oak, back in the arms of the people I loved.

Before I knew it, I was on the road leading to my home. Excitement turned to apprehension as I passed burned building after burned building. The neighbors had scattered; there was no food to be had. I scarcely noticed the hunger in my belly; I was too worried about my family to think of food. At last, I was on the road leading to the driveway of Grand Oak. I rode Providence as fast as he could go. He seemed to share my desire to make it home, for he flew with the swift feet of Mercury. One more turn in the road to go, then there she was. My heart sank. I pulled Providence to a stop so that I might take in the ruins of my home. The beautiful brick piers that had marked the entrance to the drive had been stripped of their iron gates, the posts and walls of the right side of the entrance lay burned and broken across the drive.

Fallen trees and large branches littered the once immaculate lawn. The driveway looked impassable. I prayed that God had left the house still standing. About a mile and a half down the road was a service drive that led to the storage barns and the shipping docks on the river. Perhaps this entrance would be more accessible. I had to know what had happened to my house and my family.

I spurred Providence. We rode as quickly as possible. We found the drive. It did not look used, but it was not in the condition as the main drive. We galloped past fields that had once been lush with ripening cotton; they now lay fallow and deserted. The mile-long drive never seemed so long.

Then, just ahead, I could see the river. We came around the bend in the road, and once more, my hopes were dashed. The cotton barns and the docks were no more than burned piles of rubble. Hot tears of rage began to fill my eyes. I rode on, slower now, letting the devastation sink in. There was the henhouse and the pigsty, also in ruins.

I could see the crown of the old oak over the tops of the azaleas that framed the lawn down to the river and screened the outbuildings from view of the house. I rode through a break in the shrubs onto the lawn. I stopped Providence in his tracks. Nothing could have prepared me for the sight that greeted my eyes.

My home was unrecognizable. Her once gleaming columns were black and scarred. The roof appeared to have been on fire. The windows were boarded over or looked as though they were missing altogether. The house looked abandoned. I felt the anger and resentment that I thought I had left on the long road home boiling up inside me. I choked back waves of emotion as I tried to focus.

"Think, Charles, think. This cannot be real. It's all a dream. Open your eyes and Grand Oak will be just the same as she was when you left her."

As I stared at the ruins of my home, I realized that there was someone moving on the gallery. There was only one person that big at Grand Oak; it had to be Big Jawn. I jumped from Providence's back and ran toward the house yelling, "I'm home! I'm home!"

Big Jawn stood up and looked in my direction. Suddenly, recognition flooded his ebony face. He ran to the door and opened it. He yelled inside, "Miss Josephine! Miss Effie! Everybody come quick. Masta Charles is come home."

In a flash, he was down the steps and running toward me. No sooner did he hit the bottom step than my family came flooding from the house like bees from a hive. They all ran in my direction as I crossed the lawn to them. Big Jawn reached me first. His massive arms grabbed me in a bear hug. My feet dangled like a rag doll as he wrenched me from the ground.

"Welcome home, Masta Charles. Welcome home," he cried.

"Jawn, Jawn, set me down. I can't breathe," I said.

Jawn set me on the ground. He was so excited to see me that his huge body shook like a new puppy.

"Lordy, Masta Charles. We heard you was in prison. We never expected you to make it back home so soon," he said, shaking my hands furiously.

By now, my family had reached my side. Josephine was first; she threw her arms around me, followed by Ethne and Aunt Effie and the children. Still weak from Big Jawn's bear hug, I lost my balance, and we tumbled to the lawn like a stack of children's blocks. In that moment, for just an instant, everything was forgotten. There had been no war. Grand Oak was gleaming white in the afternoon sun, we were all happy and contented, and time had not passed since we had all been together. We laughed for a second and then picked ourselves up from the grass. Josephine hugged and kissed me as Ethne extended her hand to Aunt Effie to help her up. The children skipped around us singing, "Uncle Charles is home. Uncle Charles is home."

I looked up to see Matthew helping Grandmother across the lawn to my side. Behind them, the rest of the house servants stood smiling in a row on the steps. I ran to Grandmother and Matthew. How old and frail Grandmother looked. And Matthew, he was so thin. His face looked worn and tired as he stumped across the grass with the aid of a wooden leg.

Grandmother reached out and buried her face in my chest. For a moment, she did not speak. Then she looked up at me and said, "Oh, Charles, God has brought you safely home to us. Now I can leave in peace and join your Grandfather."

"Here, what kind of talk is that?" I said. "I've just gotten home. I expect us to be together a long, long time."

Grandmother patted me slowly three times on the chest and smiled, "We'll see," she said.

Josephine and Aunt Effie looked at me as I stood on the lawn before them. It was then that Josephine realized what I was wearing.

"Why, Charles, that is not your uniform. Why are you dressed that way?" she asked.

"It's a long story." I laughed. "Let's go back to the house and I'll tell you all about it."

We walked back to the house together. We sat in the parlor, and the family entertained me with stories about of how they had come to leave the city and why the house looked the way it did. I laughed at how clever Josephine had been to making things look so bad. I told them about Hardy and our capture and of Mary Alice and her husband's visit. I told them how much I had missed them all. I was thankful—thankful to be home.

A new day was dawning. The fighting was over. The war was in the past. As a result, slavery was abolished. The old argument that had vexed our forefathers had been decided; the issue of states' rights versus national jurisdiction was finally answered. We were one nation again.

Slowly, our neighbors began to make their way back to see what was left of their homes. Here and there, all over the countryside, little pockets of humanity were cropping up. Drayton Hall was safe. The family had posted signs along the riverfront declaring, "Malaria and Typhoid." Apparently, this had frightened away any undesirable visitors. Middleton, sadly, had been mostly burned to the ground. Her beautiful gardens had been trampled beneath the hooves of the soldiers' horses. The Yankees had taken particular joy in smashing statues and burning out-buildings on the estate. Magnolia had survived, though it would be a while before the family returned.

Information began to filter out to us from Charleston; some of it was hard to bear. Aunt Effie's neighbor, Mrs. Townsend, had written of the panic that ensued as the troops had evacuated Charleston on the night of the seventeenth and morning of the eighteenth of February.

In mid-May, we received one of the most distressing letters yet from Charleston. It was addressed to Aunt Effie.

> *Dear Mrs. Scott,*
>
> It is with a heavy heart that I write to tell you the news of Charleston. As by now I am sure you are aware, the yoke of Yankee rule lays heavy upon our backs. You would scarce recognize our once proud and beautiful city. There is grass—grass, Euphemia—growing up through the middle of Broad Street.
>
> When the Yankees first arrived, they behaved as I imagine the Vandals behaved when they sacked Rome. Any house not occupied was entered and ransacked. The demons stole everything that they could lay their hands on. They stole copper downspouts and pipes and even chandeliers for the scrap value of the metal. The windows that were not broken out by shelling were broken by the first soldiers looking to loot the city. The street was lit-tered with glass. The tiny shards left behind sparkle like diamonds in the light from the afternoon sun.
>
> I suspect that there is not a pane of glass left unbroken in all of Charleston. When the authorities saw what was happening, they at least had the decency to call for an end to the looting. They ordered in more troops to help abate the violence, but, oh, Euphemia! They ordered in colored

troops. The Union officers took a great deal of pride in the spectacle of them marching up the street.

It would seem that with every passing day the Yankees find new ways to devil us. The officers have taken up residence in what is left of our once fine homes. I do not believe that any amount of cleaning will ever be able to remove the stench of them.

No person of quality is safe venturing out after dark in the city; robberies and beatings occur almost nightly. Even during daylight, the behavior of these unruly, common Yankees and trashy Negroes makes it impossible for a lady to go about the simplest of errands unescorted.

We are fortunate that, due to old Mr. Townsend's health, we could not leave our home when the city was evacuated. Our being here is all that has saved it from being looted like so many others. We are five in the house along with Basil, little Joseph's dog. He makes a great deal of racket whenever soldiers come near the house. We are so fortunate that he hates Yankees as much as we, for they are quite afraid of him.

Two or three of the old families are still here, and a few more had left their homes occupied, as you did, by servants or gardeners. Your home is safe. You were very wise to leave it in the hands of Belana and James. We were all most impressed when Belana, dressed to the nines in one of your gowns, met the Yankees at the door. The Yankees told her that they were going to set up headquarters in the house. She told them that she was a free woman of color and this was her home. She was aided in the deception by her two small nieces who clung to her skirts. The Yankees apologized and left the house alone, opting instead to occupy poor Mrs. Humphries's house, which had been left empty when she had refugeed north. They stabled their horses in your garden. The horses trampled your camellias, and there was a small fire. I am afraid the grounds are ruined.

Please tell Mrs. McGuire that her house is safe as well. Mrs. Pickney's nephew, Adam, and his wife and three little children were burned out. I knew that Mrs. McGuire's house was empty. I thought that it would help to insure that it did not fall prey to looters or Yankee occupation if it was lived in. I hope that she will not be upset with me, for it was my idea to have them take up residence there until such time as she returns or they find another dwelling.

There have been a few poor souls, mostly Negroes, trying to sell things at the market to make a little money to eat, but alas, nobody except the Yankees soldiers has any money these days.

I am sorry to say that it will be quite some time before Charleston sees any gaiety. We are, though, a strong people, and I am certain that it will take more than the Union army to lick us.

We all here hope that this letter finds you and your family at Grand Oak in good health and as positive a humor as these times will permit.

Your obedient servant,
Mrs. P. T. Townsend

As troublesome as the letter was, we were thankful that the properties in town were safe. We would worry about Charleston later.

We still had money in the bank in England, but it would be a while before we could access it. It would also be a while before the mills were producing. We needed to turn our attention to making the plantation work again. Matthew and I set out trying to find livestock, which was not easy, for so much of it had been destroyed or consumed by our invaders. We also needed to find feed for the animals and food for the family until we were able to harvest from the garden.

Somehow, we managed to make it through the summer and fall. By spring, we were so busy working to make ends meet that at first we did not notice the change coming over Grandmother. By mid-June, it was becoming apparent that her health was failing. She began to sleep most of the day, and we would catch her talking to Grandfather as if he was really there. Sometimes she would look at us, smile wistfully, and say things like, "Dear me, I have lived too long. I want to go and see Charles." Or she would say, "There is just no place for me in this new world."

We tried to make her feel comfortable and needed, but with each passing day, she seemed to slip deeper and deeper into melancholy. About the same time that Grandmother began to fade, Josephine started having bouts of nausea in the mornings and she always seemed to be tired.

I became very worried. I had seen enough illness at Fort Delaware to be concerned. One morning at breakfast, Josephine ran from the table. Ethne and Isabelle followed to assist her. Aunt Effie acted as if nothing had happened. She wore one of those all-knowing smiles that women so often have on their faces when they think they know something men do not. Matthew just squirmed in his chair and looked at his plate as if he had never seen scrambled eggs before.

Grandmother seemed to have a little of the old sparkle in her eyes as she exchanged conspiratorial glances with Aunt Effie. I stood up and threw my napkin onto the table.

"Would someone like to tell me just what is going on?" I asked.

Mammy, who had been standing in the door, disappeared. Matthew stared more intently at his breakfast.

Aunt Effie looked at me and said. "Sit down, Charles."

Surprised by her tone, I sat.

"Now, I suggest that you wait until your sister and Isabelle come back. Then you may excuse yourself and find Josephine. You need have a talk with your wife."

I just looked at Aunt Effie puzzled.

Ethne returned to the dining room. "Josephine is fine. She's just feeling a little ill; that's all. She decided to lie down for a moment."

Following Aunt Effie's advice, I excused myself. I stood up and went to find Josephine. I found her lying on the sofa in the parlor. Isabelle sat beside her with a cold cloth pressed to her forehead.

"Isabelle, would you excuse us for a moment?" I said.

"Yes, sir, Masta Charles," she answered.

I walked over to where Josephine was reclining on the sofa. She sat up and smiled at me. "Are you feeling better?" I asked.

Still smiling in a most sheepish fashion, she nodded yes.

"Josephine, I am most concerned. I have seen a lot of sickness during the war. I think we need to get you to a doctor."

"Oh, Charles!" She laughed. "It's all perfectly normal."

"I don't see how being tired and sick all the time is normal. If you were at Fort Delaware, we would have had you in the infirmary by now."

"Charles, sit down here beside me for a moment," she said, patting the sofa beside her. "I need to tell you something."

I took a seat next to her. "About what?" I asked, thoroughly confused.

She took both of my hands in hers, tilted her head to the side, smiled brilliantly, and said, "You're going to be a father."

It took a moment for the words to sink in. Of course! It all made sense now. Why hadn't I seen it? I felt rather foolish; I must be the last one to know. "Are you sure? How do you know? When?" I asked excitedly.

"Yes, darling. I'm pretty sure. It is just one of those things women know." She laughed. "Are you really happy?"

"I am ecstatic," I said as I hugged my wife close. We kissed passionately. I felt as though I was the luckiest man in the world.

A World Upside Down

By August, Josephine's pregnancy was well under way, and a dozen former slaves returned to the plantation.

In some respects, freedom was not what they had envisioned. Many former slaves went to the cities where there was a least the chance to find labor; others tried to survive on their own by farming. A few of them returned to the plantations and tried to strike a deal with their former masters.

When the call for freedom for the slaves had been on the lips of the abolitionists, they had never bothered to look into the future to see what would become of these people. It is difficult to express the effect of suddenly freeing thousands of people and turning them loose with no education and no means of supporting themselves can have on a society.

Suddenly there were tens of thousands of free blacks with no one to feed them, nowhere to live, and no way to make a future for themselves. Every day was a struggle just for them to survive. The working class detested them, for they were considered competition for jobs and resources. The white population, who had considered the Negroes a serving class, would never accept them as equals.

That summer of 1866, the entire South, and Charleston especially, was a world upside down. Unfamiliar accents, Northern and foreign, could be heard on every street corner. The city was overflowing with Yankee soldiers and poor whites. The lowest class of Yankee—carpetbaggers, scallywags, and indolent coloreds—was firmly in power.

A carpetbagger was a Northerner who moved south at the end of the war. Scallywags were Southern whites who supported reconstruction. Often they worked in tandem with freedmen to take control of their respective state and local governments. They did their best to make miserable the lives of anyone who had been a member of the upper class before the war.

The main objective of this triumvirate was to loot and plunder the defeated South. The centerpiece of their plan was known as the Ironclad Oath. The oath required every white male to swear he had never borne arms against the Union or supported the Confederacy or that he had held no office under the Confederacy. Failure to take the Iron Clad Oath resulted in the loss of voting rights. This guaranteed that anyone who had owned land or held any political office before the war could not vote.

The carpetbag rule made a mockery of justice, so the former ruling class went underground. There was a large population of shiftless, lazy coloreds from the field-hand class who had flooded into the city from the country. Most of them had been troublemakers on the plantations where they had lived. Now, with the protection of the Union army, their impudence knew no bounds. Several measures were passed to try to control the Negro problem.

First, we tried a vagrant law. It was enacted to keep the Negroes from roaming the roads and living the lives of beggars and thieves.

When this failed, we tried instituting "black codes." The black codes only served to infuriate public opinion in the North. They saw the South as creating a new order of servitude. It did not take long for the new republican government to repeal the black codes wherever they found them.

It was inevitable that we should witness the birth of a secret society, the Ku Klux Klan. Make no mistake, I am not defending the Klan or what they came to stand for, but in those early days immediately following the war, they served their purpose.

The original Klan was founded by veterans of the Confederate army. They took their name from the Greek word for circle, *kuklos,* and the old English word for family, *clan.* The primary objectives of the Klan were to defend the honor of our women, harass the carpetbaggers, destroy Union League councils, keep the unruly coloreds in place, and scare black men away from the polls.

Riding beneath the cover of darkness, hooded, white-robed men on masked, sheeted horses plied mischievous pranks upon the superstitious Negroes.

The Klan's intimidation was not limited to the imprudent Negroes; many a high-and-mighty carpetbagger and scallywag knew the fear of a nocturnal visit from the white knights.

It did not take long for the carpetbagger and scallywag politicians to notice that renegade Negroes were beginning to behave themselves, and crime was becoming drastically reduced in certain areas.

This would never do; carpetbaggers and scalawags were manipulators who, in order to insure the successful increase of their fortunes and political powers, were dependant on their ability to exploit people's fears. The Klan was obviously at the core of the reduction of crimes and violence. Thus, the Klan had to go! The Loyal League and Union League made willing allies. After all, the Klan was, for the most part, made up of ex-Confederates who were hated by both organizations.

The Union and Loyal Leagues soon joined forces and began night patrols in the name of protecting the terrified Negro population and their white sympathizers. These patrols did not hesitate to open fire on the Klansmen. The Klan responded in kind. Eventually, skirmishes broke out whenever night patrols of each side encountered each other. The intimidation of the Negroes and their allies perpetrated by the Klan had begun simply and nonviolently, but it had escalated into murder, beatings, and mayhem.

It was not long before the Southern elite came to see the Klan's excessive violence as a reason for the federal troops to continue their occupation, and they too joined the cry for the elimination of the Invisible Empire.

One day in late September, I took the buggy and traveled to Charleston. I needed to check the family properties and see to some financial matters. Matthew accompanied me. I hated leaving Josephine in her condition, but the ladies assured me that they could handle anything that might come up.

Though much had changed, it was good to be back in town. Aunt Effie's house was occupied by James and Belana. Belana continued to play lady of the manor. Her nieces were now living with her to promote the illusion of a colored family in residence. This the Yankees would respect. They left the house alone.

Adam Pickney, his wife, and their children were still living in Grandmother's house. Poor Adam! Once one of Charleston's brightest young lawyers, he was now reduced to working as a carpenter to make money for his family.

"Oh well," he said. "Jesus's father was a carpenter. It's good, honest work and I guess it's good enough for me."

I told them to stay as long as they needed. I was just grateful to have the house occupied.

The first week in October, I ran afoul of the law. I was on my way home on foot one warm evening at twilight. Returning from an errand, I had taken a shortcut through a part of town that had become very rough. As I passed what appeared to be an abandoned building, I heard someone scream. I looked into the building through the missing window. In the fading light, I could see a man holding a lady; he was shoving her back against the wall of the small, dirty room. She slapped him, and he punched her. The lady made a muffled sound as the man's fist struck her jaw.

"Let go of her," I yelled at the man as I ran into the room.

The man released the lady he was holding. Her head listed to the right, and with her back still against the wall, she slid to the floor. The man turned to face me. His white teeth shone against his ebony lips.

"This here ain't none of your business; you white men ain't got no say what I does no more!" he said.

"I do when you're hitting a lady," I said.

"She got business with me that don't be concerning you," he said, walking toward me.

"Is that so?" I said, holding my ground.

Not answering me, the man walked to within three feet of me and then swung mightily in my direction. I lurched to the right, missing his blow. I punched hard and fast, delivering a direct hit to his stomach. I stood, knees bent, shoulders forward, holding my clenched fists at chest level for a moment.

He staggered backward, landing against the same wall against which his victim sat. He looked dazed as he put his hands in front of his face. Turning my back to him, I stood between the two and offered my hand to the terrified lady sitting on the floor.

I realized that she was not a lady at all. Most likely, she was one of the prostitutes who made an easy living from the large number of soldiers in town. Still, I couldn't abandon her to this man. I helped her to her feet and asked, "Are you all right?"

Shaking her head yes, she looked up at me. Suddenly her eyes widened and she screamed, "Look out! Behind you!"

Recovering from the blow, the Negro grabbed a board that lay on the floor by his feet. He swung hard in my direction. Once again, I ducked just in time to see him hit a post behind me. I seized a piece of broken furniture that lay on the floor beside me and threw it in his direction.

As he struggled to free the board he held from the legs of the chair that I had thrown, I charged him. Grabbing the plank he held at either end, I threw my entire weight into my charge. As we struggled for control of the board, he fell backward again into the wall.

The plank was at the level of his neck. Hoping to choke him, I pressed my weight as hard as I could against the board.

Behind me, the woman screamed and ran from the building. I hoped she was going for help. We struggled for what seemed like an eternity. I watched my opponent's eyes begin to roll backward in his head. Then suddenly, he lifted his knee and connected with my groin. Pain coursed though my body. I released my grip on the board. The board fell to the floor.

While I stood doubled over in agony, my opponent put his hands on his knees and panted for a moment. Catching his breath, he picked up the board and swung at me again. This time, he struck me with a direct blow to my left leg. I stumbled then managed to stand up; now I was seeing red! I was pig-biting mad!

Forgetting my pain, I swung my right fist. It connected hard with his left eye. I followed with my left fist and a direct blow to the center of his chest. He dropped the board and leaned forward. I delivered one final punch straight to his jaw. He fell, bleeding and bruised, face down on the floor.

Reeling from the fight, I staggered two steps backward toward the door. My leg hurt like hell. I realized that my lip was bleeding. I stood by the open doorway wobbling. I wiped my lip on my coat sleeve. I had never, never hit a black man before that night, but this couldn't have been helped. Regardless of her station, I could not walk by and see any man beat a female. I realized that I must get out of here. I knew how this would look, and there were no witnesses to bear out my story.

To simply be accused of mistreating a Negro was enough to land a man in jail. Because we were under military rule, cases were heard by high-ranking Union officers. There was no telling how long a man might be incarcerated before he got his day in court. I turned to go out the door just as two Union soldiers entered the building.

"And just what do you think you're doing?" asked the first soldier.

"I...I heard a lady scream. I came to help her," I stammered.

"I don't see no woman here," said the soldier.

"She ran off when the fighting started," I said.

"There never was no woman, now was there, reb?" said the soldier.

"Yes, there was. This man was trying to hurt her. I was just trying to stop him. That's all, I swear."

The Negro on the floor moaned. He sat up and rubbed his jaw.

The second soldier walked over and squatted in front of the man.

"That so, boy?" he asked. "You have a woman in here?"

The Negro looked defiantly at me, then at the soldier.

He managed to look downright innocent as he said, "No, sir. I was mindin' my own business when that there man yells at me, 'I goin' to kill you,' an' I runs for my life. I try to hide in here, an' he follows me in an' starts beatin' me with that there board."

"Can't you see he's lying? I cried. "The woman was right here. She ran off to get help."

"We know who's lying, reb. You people gotta learn you can't be taking the law into your own hands no more."

"But I'm telling you the truth!" I swore.

"Yeah, and I'm Abe Lincoln." One of the soldiers laughed.

It was no use. They would never believe me. I decided to try to escape. I dashed across the room to the window and jumped through it into the street. I felt a terrible pain from my leg shoot through my body. I began to limp and then run as fast as my bruised and bleeding leg would carry me. I ran down an alley and through a backyard. I realized that I could never outrun them. I passed through a tangle of vines and found an old summer kitchen that was missing its roof and one wall. I ducked into the rubble of the ruined building and prayed no one had seen me. I sat panting against the cold brick. Above me, the first stars twinkled in the early evening sky.

I flattened myself against the wall, and I begged God to make me invisible. I heard the soldiers running down the alley. In my haste, I had not noticed the elderly black woman sitting in the second-floor window. She had been watching the street below. The soldiers stopped to see where I might have gone. It was then that they noticed the woman in the window.

"Did you see a man running down the alley?" they shouted.

"Yes, sir," she replied.

"Well, which way did he go?"

"He runned through them there weeds into that ole kitchen," she said, pointing in my direction.

I heard the soldiers crashing through the weeds. I looked for something, anything, with which I could defend myself. I found a few loose bricks. I waited until the men were upon me and I jumped up. Hoping to frighten them, I yelled like a madman. I threw a brick as I charged at them. One of the soldiers yelped in pain as the brick collided with his head. The other soldier rushed me. As I hurled another missile at him, he lunged, tackling me around the waist. I fell backward. I hit my head hard on the side of a crumbling wall. For a moment, I thought I heard a bugle and then a cannon fire. The stars began to swirl and run together. That was the last that I remember.

I awoke the next morning in a jail cell in town. As I sat up, I felt pain in every muscle in my body. My blurred vision began to clear, and I looked at my surroundings. I was in a small, damp cell that smelled of mildew and urine. The cell had three walls of brick. The fourth was made of iron bars. An octet of ragged, dirty men lounged on benches or sat on the floor around me. For a few brief moments, I was terrified that I had returned to Fort Delaware. I jumped to my feet. A wave of pain stabbed at my leg and then my head. I threw myself against the bars and yelled for the guards.

"Ain't no use yellin'. They don't answer," said one of the ragged old men.

"Guard! Guard! Let me out of here!" I yelled again, rattling the bars of my cage.

A couple of the other men in the cell awoke. They all began to laugh at me.

"Ain't nobody comin' to let you out. Ain't nobody gets outta here," a voice said.

To everyone's surprise, there came a rattle of iron keys. The cell block door creaked open.

The men on the floor backed away from the iron bars.

"Quiet down, you's in there!" yelled a soldier.

A second soldier followed behind him.

The first man stopped in front of the bars and leered at me. "Well now, Major, you have a nice nap?" he asked.

"I demand that you release me at once!" I said.

"That so?" said the guard mockingly. "Well, Major, I'm afraid I ain't one of your soldiers, and you ain't a major no more. I don't see as there's much you can demand."

I rattled my bars with impotent rage.

"You need to quiet down and show some respect," said the second soldier. "General wanted to talk to you as soon as you woke up."

The first soldier unlocked the door to my cell, and the second one grabbed me and cuffed my hands behind my back.

"If I had my way, we'd shackle you like you done your colored folks," said the soldier. He shoved me roughly down the hallway to the door.

As I passed from the hallway of the cellblock into the vestibule of the warehouse converted to a makeshift jail, I saw Matthew sitting on one of the benches that lined the walls. He jumped up when he saw me.

"Charles, are you all right? What have they done to you?" cried Matthew.

"I'm fine. How did you know I was here?" I asked.

"When you didn't come home last night, I got worried and I went out to look for you. When I told the authorities you were missing, someone overheard me and said that a man matching your description was arrested for beating a colored man. I rushed right down here, but they wouldn't let me see you until morning."

That explains how they found out who I am and that I have been in the Confederate service, I thought to myself.

"I'm fine, just a little bruised up from the scuffle, that's all," I said.

The guard poked me from behind. "All right, that's enough. The general wants to see you," he said.

He marched me down the hall into a small, cramped room that smelled of musty paper and cigar smoke. Matthew followed behind. The room must have been the manager's office at one time; it now served as the commanding officer's office. A large desk dominated the room, and several mismatched chairs sat along the rear wall.

The window behind the desk was propped open with a pile of books. An autumn breeze blew into the room from the river beyond. The wind animated a stack of papers on the desk. The man sitting behind the desk set a rock on top of the papers, and their attempt at flight was abated.

"General, sir!" The soldier saluted his superior. "The prisoner you wanted to see."

Without looking up, the officer finished what he was writing. I stood beside the soldier as Matthew watched from the rear of the room.

The general finished with the papers in front of him.

"That will be all, Watkins," he said. "Wait outside the door till I send for you."

The soldier saluted and did as he was told.

The general looked me up and down. He leaned forward in his chair. With his hands clasped, he rested his elbows on the desk in front of him. "When are you people going to learn that you are not in charge here? You cannot take the law into your own hands anymore. The days of mistreating your slaves are over. You cannot just beat a man when the mood strikes you."

"I beg your pardon, General," I said. "I have never beaten a Negro in my life, and I am not about to start now. I was not beating that man. I was trying to aid a female that he was mistreating."

"And how is it that nobody else saw this woman?"

"She had fled the scene by the time the soldiers got there."

"I see. And did you or did you not strike the colored man in that room?"

"All I did was defend that woman and myself."

"So you admit that you struck him?"

"I had no choice," I said. I did not like the way this interview was going.

The general took a cigar from the drawer in his desk. He leaned back in his chair and lit the cigar. The smell of sulfur and tobacco wafted through the room. He took two deep hits and blew the smoke sideways from his mouth.

"Mr. McGuire," began the general. "I am well aware of who you are. I know that your family were slave holders. I know that you were a traitor to the Union and that you were an officer in the Confederate army. As I said before, I cannot allow you people to take the law into your own hands. I have a man who is prepared to testify that you beat him for no reason other then the fact that he was a Negro. I have two officers who are willing to swear that they found you alone with him and that he was lying beaten on the floor. You also assaulted two of my men with bricks. You are in serious trouble here, Mr. McGuire."

I began to feel nauseous. My palms began to sweat. These people seemed bound and determined to prosecute me for a crime I was not guilty of.

"I'll tell you what," continued the general. "I am not an unreasonable man. I know all about the gentlemen's political association here in town, and I am aware of their midnight outings. If you furnish me with the names of these citizens and times and dates of a few incidents we are looking into, I could see to it that these accusations against you disappear."

"I have no idea what you are talking about," I said.

"Come now, Mr. McGuire. I wasn't born yesterday. I know the men of this city have taken the law into their own hands. Masks and white sheets can't hide you forever."

"I assure you, General, that I am too busy looking after my family to go traipsing about the countryside dressed in bedclothes harassing people."

"So you deny knowing anything about the Klan or participating in their activities?"

"I don't believe in the Klan," I said defiantly. "I think they are just a legend you all cooked up to blame the trouble in the city and the edge of town on us."

"Too bad, Mr. McGuire. I was going to give you an easy way out here, but you insist on making things difficult."

The general leaned forward once more in my direction. He returned his elbows to the desk and took a long drag from his cigar.

As he expelled the smoke, he rolled the cigar between his thumb and forefingers thoughtfully.

"I doubt this woman exists, but no one can say that I am not a fair man. If you can find her or anyone who saw her in the building with you, I will consider dismissing the charges of beating the Negro. But you will still be held accountable for assaulting my men. I would suggest that you find yourself a lawyer."

His expression turned to stone. He pointed the cigar in my direction. "Make no mistake, we know all about your activities. We will find all of you. One way or the other, we will put an end to your reign of intimidation. You have three weeks to prove your case. If you fail to do so, I swear, I will make an example of you."

He sat back in his chair and returned to the papers on his desk, "Good day, Mr. McGuire."

Without looking up, he called for the sentry and instructed him to let me talk to my family present and then return me to a private cell until my trial.

In the hallway, Matthew and I debated the wisdom of having him defend me at my hearing. We decided that since he was my brother-in-law, it would look too much like we were collaborating together. I wouldn't get a fair trial. We made the decision that Adam Pickney should be the one to represent me.

I thought of Josephine and my family; they would wonder where I was. I should be home to supervise the beginning of the harvest. What could I tell them so they didn't worry? I decided that honesty was the best policy, and that afternoon I wrote to Josephine and the family to tell them of my plight. I told them that Adam Pickney was representing me and that they should not worry. I would be home before they knew it.

The next day Adam came to my cell. His suit was patched, and he wore no hat. His once coal black hair was graying at the temples, and he had slicked it flat with Macassar oil. He carried with him a paper folder with some documents in it. I could tell that he was excited to be practicing law once more. He questioned me as to what had happened. He listened intently as I related the events of the previous evening to him.

When I had finished, he said to me, "Charles, I am not going to lie to you. This is very serious. As I see it, we need to find that woman or someone who saw her, and we need to make sure that the victim doesn't show up for that trial. These Yankees are eager to punish us all any way that they can."

"I don't know how to find her. I'm not even sure that I would recognize her. It was getting dark. I didn't get a clear look at her face."

I thought for a moment. "I know she was small framed and had black hair. Maybe she wore a red dress," I said. "She may have been a prostitute. Otherwise, she would never have been in that neighborhood, but beyond that, I don't remember. "

"Hmm...the girl is probably out of the picture." Adam stroked his goatee absentmindedly as he paced back and forth. "The Negro will be no problem," he muttered. "Finding a witness...let me see."

"Adam, what are you saying?" I asked.

Adam stopped his pacing and looked at me.

"What I am saying, Charles, is that the Yankees will not fight fair. They want someone to make an example of. I am afraid that they have found the perfect person in you. You and your family represent everything they hate about us. You're rich and well-connected. Your family epitomizes the Old South. To make matters worse, you didn't lie down and die like the rest of the good townspeople; and you still have money and businesses in

England. They won't be happy until they have seen you suffer. They want to destroy you."

"But, Adam, I am innocent!" I exclaimed.

"The jails are full of innocent people these days. It doesn't matter; they have already tried and convicted you in the court of popular opinion. You are guilty in their eyes."

I looked at the floor of my cell. Adam was right. I would be doomed if I fought fair. They were telling lies about me. The only way to defend myself was with more fabrication.

"So what do you have in mind?" I asked.

"The Negro can be made to change his mind or he can disappear altogether," began Adam.

I looked quizzically at him. "But..." I began. Then I saw the look in his eyes and I understood. "Oh, Adam, how could you get mixed up with the Klan?" I asked.

"Charles, I never mentioned anything about the Klan. You have been away from the city. You don't know how things are here now. There are many ways of persuading a person to change his mind."

Adam patted me on the back. "Anyway, it is better if you don't know some things. Just let me worry about it." Adam shook my hand and said, "I have a lot of preparations to take care of. I will see you tomorrow."

Three weeks later, the first chilly air of autumn blew across the harbor and through the streets of Charleston. It rattled the doors and shook the windows of houses all over town. I was taken from the jail to the courthouse in handcuffs like a common criminal. I was led into the courtroom and seated at a table with Adam. We faced the general who was to hear the case. Since we were still under marshal law, my case was to be heard by the officer who was in charge of the city.

The courtroom and balconies were filled to capacity. People who could not find seats lined the back walls. The importance of this trial was not lost on the residents of Charleston. We were all on trial here. Would the average citizen be able to protect his property and his family, or would we all just have to sit back and bow to Yankee rule, no matter how vindictive?

I spied Josephine and Aunt Effie sitting toward the front of the room. Once she had learned of my plight, Josephine insisted that Big Jawn take her to town to see me. No amount of protesting could persuade her to change her mind. She, Aunt Effie, and Big Jawn set out for town leaving Ethne with Mammy and the house servants to care for the children and Grandmother. I smiled helplessly at my wife and aunt. They smiled back. Aunt Effie dabbed her eyes with a handkerchief as Josephine patted her on the shoulder.

The general entered the room and took a seat at the big table across from us. His assistant carried a large ledger and took the seat beside him. The assistant opened the ledger and began to record the conversation.

"Charles McGuire, you have been charged with assault on a citizen of this city and with assaulting two soldiers of the United Sates Army. How do you plead?"

Adam stood and addressed the general. "We plead not guilty by reason of self-defense," he said.

"Very well, gentlemen. Shall we proceed? Bring in Jefferson Roth."

"General, sir, I am afraid that will not be possible," said Adam.

"What?" said the general obviously angered.

"I'm afraid that whereabouts of Mr. Roth are…unknown, sir," said Adam.

"Unknown? How can his location be unknown? Where is he?"

"Well, sir, if you will permit me, I have a man here who can explain that," said Adam.

"Bring him forward," ordered the general.

The doors in the rear of the courtroom opened, and an elderly black man shuffled in. He was escorted to the table where the general sat. The man was bent and gray; he wore an ill-fitting sack suit. The toes of his sockless feet poked through his worn-out shoes. In his hand, he carried a tattered straw hat. He stood at the desk in front of the general.

"State your name and tell us what you know about the disappearance of Mr. Roth," instructed the general.

The old man straightened up and smiled a crooked smile. He was obviously pleased with the attention he was receiving.

"My name be Moses Drayton," he said. "I was a slave, but now I is a free man." He grinned with pride. "I is livin' out at the end of town in a camp with a bunch of other free colored folks. The man you be talking about, he live out there too. He just plain bad news."

"How do you know this man?" asked the general.

"I told you. He live in the camp with us," said Moses.

I suspect that the general did not believe Moses, for he asked, "What is his name?"

"Jefferson Samuel Roth," said Moses.

"Describe him for me," ordered the general.

Moses described the man to the general's satisfaction.

"Continue," ordered the general.

"Well, late one night 'bout three weeks ago, after it get dark, Jefferson, he come home, all drunk, and he be bragging on how he just beat up on a white man. He say the white man in trouble and now he goin' to jail. Well, sir, one of the other men at camp he calls ole Jefferson a liar. An' ole Jefferson he say the devil with you. I ain't no liar. An' the other man say you is too. Then they get in a fist fight. Ole Jefferson, he knock the other man down, and he turn and walk away, only the man on the ground, he pull a knife out of his shoe an' throws it at Jefferson. An' Jefferson he falls down dead, stabbed in the back."

"Is this the truth? Do you swear?" asked the general.

"Yes, sur. I be speakin' the gospel," said Moses.

"Did anyone put you up to this or pay you to say this?" asked the general.

"No, sir. I just don't wanna see anyone get in trouble on account of that worthless Jefferson, that's all."

The general looked agitated. He dismissed Moses Drayton and called the two soldiers who had found me in the building that night. They related the story of how, while on patrol, they had heard a noise coming from the building. They told how they had gone to investigate and found me standing alone in the room over the body of a black man who had been obviously beaten.

"Did Mr. McGuire offer any explanation?" asked the general.

"Yes, sir," said the soldier. "He said he was defending a lady, sir."

"Did you see anyone else in the room?"

"No, sir."

"And what happened when you questioned Mr. McGuire?" inquired the general.

"He ran from the premises, sir. We followed him to an old building, where he attacked us with a couple of bricks. That's when I tackled him and he fell and hit his head."

"Thank you. That will be all," said the general. "Mr. Pickney, do you have any questions?"

"No, sir. But I do have a witness who can verify Mr. McGuire's story."

A murmur of surprise went through the room.

The general's face registered surprise. "All right, let's quiet down now. Very well, Mr. Pickney. Bring them in."

The soldiers exited the room and in walked an attractive mulatto girl of about nineteen.

"State your name, please," said the assistant.

"Lavinia Jones," answered the girl.

"And what do you do?" asked the general.

"I works for the Alston family on Saturdays, I sells flowers and sweet grass baskets at the market," she said.

"Miss Jones, I would like you to tell the general here the story that you told me the other day," requested Adam.

"Yes, sir. I was returning from an errand my mistress done sent me on. I went home by Chalmers Street 'cause I remembered that there were several old rose bushes behind one of the houses there. They sometimes put out a few flowers in the fall, and if there was any, I would pick 'em an' take 'em to market the next day.

"I went round the back of the house and was looking for flowers when I heard a lady screamin'. I went to the front of the house, but I couldn't see into the buildin' across the street. I stood and listened for a moment, and the woman screamed again. That was when I saw a man come runnin' down the street and into the buildin'."

"Do you see that man here today?" asked Adam.

"Yes, sir. He's sittin' right there beside you," answered the girl, pointing at me.

"I see. And what happened next?"

"Well, I was too scared to run, so I hid by the wall of the house and watched. I heard things crashin' and breakin', and the woman screamed again, and then she ran from the house. A moment later, I saw the soldiers come, and not too long after that, the man beside you, he jumped through the window and ran down the street followed by the soldiers."

"Did you recognize the woman?" asked Adam

"No, but I think I seen her down by the docks before."

"Did you see what she was wearing?" he asked.

The girl thought for a moment. "A red dress. Yes, a red dress, and she had a black shawl with her, and her hair was long and dark."

"Why didn't you come forth with this story earlier?" asked the general.

"Well, sir, I was scared I wasn't supposed to be there, and I didn't want my mistress to find out where I had been."

"What made you change your mind?"

"My mistress. She overheard me telling one of the other maids, and she said I had to tell you what I seen," said the girl.

"Thank you, Lavinia," said Adam.

The girl curtsied, turned from the desk, and walked out of the room.

"Are you finished, Mr. Pickney?" asked the general.

"No, sir. I would like to call one more witness today," said Adam.

"Very well, but make it quick. I have heard enough," said the general. He was becoming irritated. He could feel his case against me slipping away.

Adam called for Henrietta Charles to come forward. A diminutive, arthritic, black woman made her way to the table. She walked with the aid of a cane that was nearly as bent and twisted as she.

"Thank you for coming down here today, Henrietta," said Adam. "Do you know why we asked you to come here today?"

"Yes, sir. You be wantin' me to tell you 'bout what I saw that night a few weeks back," she said.

"That's right, Henrietta. Can you tell us what you saw?"

"Well it was a warm night, I was sittin' in my window takin' in the night air. The breeze always comes real nice off the river, so I sits there to keep cool. After a spell, I sees this here woman runnin' down the street. She be cryin', an' her dress be all tore up."

"Did you see what she looked like?"

"I couldn't see her face so good, but she had long, black hair, an' she was wearin' a red dress with a fancy black shawl pulled round her shoulders. She weren't very tall neither."

"What happened after you saw the woman?"

"Well, I just sit there for a spell an' pretty soon I sees that there white man come runnin' down the street like he being chased by Satan himself. He runs into the old kitchen an' hides. Pretty soon the soldiers comes runnin' down the street. They ask if I seen a man runnin' this way, an' I tell them yes an' point to where he run to."

"Then what happened?" asked Adam.

"Then the man I see, he tries to run off, only the soldiers, they trying to knock him down. The next thing I knows, they is soldiers all over the place, an' I see them carry the man off like he dead."

"What about the rocks or bricks? Did you see the man throw anything at the soldiers?" asked the general.

"No, sir. I didn't see the man throw no rocks. Besides, he was too beat up. He was limpin' real bad an' bleedin' too when he run into the kitchen."

"If it was dark, how could you see that well?" questioned the general.

"It weren't that dark, and I sees just fine!" said the woman.

The crowd broke into an amused murmur.

"Silence," said the general as he banged his gavel on the table.

"That will be all. You are free to go," said the general curtly. He looked first at me then at Adam. His face was red with rage. He shook his gavel at us.

"Don't think I don't know what's going on here," he said. "I know you are all covering for each other. I don't understand you people. After all you have been through, you still stick together and lie for each other. Well, damn it, you don't run this city anymore! The United States government and I do, and someone will be held accountable. As to the matter of the beating of the Negro, that we may have to overlook, but there is still the matter of assaulting the soldiers. My soldiers do not lie. Mr.

McGuire, I find your conduct and your attitude unacceptable. I am sending you to—"

"General, sir, may I speak?"

An excited chorus of voices washed over the room courtroom as everyone turned to see where the voice originated. The voice came from a man in the rear of the hall. He wore the black uniform of the clergy. As he walked toward the front of the room, I looked in his direction. He lifted his head and I saw his eyes. Even across the room, there was no mistaking that shade of Yankee blue. It was Thomas Hallowell!

"General, if I may?"

"And who are you?" asked the general.

"The Reverend, Thomas Hallowell, sir, from Fall River, Massachusetts. Before I became a minister, I was a captain with the first Massachusetts."

"Very well, but make it brief," said the general.

"When my unit transferred south, I was involved in the fighting not too far from Mr. McGuire's home a few miles up the river from here. We set up our field hospital on the grounds of Mr. McGuire's plantation. I can honestly tell you, sir, that if it were not for the help the ladies of his family gave us, many of my men would not have made it. And when I fell in love with a member of Mr. McGuire's family, they welcomed me with open arms, even though I was a soldier in the Union army. It was their hospitality that helped me to realize that I had a calling to serve the people. I have lived here among these people on and off for over three years now. I have found that, yes, sometimes they can be a bit clannish."

Adam and I smirked to ourselves at the reverend's unintentional play on words.

"But look at what they have been through," continued Reverend Hallowell. "Their whole way of life is gone. Their economy has suffered, and every day is a struggle just to survive. How would you feel if someone came into your home and turned your world upside down? These people mean no malice. They are just trying to return to some form of normalcy in their lives.

"I feel fairly certain, sir, that there is no purposeful intent to deceive here. This is only a community trying to see that one of their own gets a fair trial. General, sir, the war is over. It is time to put *us* and *them* behind us. We are all God's children. We need to reunite this country and remember that we are all just Americans. It would go a long way to helping to heal this community if you could find it in your heart to believe Mr. McGuire and let him go home to his family."

"Are you trying to tell me that you believe that this man and these people are not all in cahoots? That you believe this fabrication?"

"I am saying, sir, that I believe Mr. McGuire to be an honorable man. I would trust him with my life, and if he says he was defending the honor of a lady, then I believe him!"

"Reverend Hallowell, may I have a word in private?" requested the general, rising from his chair.

The general motioned to a corner in the back of the room. Thomas nodded his head once and followed. The crowd broke into a nervous twitter.

After a few moments of animated conversation, the general returned to his table. He began to speak slowly as though he had weighed the meaning of each word carefully.

"It is the decision of this court to be moved to leniency," began the general.

The crowd began to buzz.

"Settle down. Settle down. In the interest of fairness, Reverend Hallowell has caused me to reconsider my opinion. I believe that Mr. McGuire was acting on behalf of the welfare of one of the citizens of Charleston.

"I have also considered his family's contribution to their country by helping our soldiers when they were camped around their home. Therefore, I am willing to overlook certain incidents. I find you, Charles McGuire, not guilty. You are free to go. Private, release the man please."

The crowd erupted into an excited roar. The soldier standing behind me unlocked my handcuffs. Adam Pickney slapped me on the back as Thomas shook my hand vigorously. Josephine and Aunt Effie pushed their way to my side. I hugged Aunt Effie and then kissed my wife. I looked up, and standing behind her was Mary Alice. She held in her arms a beautiful baby boy. She beamed at me.

"Congratulations, Cousin Charles," she said.

I made my way to my cousin's side. I smiled. "It would seem that the two of you are my guardian angels. You always seem to show up just when I'm up to my neck in trouble. Once again, I find myself in your debt," I said as I hugged her.

"Nonsense, Charles. We're family. You would do the same for us."

The general was correct about our looking out for each other. Although neither the good reverend nor I was aware of it at the time, my accuser had not been done in by one of his compatriots at the settlement outside of town. The gentlemen's "political association" had paid a visit to the camp and made sure that he posed no threat. Whatever happened to Jefferson Samuel Roth, only those who were there that night know. The mulatto girl who claimed to have seen the woman running from the building was an actress from New Orleans. Unable to make a living there, she moved to Charleston, where she found it very profitable to perform privately for certain gentlemen about town. Moses Drayton had no problem recounting events that never occurred. He went home with a bottle of fine bourbon and four silver dollars. Henrietta returned to her window. She felt safe and secure. She smiled to herself every time she thought about the little box containing that money beneath her bed.

Camellias Have No Memory

"Charles, you're going to wear a hole in that carpet if you don't stop pacing back and forth," said Matthew.

"He's right, you know. You could have walked to Charleston and back by now." Thomas laughed.

"I don't know how you all stood it. Does it always take this long?" I asked.

"Longer sometimes." Matthew shrugged. "Ethne was in labor for fourteen hours with little Matthew."

Josephine woke me at six thirty in the morning to tell me it was time and request that I fetch Aunt Effie. Aunt Effie came scurrying with her medical bag, followed by Ethne and Mary Alice.

"You run along now, Charles. You'll only be in the way! Why don't you go for a ride with the other men? When you come back, you'll be a father," said Aunt Effie.

I turned to leave the room.

"Oh, and Charles, be a dear and send Isabelle upstairs to us, please."

With that, I was dismissed from the presence of my wife and soon-to-be-born child.

It was now two fifteen in the afternoon of February 21, 1867. I was much too nervous to take the prescribed ride in the country.

I was on my fourth scotch, trying to relax. The week had been difficult. Grandmother was not doing well. She was not eating, and she kept calling for Grandfather. We hadn't the heart to tell her he wasn't coming. We just smiled at her and said he would be there soon.

The weather had been rainy, making it difficult to get the crops planted. Just when the sun had come out and begun to dry the fields enough to plant, one of our mules threw a shoe. We had not discovered it until it was too late. Fortunately, the damage to his hoof would heal, but in the meantime, that left us with only one mule, so plowing would go slower.

Isabelle came into the room to check on us.

"Masta Charles, can I get you anything?" she asked.

"No, thank you, Isabelle," I answered for all present.

"How is Miss Josephine doing?"

"Miss Josephine, she doin' just fine. Your Aunt Effie say it won't be long now. An' Mammy, she say you got 'bout a half a hour. She says Young Masta Charles, he come in on the tide."

Mammy insisted that the baby was going to be a boy. She had taken to calling him "Young Master Charles."

"How about Grandmother? Is she all right?" I asked.

"Old Miss, she sleepin'. She done slept for most of the day," said Isabelle.

"Isabelle, I want you to promise me that you will let me know as soon as the baby gets here," I said.

Isabelle giggled and rolled her hazel eyes. "Don't you be worrin' none, Masta Charles. You be the first one to know."

Isabelle left the room. I redoubled my efforts to wear a path through Grandmother's oriental rug. At two forty-five, the tide began to wax. Fifteen minutes later, Ethne called for one of the servants to bring some boiling water to Josephine's bedside.

"What do they do with the boiling water? Make tea?" I asked. Both Matthew and Thomas just shrugged and shook their heads.

"Beats me!" offered Matthew.

Several minutes later, the sound of footsteps on the stairs was followed be a sharp cry and then the sound of a baby crying.

We all looked through the door into the hallway.

I was first out of the door. Isabelle stood on the second step, arms crossed, fiercely blocking my way.

"Get out of my way, you fool woman. I want to see my baby!" I cried.

"Oh no you don't! I got orders from Miss Effie not to let you up them stairs till they gets that baby all cleaned up and Miss Josephine is ready for to see you," she said.

"But this is my house, and that's my baby up there," I said as I ducked to the left, trying to pass the maid.

She anticipated my move and blocked my assault, but not before I gained four steps up on her.

"No, sir, Masta Charles. Mammy will skin me alive if I let you up them stairs before they is ready for you."

By this time, Matthew and Thomas had reached my side.

"Come on now, Charles, you've waited this long. What difference is a few more minutes going to make?" said Thomas.

"Thomas is right," said Matthew.

I sat down on the second step. Matthew and Thomas sat on either side of me. Thomas patted me on the back as Matthew smiled up at Isabelle as if to say, "It's okay; we got him."

After what seemed like an eternity, Mammy appeared on the top of the stairs.

Grinning from ear to ear, she called to Isabelle, "It's okay. You can let Masta Charles upstairs now."

I jumped to my feet and passed Isabelle like a man possessed. I took the steps two at a time. I burst into the room where Josephine lay propped up on the bed. Her auburn hair fell in soft waves about her shoulders. Her alabaster skin was pink from the trauma of birth. I had never seen her look more beautiful. In her arms, she held a tiny, red, squirming baby. Our baby! I walked over to her. I bent and kissed her on the forehead. The baby gurgled and put its fist in its mouth.

"Are you all right, my dear?" I asked.

She nodded her head to me and smiled.

She opened the blanket wrapped around the baby and said to me, "Look, Charles. You have a son."

Mammy beamed smugly from the corner.

"I done told you, you was goin' to have a boy." She smiled.

"A son…how wonderful! Mammy, you were right," I said.

I sat on the bed next to my wife. I took the baby from her arms and held him. He was so tiny and fragile. As if on cue, he opened his eyes and smiled at me. He squirmed and gurgled.

"He knows who his daddy is," I said. "Don't you? Don't you? And look at those eyes, they are Rutledge blue!"

Aunt Effie and Ethne smiled at each other.

"I believe his eyes are more Everson blue than Rutledge blue," said Aunt Effie.

"Oh well, just look at that red hair. It's a better bet that he's a McGuire through and through!" I laughed.

"Now, wait a minute!" scolded Josephine, putting her arms out for the return of her child.

I passed the baby to her.

Taking the baby in her arms, she examined his hair. "Let's not forget the St. Johns. That hair is St. John red, not McGuire red."

We all laughed together.

"Have you thought what you are going to name him?" asked Aunt Effie.

I looked at Josephine; she smiled back at me. I knew she was reading my mind. I could hear Hardy's voice in my ear saying, "As long as the people you love remember you, you will live on in their hearts."

"Hardy Stewart McGuire," I said without hesitation.

Josephine smiled her approval.

"Hardy Stewart McGuire." Ethne smiled, repeating the name.

Isabelle came into the room to inform us that Grandmother was awake.

"Josephine, why don't you get a little rest? Ethne and I will take little Hardy to meet his great-grandmother," I said.

Josephine kissed the baby and handed him to Ethne.

"Thank you, Charles. I am a little tired," she said.

My sister and I walked down the hall to Grandmother's room. We entered the room softly. Isabelle had opened the drapes, and the late afternoon sun bathed the room in a golden glow. Grandmother lay propped up on a pillow. Her eyes were closed and she looked to be at peace.

"Grandmother, it's Charles and Ethne," I said softly. "We have someone who wants to meet you."

Grandmother opened her eyes and turned her head to us. She smiled slowly and made an effort to sit up. She seemed to be much more alert than I had seen her in several days. I walked over to her side and placed another pillow behind her head.

"Well, it's about time you arrived, little fellow," she said. "Let me get a good look at you."

Ethne held the baby close to the bed and opened the blanket so Grandmother could see him. "Hardy Stewart McGuire, meet your great-grandmother, Charlotte Rutledge McGuire," she said.

Hardy chose that moment to let out a loud wail and kick his legs and arms.

Grandmother smiled approvingly. "Good set of lungs on that one. And look at those legs—they'll take him far! You can tell he's a thoroughbred."

Grandmother laid her head back on her pillow. She paused as if thinking for a moment, then, as the smile faded from her lips, she said, "He came in on the tide, didn't he?"

"Actually, he did," I said.

"Good." She paused for a moment and looked toward the window. "And a new moon too," she said. "That means that he will be strong and healthy; you need never worry about him. The McGuire name will live on. Your grandfather would be so proud."

"And you can tell little Hardy all about his family history," I said.

Grandmother smiled. "I'm afraid that job will have to fall to you and Ethne," she said.

"What do you mean?" I asked.

"I plan on leaving with your Grandfather on the next tide," she said.

I felt a shiver run down my spine.

"Don't talk like that," I said.

"Don't be ridiculous, Charles," said Grandmother. "We all know my time here is done. I want to be with your grandfather. I have had a good life, and I have lived to see my great-grandson born. But now I am tired. I want to see my husband." She smiled up at us and raised her hand to me. I took it and she squeezed it.

"Don't worry, Charles. I'll be all right. The captain will be here for me shortly. I saw him just this morning." She dropped her hand to her side and snuggled her shoulders into the bed. She took a deep breath. "Now, I need a little rest. Be a dear and send Isabelle in with a little water." She smiled and closed her eyes.

A little less than six hours after Hardy was born, the tide began to wane. Just as Mammy had predicted, Grandmother passed with the tide. I felt great solace picturing her last moments in my mind. I could see grandfather standing beside her bed. He was smiling down at her. He was young and handsome once again.

Behind him in a bright beam of light stood the old oak tree, its leaves dancing in the sunlight. Grandmother stretched out her hand to her husband. She saw the wrinkles fall from her body. She too was young once more. As she got out of bed, she realized that she was wearing the blue silk gown she had worn to meet Grandfather upon his return from England so many years ago. Grandfather took her hand and led her to a silver boat on a shining blue river. As the tide began to wane, the boat pulled slowly from the shore, and I watched my grandmother leave with the man she loved.

Three days later, we laid her earthly remains to rest on the plantation beside Grandfather. I was struck by the thought, *The Lord giveth, and the Lord taketh away.* I had lost my Grandmother, but I had gained a son.

At the end of June of the following year, as the heat of July approached, the crops were in, and work on repairing the house was coming along nicely. I decided that it was safe to plan an overseas voyage. It was time to get the mills in England back in full production. With the absence of Southern cotton, the mills had switched to producing wool. They were doing well, but they were not living up to their full potential. I needed to find new management and hire more workers.

Thomas, Mary Alice, and their two little boys were living in town. Saint Phillip's regarded their new Yankee rector with cool aloofness. The efforts of his Southern wife in the service of the restoration of their church building, together with her tireless work for the congregation and her devotion to her two adorable little boys, soon melted the sternest of hearts.

Ethne, Matthew, and their children would stay at Grand Oak to oversee things until I returned. Adam Pickney was rebuilding a home for himself and his family. He would not need Grandmother's house much longer. When the Pickneys moved out the following spring, Matthew and his family would move to town, where it was hoped that he could return to his law practice. James, Belana, and her nieces still occupied Aunt Effie's house.

Aunt Effie had sadly made some unwise investment choices just before the war. It was decided that she should sell the warehouses she owned and also the Kaolin mines. We tried to talk her into selling Sycamore Hill as well, but she insisted on keeping the property. The money made from the sale of the warehouse and mines would be enough to see to it that she was able to fix up the townhouse and run it the way it should be run for the rest of her days.

I set sail for England the first week of July. Josephine, Hardy, Aunt Effie, and Hardy's nurse accompanied me. Josephine was eager that Hardy should see the land of his mother's people.

"But he won't remember a thing," I said.

"It doesn't matter. I will remind him later," said Josephine. "Remember, he is one-half St. John, after all!"

We all needed a break from the difficulty of the previous few years. I must confess that it was nice to be in a world not torn apart by war. Here, surrounded the gaiety of London, it would have been easy to forget the trials and tribulations of home. It would have been so simple just to remain in London without any cares or politics. But there were responsibilities at home, and I had work to do here.

While I set about the task of getting the mills back to full production, Josephine and Aunt Effie wore out their shoes perusing the shops and boutiques of London. They informed me that hoops were flatter in the front this season and trains and overskirts were all the fashion.

I laughed as they returned to the flat that I had kept in town. The poor valet I had hired for them was laden with a huge collection boxes and packages. Together with the previous day's purchases, the sitting room was strewn with a kaleidoscope of dresses, bonnets, parasols, shoes, and gloves.

"Why didn't you just have them delivered?" I asked, taking a couple of the boxes from the valet.

"What, and miss trying them all on with our new gowns?" they chorused.

I realized the foolishness of my question.

In November, we returned to South Carolina, just in time to see Ulysses Grant become the eighteenth president of the United Sates.

One afternoon in March of the following year, Aunt Effie announced that she wanted to visit the remnants of Sycamore Hill.

"Charles, I have given this a great deal of thought. I have decided to sell Sycamore Hill. I would like to see the property once more before I do," she said.

"Are you sure, Aunt Effie?" I asked. "There is nothing much to see. There cannot be much left standing after four years. All that is left are ruins. It is a very long trip overland for nothing."

"It will not be a trip for nothing. The land and the hills are still there, so are the orchards my father planted. Both my parents and my brother are buried there. I need to see them and my home once more."

"But, Aunt Effie, wouldn't you rather remember Sycamore Hill the way it was?"

"Charles, my mind is made up! Please do not try to dissuade me. I shall get James to take me if you will not."

"Aunt Effie, you know full well that James is not capable of protecting you on a journey as long as the one to Goose Creek. Why, I am sure that he couldn't even find his way there," I argued.

"I assure you that I am quite capable of finding Goose Creek and Sycamore Hill, young man, and I will have Lizzie with me. Together, with James, we are quite able to take care of ourselves."

I laughed at Aunt Effie's pluck. I started to feel that I might not be able to win this argument.

"But, Aunt Effie, the house is gone, and Mrs. Hammond said that the army had burned the outbuildings. Where would you stay?"

"Charles, this matter is not open for discussion. My mind is made up. I am not asking you to take me. I am telling you that I am going. I have never asked you for anything in your life. What I am asking you now is, will you please go with me?"

"I cannot talk you out of this?" I asked.

"Absolutely not!"

"All right then. I'll tell Josephine. Let me make the arrangements, and we will leave Monday morning."

Josephine had never visited Sycamore Hill. When she heard of our plan, she insisted that she accompany us for moral support. She left little Hardy with his nurse and joined us on our voyage.

We left at first light the next morning. The trip overland took three days. Travel was still not easy. A few bridges had been rebuilt, but many of the roads were still in a deplorable state. Fortunately, the weather cooperated. We reached Goose Creek late in the afternoon on Wednesday. There was, luckily for us, one small inn operating in town. They had a room for Aunt Effie and Lizzie and another for Josephine and me. I was grateful for the break. We would be fresh for the trip to the ruins of Sycamore Hill in the morning.

I had my doubts about this trip from the moment Aunt Effie had proposed it, but now, I was feeling guilty for not having been more agreeable when she had first suggested it. It seemed that even God approved, for the next day dawned with brilliant blue skies and warm flower scented breezes. A groom from the stable pulled the carriage around to the front of the inn. Before I climbed into the carriage, I instructed him to put the top down on the buggy so we could enjoy the view of the countryside. I helped Aunt Effie, Lizzie, and Josephine into the carriage. The ladies arranged their dresses and sheltered themselves under dainty parasols to protect their complexions from the warm spring sunshine.

I had visited Sycamore Hill several times during my youth. I had many fond memories of fields of neatly planted peach trees, painstakingly ordered gardens, and a wonderful little stream that was perfect for wading on hot summer afternoons. Lizzie did not share my pleasant recollections. She had been there only once when she was a child. That had been the day we buried Uncle Philippe.

As we drove to Sycamore Hill, Aunt Effie shared memories of her home.

"The day your Uncle Henry and I were married was just like this," she said. "The grass was green and the sky was the bluest I had ever seen. And the peach trees, I will never forget the peach trees. They stretched as far as the eyes could see. Each one was covered in the loveliest fragile pink blossoms. My sisters had filled the house with bouquets of them. The house was so alive! It was bursting at the seams with family and friends. It is hard to believe that most of them are gone now, even the house and mother's beautiful parlor, all gone."

For a moment, Aunt Effie looked as though she might cry. I began to think maybe this wasn't a good idea after all. I tried to think of a topic to take Aunt Effie's mind from her loss.

"Do you remember Uncle Henry teaching us to carve baskets from the peach pits?" I asked.

Aunt Effie smiled. "I had forgotten he used to do that. You were so proud of yourself when you gave me that first lopsided little basket. I remember how worried your mother was that you might cut yourself with the knife."

"And the cobblers and peach pies, do you remember those?" I asked.

"Yes indeed. Nobody could make a cobbler like Kizzie, and her preserves, they were the best in three counties! I can almost taste them. Slow down, Charles. The entrance to the drive is just around this bend," said Aunt Effie.

Goose Creek varied from Charleston in that it was slightly hilly, not as hilly as the northern part of the state, but compared to the coast, it was not flat. We came around the bend onto a slight rise. There was a pleasant view of a shallow valley with another hill beyond. I stopped the carriage so that we could take in the view. Once upon a time, the valley would have been a sea of warm red soil, rich, green grass, and hundreds of blooming peach trees.

Despite the ravage of war that had swept over the land, one could tell that the orchard had once been a scene of great beauty. Gone were the neatly ordered rows of trees with the cultivated furrows between them. Many of the prized trees now lay gnarled and broken in the field. Tall grass and a tangle of vines had begun to reclaim the land. Here and there, in pairs or small groups, some of the trees remained standing. The peach trees, like ladies of fashion raising their hems from the mud in the streets, did their best to lift up their branches above the disarray at their feet. Nature rewarded their efforts by covering the trees in petticoats of delicate pink flowers.

At the foot of the hill was a brick wall with a wooden entrance gate. The gate stood open, lazily keeping watch over the drive leading to the house at Sycamore Hill. The drive beyond the gate was clear but deeply rutted.

I turned to look at Aunt Effie. Josephine sat holding both of Aunt Effie's hands in hers. The two women gazed across the fertile valley. Lizzie, unusually quiet, sat on the seat beside them staring blankly straight ahead. Aunt Effie wore a smile of peace and happiness on her face.

I could tell that she was not seeing the orchard as it looked today. She was seeing it in the heyday of her youth. I believe that she fully expected to see Philippe or her father come galloping down the driveway to greet her.

"Oh, Aunt Effie, it is breathtaking," said Josephine.

"Thank you, my dear. This is always the most beautiful time of year to see Sycamore Hill."

"Are you sure you want to do this, Aunt Effie?" I asked.

"Yes, Charles. I need to do this," said Aunt Effie softly.

I flicked the reins and the carriage lurched forward. We descended the hill and drove through the gate to the house. Halfway up the drive, a large clump of peach trees stood very near the road.

"Stop, Charles, stop!" cried Aunt Effie.

I quickly pulled the buggy to a stop.

"What is it?" I asked.

"I want to pick some flowers for Mother and Father and dear Philippe," she said.

Not waiting for me to assist her, Aunt Effie was out of the carriage in one jump. With the agility of a twelve-year-old, she took her skirts in her hands and ran toward the trees. Josephine quickly followed. Even Lizzie's spirits seemed to lift as she joined her mistress running through the grass.

I sat in my seat and watched. A smile crossed my lips. As the trio picked armloads of blossoms, they laughed and giggled like school girls. I wondered how many times this scene had played itself out in the past. I could see the three sisters, the graces of Sycamore Hill, running through the sweet grass, collecting flowers and butterflies. I could hear their father good-naturedly scolding them for picking the profits from his trees.

The ladies, with armloads of flowers, flitted back to the carriage. I jumped from my seat to assist them back into the buggy. Quite out of breath, Aunt Effie said, "Oh, Charles, thank you so much. These are so beautiful. We must hurry and take them quickly to Mother and Father before they wilt."

Once everyone was seated, I tapped the horse with my crop. He plodded up the rise to the spot where Aunt Effie's family was buried. I stopped him by an ornate cast iron fence surrounding a grove of cedars. I knew these cedars; almost every plantation and homestead had a clump of them somewhere on the property. They had come to be known as funeral cedars because they usually surrounded family burying grounds.

We stopped in front of the fence and all dismounted from the carriage. The gate to the cemetery, like the gate to the driveway, stood open. This, to me, was not a good sign. I thought for a moment that I should go first. There was no telling what desecration the Yankees may have visited on the graveyard.

As I peered over Aunt Effie's shoulder, I breathed a sigh of relief; the graveyard was undisturbed. I helped the ladies pull some of the grass that had grown up around the stones; then the ladies decorated the graves with the flowers they had gathered. We all offered a prayer and continued our journey to the site of the house.

Just a few minutes later, we were standing at the site where Euphemia's home had once stood. The grove of fire-damaged sycamores, from which the house took its name, stood around the pile of rubble that had once been the big house.

It had been just two months shy of four years since the house had been burned. Four years worth of rain from spring showers and summer storms had washed much of the soot from the walls and columns. Nature was doing her best to cover the scars on the trees with green. In the dappled late morning sunlight, the ruins looked soft and peaceful. The scene reminded me of the ruined cathedrals I had visited in Europe. It was hard to imagine that the house had ever looked any other way.

The steps and gallery floor were still recognizable. The six Corinthian columns that had once supported the gallery roof stood like silent sentinels, steadfast in a row. They guarded the remains of the once proud house. The four walls of the original center section were still standing, as were the walls of the west wing. A small portion of the front façade of the east wing now lay shattered and broken, like a child's toy, across the drive. The other three walls remained in place.

As the house had burned, she had been consumed from within, collapsing in layers onto the foundation. I could see in my mind the once elegant rooms lit by the glow of terrible, crackling, red and orange flames. I could hear the groan of the support beams as they pulled free from their foundations. I heard the breaking of glass as the windows blew out, and tinkle of the chandeliers as they pulled from the ceilings and crashed to the floors. I could hear the final, awful chord that the pianoforte sounded as the ceiling came crashing down upon it. I could smell the acrid smoke and the burning wood. And then there was silence and peace. Like the grand lady Sycamore Hill had been, she grew weary and simply laid down and gone to sleep.

I shook the images of the mansion's final moments from my head. It was obvious that at some point, scavengers, realizing that the property was abandoned, had visited the ruins. They most probably had been looking for bricks or wood to use in repairing their own ruined homes. Others came in search of metals or materials that could be salvaged and resold for scrap value. Then there were the fortune hunters, mostly poor whites and ne'er-do-wells, who came to sift through the rubble hoping to find jewelry or valuables that had escaped the inferno that had laid waste to the house.

I turned in my seat to look at Aunt Effie. It was difficult to read her expression. She did not wear a look of sadness, but rather her face gave the impression of being at peace. A haunting, winsome smile crossed her lips as she said, "Sycamore Hill was the finest home in the county. How we laughed and enjoyed ourselves. So much life and so much love within these walls." Aunt Effie closed her eyes. "Listen. Can you hear that?"

"Hear what?" I asked.

"In the breeze, listen. You can hear the laughter as my sisters tease Papa, and my mammy scolding Philippe to take his boots off before he goes into the house. I can hear the sound of mother's piano in the parlor."

Aunt Effie smiled again and tilted her head toward the music. She began to weave side to side as she hummed some tune recognizable only to her.

I smiled at Aunt Effie. I didn't want to disturb her daydream.

Lizzie had grown irritable and morose once more. She looked at her mistress as though she had lost her mind. "I don't hear anything," she said. "And furthermore, I don't see anything neither. This place scares me. There's too many ghosts here."

Josephine gave Lizzie a cross look. "Lizzie, your grammar," she scolded. To Aunt Effie, she said, "Oh, Aunt Effie, I hear it too. It's Chopin."

"Yes, yes. That's it, Chopin," said Aunt Effie.

Completely lost in the moment, listening to music only she and Aunt Effie could hear, Josephine said, "How lovely and how beautiful the house must have been."

I turned to watch the ladies in the backseat of the carriage. I regretted not being able to shelter them from all that had happened. They should have lived their lives surrounded by garden parties and balls. Their only worries should have been what to wear or what to have the servants serve for supper.

Nevertheless, the war had come. The ladies were forced to see the ugliness that can be reality; they were forced to work like field hands. They were forced to witness the destruction of their homes and villages, forced to bury their families and friends. Yet, in spite of the hardships, they hitched up their skirts, rolled up their sleeves, and did what needed to be done. Yes, before the war, the women of the South had been pampered and spoiled, but when hard times had come, they had shown what they were made of. Now they were the backbone of the South, encouraging their men and finding ways to care for their families and communities.

"Well, have we seen enough?" I asked.

"No. Wait here for a moment," said Aunt Effie. "I want to get a few bricks to take home and put in my garden. Would you please help me from the carriage?"

I pulled the buggy to the carriage block that was still in place near the steps. I helped Aunt Effie and then Josephine from the vehicle. I offered my hand to Lizzie. She looked at me defiantly. She was usually better behaved than this. I really couldn't blame her for her attitude. To her, this place must seem very unpleasant. She had come here once as a small child to bury her father, and her life had been forever changed. Now the house was in ruins, and the trip to the graveyard was only a reminder of her loss.

"I hope you don't think I'm going anywhere near that place," she said. "There's bound to be snakes or rats crawling around them ruins. I am not going anywhere near them."

"Very well. Suit yourself. But don't come crying to me if one of those snakes or rats you're so afraid of comes running from the ruins and carries you off." I laughed.

"Just leave her be, Charles. We'll be better off with out her anyway," said Aunt Effie.

Lizzie crossed her arms and glared at me. I turned from the carriage and walked toward my aunt and Josephine.

"Wait! Wait!" screamed the girl.

I walked back to the buggy and picked Lizzie from the seat. I sat her on the ground. As we walked to the steps of the gallery, she grudgingly followed several paces behind us. We stood on the bottom step looking up at the columns. They were still in excellent shape despite the fire. We looked in through the gaping hole that had once been surrounded by an oak door and transom. We could see into the shell that had once been such beautifully appointed rooms.

"Oh, this just breaks my heart," said Aunt Effie. She began to cry.

Josephine offered solace. "Don't be sad, Aunt Effie. Think of how lucky we are to still have each other."

"I know," said Aunt Effie. "It is just that I suddenly realized today would have been our forty-sixth wedding anniversary. Forty-six years ago today, I was standing in the parlor surrounded by my family and friends. I am so glad none of them are here to see this. Who could ever have thought, on that happy day, that it all would have ended this way?"

She stooped, picked two bricks from the rubble, and turned from the door. "I've seen enough, Charles. Let's go."

I offered my arm to her.

"Wait! Aunt Effie?" said Josephine.

"What is it, my dear?"

"Do you remember the letter that Mrs. Hammond wrote to you? Do you suppose that there is anything in the hole in the wall she mentioned in her letter?"

"I don't know. I had quite forgotten about it."

"Mrs. Hammond said the hole was on the wall between the original house and the west wing addition. Do you know what she was talking about?" asked Josephine.

"Actually, yes, I do," answered Aunt Effie. "There had originally been three windows on the west wall of the parlor. When the addition was added, the center window was made into a doorway to the new rooms. The two windows on either side were turned into niches. Mother kept statues of comedy and tragedy in them. There was a gap between the walls to allow for the depth of the niches. There was a marble base in each niche. But the gap in the one on the right was not filled in. The base was never adhered to the wall. Mother used to hide things in there. I am sure that was what she must have been talking about."

"Can you see the spot through the door?" asked Josephine.

Aunt Effie, her curiosity aroused, turned and walked back to the door. Josephine and I followed closely. Aunt Effie peered into the shell.

"Let's see…yes…over there to the left. See the three holes in the wall? The middle one was the door to the music room in the addition. The holes on either side are the windows that had been made into the niches. The windows are burned out, but the sills were marble. I'll bet they are still there."

"Charles, do you think you can make it through the rubble to the window?" asked Josephine.

"I don't know. It looks kind of unsafe," I said.

"But aren't you curious whether or not there is anything there?" she asked.

I had to admit I was.

"Okay, I'll try. You both wait here. I'll see how close I can get."

I picked my way cautiously across the debris field. Boards and bricks tottered beneath my feet. Twice I slipped, and the ladies called to me to be careful. I finally reached the wall of the house. There was a considerable amount of debris piled up by the window. The sill was not visible.

I picked through boards and debris until finally there came into view, just as Aunt Effie said, a marble sill.

"I found the sill," I called.

"Wonderful. Now see if you can lift it up and look inside," called Aunt Effie.

I did my best to dislodge the marble from its resting place. The heat from the fire must have done something to swell the brick and mortar, for the marble was stuck firmly in place.

"I can't seem to move it. Are you sure that this is the one? I called.

"Positive," answered Aunt Effie. "See if you can take a brick and whack it from underneath."

I searched the area around me for a brick. Finding one, I did as Aunt Effie suggested and gave the sill several good hits from beneath. On the fourth blow, the marble broke loose. I lifted it from its place and peered into the opening. Sure enough, there was a large, gray, flannel bag resting on the bottom of the compartment. Also in the space were five rolls of canvas and two more smaller burlap sacks.

"I found something," I called.

"What is it?"

"I don't know. I'll bring it back, and we can find out together."

I made my way back to where Aunt Effie and Josephine waited impatiently for me. When I reached them, I handed Aunt Effie the rolled canvases, and then I returned for the sacks. To Josephine, I handed the smaller bags; I carried the larger gray flannel one. We sat the bags down on the lawn. Opening the large, gray, flannel one, we found, carefully wrapped in cheesecloth, Aunt Effie's family silver tea service. It had belonged to her mother Aunt Effie wept tears of joy when she saw it.

"Oh, I thought this was lost forever," she cried.

The second sack contained a pair of silver candelabra, and the third contained two hundred and thirty-seven dollars in Confederate money, two photo albums, and a fancy wooden box containing an ornately woven bracelet. The bracelet was woven from hair and fastened with a beautiful cameo clasp. On the face of the cameo was carved a representation of the three graces. The reverse was engraved, "To mother with love, Euphemia, Rebecca, Louisa."

"I remember when we gave this to her. We were so afraid Mother would notice the swatches of hair we cut so that we could have this made for her birthday," said Aunt Effie.

Next, we unrolled the canvases. We were delighted to discover that two of them were the wedding portraits of Aunt Effie's mother and father. The other three canvases were landscapes that had been particularly treasured.

"Well, this was certainly worth the trip," said Aunt Effie. "Josephine, I am so glad that you came with us. I would never have remembered that letter."

Josephine hugged Aunt Effie. "I'm just thankful that the Hammonds had the foresight to hide a few of your family's things away."

As I loaded the sacks into the carriage, Aunt Effie and Josephine walked around to the rear of the house where the gardens had once been. Lizzie, as she had done all afternoon, followed behind.

When I had finished loading Aunt Effie's treasures, I went to find the ladies in the garden. I walked around to the back of the house. Grass and seedlings had begun to sprout between the brick floor of the terrace. The original balustrades still separated the terrace from the overgrown lawn and the formal gardens beyond. I walked down the steps to the lawn and into the camellia beds that had been Mrs. Everson's pride and joy.

The Yankees had toppled and broken the life-size statues of the four seasons that, at one time, graced the corners of the garden. The oyster shell paths needed to be raked, and the reflecting pool in the center of the garden was filled with leaves and debris. The army had apparently camped in the garden. It was obvious that before their departure, they had tried their best to destroy it. They had ridden their horses through the beds and smashed or pushed over anything of value. They had cut down what of the bushes they could. Hoping to catch the area on fire, they had thrown burning logs and lumber into the garden. I was struck by the madness of their cruelty. It was bad enough to leave us homeless and hungry, but what kind of animal steals away beauty and hope?

Lizzie stood in the center of the garden mindlessly kicking bits of oyster shell into the stagnant green water of the reflecting pool. The shells made little plopping sounds as they landed in the water.

Aunt Effie and Josephine sat on the only stone bench not broken by the Yankees. On the seat between them was an assortment of the last camellia blossoms of the season. Aunt Effie was naming them off to Josephine, who sat admiring each one as if it were an exotic butterfly.

"The white ones are Alba Plena. They were mother's favorite. The lovely dark rose one is Aunt Jetty. The pink one is Mathotiana," said Aunt Effie.

I will always remember the pretty picture they made sitting there in the afternoon sunlight in the ruined garden. They had decorated themselves with colorful blossoms, tucking the flowers into their hair and the necklines of their dresses. Upon seeing me, Josephine jumped up and ran in my direction. A shower of blossoms tumbled from her skirt and fell to her feet.

"Look, Charles. Aren't they beautiful?" she gushed as she tucked a flower into the lapel of my coat.

I smiled at her. So much like Josephine—ever the optimist. How could she sit here amid this ruination and see only beauty? All I could see was the cruelty of our aggressors.

Aunt Effie smiled up at me from where she sat. "It's a miracle," she said. "The Yankees rode through here and did their best to destroy all of this. The camellias have been burned, broken, and crushed, but they have thrived. They are prettier than ever."

Josephine stood with her arm around my waist. She laid her head against my shoulder.

"Wouldn't it be wonderful if we were more like the camellias, and we could go on with our lives and just forgive and forget?"

I gazed down at Josephine by my side. I grinned at her naiveté. I thought about all that we had been through to get to this moment. I recalled the war and my incarceration at Fort Delaware. I thought about the Yankees invading Grand Oak. I thought about the friends I had lost. I remembered Hardy. I may be able to forgive in time, but I would never forget!

I looked lovingly at my wife. Not wanting to spoil the moment, I smiled sadly and said, "Yes, my love. That would be nice."

I stroked Josephine's hair and kissed the top of her head. "But then it's easier for them to forget; camellias have no memory."

EPILOGUE

I have chosen to end Charles Everson McGuire's story here. I like to think of him surrounded by Aunt Effie, Lizzie, and Josephine. I can see the four of them happy and contented, admiring the flowers, on a warm spring day in the ruined garden at Sycamore Hill. I like to believe that, based on his diaries and letters, Charles was able to follow Josephine's advice and put all of the trials and tribulations of the war behind him.

After I finished reading the diaries and manuscripts, I returned to the trunk and the secrets it had held for all those years. The items now seemed to be like holy relics.

The watch chain wasn't made from thread; it was made from human hair. I couldn't believe that I had been holding a watch chain actually made from Josephine's hair. It was almost like touching her in person. I had to wonder how many times Charles had held this very watch and chain in his hand as he thought of the woman who gave it to him.

The photographs or tintypes were the actual pictures taken on Josephine and Charles's wedding day. Hardy's bugle was there too, along with the money Aunt Effie had found hidden in the wall at Sycamore Hill.

And at long last, the riddle of the damaged epaulets was solved. They were the very ones that had been shot off the major's jacket on that summer day so long ago. All of the items in the trunk took on a new meaning. It was like holding the hands of the people who had treasured theses items and each other so long ago.

It was apparent from the volume of writing that the Charles left behind that he had planned at some point to have his memoirs published. Many veterans of the war, from both the North and the South, later in their lives felt the need to document their experiences. Some did it for money, others for fame, and some, like Charles, simply wanted to leave a written record of their experiences for the next generation. Why Charles never finished his work on his memoirs I will never know. It is fortunate that all of the diaries and letters stayed together in his campaign trunk. Without them, I never would have been able to tell his story.

I was curious as to what happened to Charles McGuire and his family. I was able to piece together the latter part of their lives by searching the newspaper archives and files in the historical society in Charleston

In the years following the war, accompanied by Josephine and Hardy, Charles kept himself busy with yearly trips to England. They would spend the late spring and summer enjoying the cooler European climate, returning to Charleston for the fall and winter. Charles spent a great deal of time in the years immediately following the war in rebuilding his family's mills.

He foresaw the decline of the American cotton crop and moved to producing fine woolens and silks. Cotton production was not cut out entirely, for, true to his word, Charles McGuire divided a sizable portion of the original plantation acreage and parceled it out to the families of the slaves who returned after the war. He wanted to make sure that the landholders had a market for their cotton until other crops were introduced. Some of that land parceled out by Charles McGuire remains today in the hands of the descendants of the former slaves.

With the mills running smoothly and his family taken care of, Charles devoted much his time in his later years to horse breeding and racing. I suspect that Charles's return to horse breeding was influenced by the love of horses instilled in him by his Grandfather and by the time he spent in England. Both he and Josephine were frequent guests at the Royal Ascot. In addition, Charles is known to have enjoyed both flat racing and hunt racing.

Charles lived to be one hundred years old. He died at Grand Oak, on his birthday, August 21, 1923, in the Charleston rice bed in the same room in which he had been born. He was laid to rest beside Josephine in the family mausoleum in the churchyard at Saint Michael's in Charleston.

Although Josephine lived until 1911, her diaries ended about the time her husband returned from the war. Perhaps her pen was silenced by the need to care for her family, or perhaps it was because she wanted to put the past behind her and look to the future.

It is interesting that she kept every one of the letters that her husband had written during his incarceration at Fort Delaware. She also kept the letters she had written to him but had never mailed. They were all tied together with maroon ribbons and laid away in the major's campaign trunk. I must confess to feeling guilty at reading such personal correspondence, but I kept telling myself that neither Josephine nor Charles would have minded my eavesdropping if it aided me in telling their story. It is evident from the content of the letters that Josephine never regretted her decision to remain in this country and marry Charles McGuire.

Her life surely would have been much more comfortable had she returned to England during the war. What is certain is that the future of Grand Oak would have been greatly altered had she not been there during the war years.

After the end of the war and reconstruction, Josephine worked to build a better world for her son and for the next generation who would succeed her. She believed that education was critical in this pursuit. Josephine championed educating the children of former slaves. She donated a lot of time and money to Belana's school for colored children. In addition, she reached out to any adult who wanted to learn to read and write in order to improve his or her life. Many people in town were uncomfortable with her work on the behalf of the Negroes, and they voiced their disapproval freely; but as Josephine had always done, she shrugged them off and followed her heart.

Josephine was truly a woman ahead of her time. The belief that all people should be treated equally and fairly had just recently been extended to include the former slaves. As she struck a blow for recognition and education for others, she realized that she, as a woman, and indeed all of her sisters, was still being treated as second-class citizens. The irony that the Fourteenth Amendment, passed in 1866, guaranteed black men the right to vote while still denying women this same basic freedom was not lost on her.

It was a natural progression that she would become involved in the women's suffrage movement. Her passion for the issue must have worn off on her granddaughter, for Maggie-Joe took up the torch and became, at a very early age, a champion for the issue of women's suffrage. Josephine would not live to see her twenty-year-old granddaughter proudly become the first woman in South Carolina to vote for republican Warren G. Harding for president. I suspect that neither Maggie-Joe's Democratic father nor her Democratic grandfather was very happy with her choice.

The last entry in Euphemia's diary was dated May 21, 1868. She spoke of selling Sycamore Hill and the remorse she felt at letting go of the last of her family's properties. Euphemia lived another twenty-one years after her last diary entry. She died in the autumn of 1889, at the age of eighty-seven in the house on Legare Street. She left the house, all the furnishings, and the remainder of the money from the sale of the plantation, to her faithful servant Belana. Belana turned the house into a school for colored children. The house remained a school until 1912 when it was sold to a banker from New York who wished to retire in the South. Beautifully restored, the house still stands behind the same wrought iron gates and brick piers crowned with pineapple finials.

The gardens, their abuse at the hands of the Union army no more then a footnote in history, are alive once more with roses, camellias, and a progression of seasonal flowers. Mrs. Humphries's house, too, still stands. It is also beautifully restored. One can stand on the second-floor landing and look across the former Scott family gardens to the piazza where Euphemia and Henry took their afternoon tea. I have heard it said that occasionally, on a warm spring night when the moon is full, if one looks out the second-floor window of the stair landing of the Humphries house, one might see a lady in a blue silk dress waving a handkerchief from the Scott family's piazza to someone on the street.

Hardy, following in his father's footsteps, received his education in England and went to work for a time in the family's mills. Like his father, Hardy married late in life at the age of thirty-one. Also like his father, he fell in love with and married an Englishwoman.

The couple split their time between England and South Carolina until the birth of their daughter, Josephine Margaret McGuire, in 1900.

Wishing to follow in the family's tradition of having the heirs to Grand Oak born on the plantation, Hardy and his wife, Margaret, returned to Grand Oak for the birth of their first child. Whether or not the family was disappointed that Josephine was not born a boy was not recorded. I suspect Hardy and his wife were just happy to have a healthy child born to them.

Family lore says that Hardy chose to name the baby girl after the two most important women in his life: Josephine, for his mother, and Margaret, for his wife. For most of her life, young Josephine Margaret would be known as Maggie-Joe.

One year later Margaret gave birth to a son. Sadly, the child lived only one week. Two years later, she was pregnant with her third child, but she died with the infant in her eighth month. Hardy was inconsolable and never remarried.

Grand Oak house still stands majestically in a grove of live oaks on the Ashley River. The estate was purchased by a development co-op, and today is the home of the Grand Oak Golf and Tennis Club. Except for the addition of electricity and modern plumbing, much of which was added by the home's last occupant, Josephine M. McGuire, the original house remains pretty much unchanged from the major's time. The mansion serves as a clubhouse for the golf club. The club boasts a four-star restaurant, named Miss Lottie's, in honor of the woman for whom the house was built. The ballroom can be rented for weddings and special events. The upstairs rooms are available for conferences and meetings.

While the house remains relatively unchanged, I doubt the major or his family would recognize the grounds. The original driveway is much the same, although it has been widened and paved. Much of the original land once cultivated for cotton is now part of an eighteen-hole championship golf course. Of the once lush gardens that surrounded the house and ran to the river, very little is left. Only a small portion of Miss Louisa's garden remains. A putting green and outdoor terrace now occupy the spot that once was home to Louisa's famed roses.

The former site of the barn, chicken coops, and cotton sheds now is home to the tennis courts. On the site once occupied by the major's grand stable is a large indoor tennis court. Most of the members of the club are unaware of the little stream running just west of the building. They have never seen the grove of trees and the curious unmarked stones that dot the cool, mossy earth. Only the ancient trees remember the brave young men who fought for their country and now lay sleeping in the cool, green woods.

Where the slave cabins once "squatted on the ground," Charleston's elite now lounge by the aquamarine waters of an Olympic-sized pool. Blissfully unaware of the suffering of the people who once lived on this land, they order bourbon straight or juleps from handsome, young servers dressed in club colors. The sound of the plantation bell calling the men from the fields has been replaced by the ringing of cell phones, the tinkle of ice in frosted glasses. The smell of dinner cooking in the cabins has been replaced by the smell of suntan lotion and chlorinated water.

To the right of the main house on what was once open lawn is a new Georgian revival building that houses the offices and maintenance buildings for the club. If one ventures behind these buildings, one will find, winding through the moss-laden oaks and subtropical foliage, a narrow path leading to a grove of cedars. There is an old wrought-iron fence surrounding the little cedar grove. In the middle of the fence is a creaky rusted gate, which can only be opened with a small degree of difficulty.

In the middle of the clearing surrounded by the century old cedars are two beautiful stone monuments. One is inscribed: "Captain Charles Everett McGuire, born Charleston South Carolina 1775, died Grand Oak Plantation October 21, 1853." Next to that stone is another, which reads, "Charlotte Rutledge McGuire, born Charleston, South Carolina, 1781, died at Grand Oak Plantation, February 21, 1867."

Somehow it seems only fitting that after all of these years, the captain and Miss Lottie are still together welcoming visitors to Grand Oak.